The Queen of Second Place

The Queen of Second Place

Laura Peyton Roberts

delacorte press

Published by
Delacorte Press
an imprint of
Random House Children's Books
a division of Random House, Inc.
New York

Visit us on the Web! www.randomhouse.com/teens
Educators and librarians, for a variety of teaching tools, visit us at www.randomhouse.com/teachers

Library of Congress Cataloging-in-Publication Data
Roberts, Laura Peyton.
    The queen of second place / Laura Peyton Roberts.
        p. cm.
    Summary: Smitten with a new boy at school, California high school sophomore Cassie Howard spends months trying desperately to win him over before she finally regains some perspective.
    ISBN 0-385-73162-0 (trade) — ISBN 0-385-90200-X (glb)
    [1. Identity—Fiction. 2. Interpersonal relations—Fiction. 3. Competition (Psychology)—Fiction. 4. Friendship—Fiction. 5. Family life—California—Fiction. 6. High schools—Fiction. 7. Schools—Fiction. 8. California—Fiction.] I. Title.
    PZ7.R5433Qu 2005
    [Fic]—dc22
                                                    2004011107

Book design by Kenny Holcomb

Printed in the United States of America

August 2005

10 9 8 7 6 5 4 3 2 1

For Lindsay, Megan, Renee, and Chelsea,
my favorite teenage girls

And for Dick,
whose support and sense of humor
make writing for them possible

The Queen of Second Place

My Personal Philosophy of Talent
by Cassie Howard

I have this theory that everybody has a talent. Rich, poor, clueless—it doesn't matter. I honestly believe that every human being on earth is born with one special gift. The problem is, not all talents are created equal.

People think that talent means you sing, or dance, or act. But those are the glory talents, the ones that everyone wants, and for every diva out there, about a million other people are walking around with one of the lesser talents, the kind that <u>don't</u> get their own videos.

This guy I know, Fitz, his talent is always choosing the longest line—not the one that looks the longest, the one that takes the longest. There can be twenty people in one line and two in the other, and if Fitz gets in the two-person line, that's all it's going to take. Say he's at the store—the cash register will break. When they finally get it running again, the person first in line will want to use about five hundred coupons. Then the next guy will try to write a check with no ID and the cashier will call the manager but no one will be able to find him because he's on a break and . . . you get the idea. Fitz's is definitely not the kind of talent you'd love to have, but maybe it will come in handy if he ever has to choose a line for something bad. Like a firing squad.

This other guy I know—actually, we used to kind of go out, but that's another story—his talent is finding parking. There's no place too popular, no lot too crowded. Quentin parks in front at school, at the beach, at the movies. If the hottest band in the country were playing a free concert somewhere with only a hundred spaces, Quentin would get there ten minutes before the group went on and still get a place right in front. His theory is that other people don't believe there will be a good space left, so they don't look. Mine is that parking is that guy's gift.

Which brings us to me, I guess. I have a talent too, and it's definitely <u>not</u> of the glory variety. My talent is coming in second.

I am the Queen of Second Place, the poster child for close-but-not-close-enough. And I'm not saying that to make you feel sorry for me—although, you know . . . feel free, if it helps. I swear it's completely true.

I have a drawer full of second-place ribbons—for the science fair, for youth soccer, for a three-legged race I entered at camp. And unfortunately, my deal doesn't end with contests. I take second place in <u>everything,</u> in every little aspect of life.

In eighth grade I had hair past my waist—so long I

could practically sit on it. It would have been the longest hair in school, except that Amber Brooks <u>could</u> sit on hers. So last year I cut it, and I mean really cut it. The stylist only left these spiky little tufts. The first day I went to school like that, Kirsten Kirk came in with a buzz cut. You could see the girl's scalp. And in case you don't think hair's such a good example, believe me, I've got others. It's just that some of them get pretty personal, and anyway the bell is going to ring . . . right . . . now!

Welcome to My Nightmare

Hayley was waiting for me when I got out of detention. I had writer's cramp from my middle finger to my elbow and I'd been concentrating so hard I felt like I'd been breathing underwater, but I still couldn't wait to tell her what I'd been up to.

"Get this!" I said. "I had to write an essay about talent!"

"You're kidding me." Hayley shook her head, her scores of tight bouncy ringlets barely brushing her shoulders. We were both going through kind of a tufty thing last year—the difference is, her hair looks good now. "You didn't give Conway the theory?"

"Of course. What else?"

Hayley knows the theory. In fact, she's intimately familiar with it, since she's been my best friend, like, forever. And in case you're wondering, Hayley's talent is whistling.

Again, not in the glory category, but I've at least *seen* whistling in videos. Luckily for Hayley, she's so smart she'll never have to rely on talent. The girl gets solid A's. I get mostly—you guessed it—B's.

"That ought to be good for another ten weeks of detention," she said.

"What? Oh! I didn't tell Conway *her* talent. I may be dumb, but I'm not stupid."

"You're not dumb, either," Hayley told me loyally.

You can see why I love her, but getting detention was pretty dumb. Even if it wasn't my fault. Exactly. Even if the forces that conspired against me were so far beyond my control that I was practically their sock puppet. Even if it ought to be someone else sitting in that absurdly hard chair every afternoon writing Conway's essays instead of me.

Because I have excuses, believe me. I could make any sane person—which obviously excludes Conway—see my side in less than five minutes.

You know, now that I'm thinking about it, I'm *not* dumb for getting detention.

I'm dumb because I'd do it again.

Oops. Backing Up Now.

You know what I just realized? You don't have the first clue what I'm talking about. I mean, hopefully you've deduced that Hayley is the perfect friend while Mrs. Conway takes all the fun out of being a sophomore, but you still don't know what *happened*. You can't begin to comprehend how the fabric of my previously ordinary life has unraveled to the point that I'm dodging around school wearing sunglasses and a ski cap, counting the days until graduation lets me sink into oblivion. Unfortunately, there are seven months, a summer, and two whole school years left before that happens.

But I digress. I still haven't even mentioned Fourteen-Karat Carter. Probably because even thinking about that phony, scheming soc makes me want to hurl. If there were any way to leave her out of this story, you'd better believe I'd take it. Seriously, I'd *pay* to take it. Maybe it's true that we don't always get to pick our friends, but we never pick our enemies. They just kind of find us somehow.

Fourteen-Karat Carter found me in the lunch line the fall of our freshman year.

"Geez la-weez," she announced from behind me, in the loudest possible voice. "They ought to make people get a license before they sell them Sun-In."

My hair was still long then, and the sad truth is I *had* gotten carried away with Sun-In over the summer. Anyone with truly red hair should be automatically forgiven for anything they do to it anyway, but the roots I had going by October were seriously noticeable. The strawberry blond I'd been trying for had come out brassy orange, and my new growth looked almost brown in comparison. My mom wouldn't take me to a salon to have it fixed because she'd told me not to mess with my hair in the first place, and being a lawyer and all, she's big on crime and punishment. My friends said it didn't look that bad.

Fourteen-Karat Carter said, "You take carrottop a whole new place."

Then she tossed her perfect blond mane, rolled her blue eyes, and cut right in front of me, her short, preppy skirt twitching across her perfect behind. I just stood there with my mouth hanging open, completely without a comeback. I didn't even know who she was yet, but that was the moment I knew I hated her and that I'd hate her the rest of my life.

"Who *is* that?" I whispered to Hayley. "And how can we kill her with no one finding out?"

"Sterling Carter," Hayley whispered back. "She's in my Spanish One class, and so far all the guys have learned to say is *sí, señorita* and *muy caliente*."

"You're telling me someone would miss her, then."

"Afraid so."

I just stood there, grinding a clog into that rock-hard cafeteria linoleum and staring daggers at the back of Miss Perfect's Izod shirt. By then she had walked too far off to hear us, but she cast one last condescending look my way, tossing her hair as if the guy behind the cash register were filming a shampoo commercial.

"Sterling!" I spat. "What kind of name is that, anyway?"

Hayley shrugged. "You have to admit it fits her."

Which, being true, irked me even more. I mean, what kind of person gets named for a precious metal and actually carries it off?

"More like Fourteen-Karat," I grumbled. "At least, that's what *she* thinks."

"Oh, she thinks she's *all* of fourteen," Hayley agreed, laughing. "Just ignore her. The girl's a soc."

Which was practically a compliment compared to the things we call her now. Fourteen-Karat Carter is the most obnoxious, scheming uberwitch in the history of Hilltop High School. If Mrs. Conway weren't currently hogging all my free time, I'd send the girl's picture to Webster's, in case they need an illustration for *psychopath* in their next edition. Or, for that matter, one for *soc*.

Maybe you don't have socs at your school—which is to say you probably do but you might call them something else. Snobs, preps, enormous pains in the butt . . . a soc (pronounced *sōsh*) is all those things and more. The word is short for *social*, as in *socially* elite and not afraid to let you know it. As in diamond-dripping debutante and future *socialite*. As in cross her and she'll ruin your social life for the next four years. Are you with me now? You do have socs, right?

Anyway, that's the story on Fourteen-Karat and all the good and legitimate reasons I hate her. Or actually, I've barely scratched the surface, but you get the idea. The thing is, I have to hurry home now, before my mom finds out I'm not there yet and the proverbial brown stuff hits the fan.

Okay. New Plan.

This whole in medias res approach might have worked for the Greek poets, but it's confusing the heck out of me. Not that it can be helped, since you showed up right in the middle of things. It's just that I can't remember what you already know and what I haven't told you yet. I'm pretty sure I haven't even *mentioned* Kevin, and he's the most important part of this entire story.

You know what? I'm going to skip right to him—to when I first saw him, I mean—because even though I could fill a book with all the ways I loathe Fourteen-Karat (not to mention all the stuck-up, petty things she did while we were freshmen), things didn't get really ugly between us until this year, until Kevin Matthews transferred to Hilltop High and stepped into Mrs. Conway's otherwise relentlessly heinous sophomore honors English class.

Okay, you know what again? I'm going to cover that momentous day in really complete detail, but before we move on, you deserve at least five good reasons why Fourteen-Karat Carter shouldn't be popular, believed, or even tolerated:

1. Because never, not once in her entire life, has she ever had a zit, stubbly legs, or a close encounter with Sun-In.
2. Because being better-looking than I am does *not*

give her the right to move in on a guy I so clearly claimed first.

3. Because Jeannie Patrick said that F.K. called me pushy, desperate, and completely without shame. Which is a joke, because everyone knows how Carter gets *her* boyfriends. Four already this year. If I were counting.

4. Worse, Hayley heard F.K. tell Quentin she pitied him for ever being seen with me and that he ought to aim higher next time if he doesn't want the whole school to think he's a loser. Who's desperate now? It's so obvious what she's up to. Not that I care. But still. Poor Quentin's so clueless he didn't even realize he was only her backup plan.

5. Are we up to #5 already? Because I could go longer, believe me. All right, then: I happen to know for a fact that F.K. cuts the tags out of her clothes so no one will find out she's not really the size four she claims.

Whew! I feel better. Now back to Kevin.

In the Beginning . . .

Tuesday, October 14, 9:16 a.m.

I'm not normally an obsessive person—not *very* obsessive, anyway—but I'm positive that's the exact day and time I first laid eyes on Kevin Matthews. I know this because I wrote it on the cover of my blue notebook and it's been there ever since. It's almost as if I guessed how important this moment would turn out to be, as if my entire future flashed in front of my grammar-glazed eyes.

Anyway, the classroom door flew open and Kevin walked in a few paces behind Principal Ito, who went straight up to Conway and started whispering with this intense look on his face. The thing is, Ito always looks like the world is counting down to nuclear war. No one pays attention anymore. Besides, suddenly there was something much better to pay attention to.

"Oh. My. God," Cyn Martin whispered, leaning across the aisle between her desk and mine. "Is it hot in here, or is it him?"

"Shhh!" I whispered back. "You're talking about the man I'm going to marry."

We both laughed, clapping hands over our mouths when Conway broke off her summit with Ito long enough to shoot us a dirty look.

But even though I was laughing, I was completely serious. I mean, not about marrying him. Probably. But I knew. Somehow I just *knew* that Kevin was the guy I'd been waiting for, the one who was going to make everything right. If he wasn't, why did my heart leap around in my chest until my blood felt carbonated? I could tell my cheeks were purple, too—another special bonus of being born redheaded. When Hayley blushes, her brown skin glows like she's wearing makeup. I blush so hard I turn splotchy. Life is not fair. Which is kind of my point, but I'm getting off track again.

Anyway, Conway and Ito were yakking on, and Kevin was just standing there, looking like he wished he were anyplace else—which is pretty standard in Conway's class. He kept shifting his weight from one scuffed Adidas to the other, his hands stuffed so far into his pockets that the hem of his blue T-shirt hovered an inch above the waistband of his jeans. And not that I was staring (much), but his abs were incredibly tan—something we appreciate here in California—and a line of curly brown hair ran straight down from his navel. The hair on his head was brown too, which I probably should have mentioned first, and all spiked through with the kind of highlights that suggest a long, close acquaintance with salt water.

What else? Straight brows, high cheekbones, chiseled jaw, and a completely perfect nose. I couldn't see his eyes then, but I can tell you now they're green. Sea green. Picture Michelle Pfeiffer as a totally hot teenage guy.

Unless that seems weird. In which case, don't.

Eventually Principal Ito left and Conway turned to address us: "Class, this is Kevin Matthews. He just transferred here from Orange County and I hope you'll make him feel welcome."

A little more detail would definitely have been appreciated. For instance, *where* in Orange County? People act like that place is a dot on the map, but it's the size of a small country. Why did Kevin's family move? What did he think of Hilltop? And, most importantly, did he have a girlfriend back home?

But that was all we were getting. Her introduction complete, Conway pointed Kevin toward two adjacent vacant desks at the back of the room. He started walking, dragging his feet like he already suspected the horrors her class had in store. For me, on the other hand, sophomore honors English had suddenly developed the potential to become a truly rewarding learning experience.

I'll make him feel welcome, I thought, cranking up my smile as he walked past. *I'll make him feel* very *welcome*.

(Love at First Sight)²

I could barely wait to find Hayley at lunchtime and tell her that I was in love. Truly, deeply in love. And in case you don't think it's possible to meet a guy at 9:16 and be so head over heels you're in pain by 11:50, just wait. It'll probably happen to you someday.

Not that I'd technically *met* Kevin yet, but if I'd moved my knee I could have bumped it into his when he walked past my desk. You have to admit that simply smiling at him was a lot more mature. I should probably confess that I might also have tossed my hair, but that was a reflex or something. He noticed me, too, because he smiled back.

Did I mention? Perfect teeth.

Anyway, somehow I survived third-period algebra and the massive yawn known as Western civ, and the minute the lunch bell rang I ran off to find Hayley.

She was waiting at our new favorite place on the edge of the quad. Now that we're sophomores, we never eat in the cafeteria unless it's raining. Anyone who's remotely cool either brings a lunch or goes off campus. The school board actually figured this out, so in order to keep the lunch ladies busy, they built two grab-and-go kiosks outside in the quad to sell the school's version of fast food. We usually buy diet sodas there, and sometimes pizza or these killer fresh-baked cookies.

I ran up and yanked Hayley's arm so hard I practically pulled her over. "You aren't going to believe this!" I cried.

"If this is about you marrying Kevin Matthews, I already know the whole story," she said with a smug little grin.

My jaw dropped. Hayley's a good friend, but she's not clairvoyant. I mean, not as far as I know.

"How . . . how . . . ?"

"Cyn Martin's in my fourth-period Spanish class, remember? She went on about the guy for fifteen minutes. In Spanish." Hayley's eyes got a faraway look. "Which was kind of impressive, I have to admit."

"In front of the whole class?"

"Señora Gomez is so desperate to get us to speak in whole sentences now, she doesn't much care what the topic is. She made the mistake of asking Fourteen-Karat who the most handsome celebrity is and F.K. said Brad Pitt. So then Cyn broke in and said this guy who showed up in her English class this morning could be Brad's younger brother. Fourteen-Karat said *mucha duda* and they got into this whole feature-by-feature comparison thing. He sounds pretty cute. Kevin does, I mean."

"In front of the whole class?" My voice had gone up an octave, but that's what happens when I can't breathe.

"Geez, calm down—you're turning purple, Cass. We had discussion groups today. It was just me, Cyn, Fourteen-Karat, and Ellie Marx."

My heart started beating again, but I still wasn't positive I wanted it to.

"I was only kidding about marrying him," I said.

"I know that. Why are you getting so—" Understanding dawned in Hayley's brown eyes. "Oh! You think Cyn told *everyone* about you lusting after Kevin? Relax. She only told that part to me."

"It's not lust," I protested, but that was just a reflex. I was so relieved I didn't care what she called it.

"No, I'm sure it's the purest love," Hayley teased. "It must be, if you're planning to marry the guy."

"Well, first I'll date him. Then we'll have a long engagement while he saves up for a big rock from Tiffany's."

We both laughed, but the weird part was that I sounded confident. Which was ridiculous, because when it comes to my record with guys, there was absolutely no reason to think this time would be any different.

You know what the Queen of Second Place gets when it comes to boyfriends?

I'll give you a hint: *Boy+friend*. Which part comes second?

Remember Quentin, that guy I mentioned before? We dated freshman year. Okay, "dated" might be overstating things. We hung out. A *lot*. Sometimes at night. At the movies. Or over pizza. I had his phone number memorized, his name doodled all over the inside of my notebooks, and his picture hidden under the books in my locker, just waiting to be taped up inside the door the moment we made it official.

Then one night we're at a basketball game against Simi

Valley and practically the whole school is in our gym. I'm thinking we're really putting ourselves out there for everyone to see and this time he's for sure going to kiss me when we say good night. Finally our team wins and everyone is screaming and hugging each other, celebrating the victory. Quentin wraps his arms around me, and do you know what he says?

"It's so much fun doing stuff with you. I never thought I'd have such a good girl friend."

You heard me: Girl. Friend.

So of course I said what a great boy friend he was. And the next day I dug his picture out of my locker and ripped it into confetti. Which made me feel better for about two seconds, and then I felt even worse.

It's okay now, though. I'm pretty much over him. And Will Malone from eighth grade. And Jeffrey Avila from sixth. Hayley and I don't even *mention* my humiliating crush of last summer, so I'm sure not going to spell it out for you. Let's just say that when He Who Shall Remain Nameless moved to Florida this fall, it was the biggest relief of my life. I mean, now I probably made it sound sexual or something, which is so far from what happened it's ridiculous. Forget about second place—the queen didn't get to second *base* on that one.

Anyway, there I was in the quad with Hayley, sounding inexplicably confident, and who do you suppose walked right in front of us on his way into the cafeteria? Kevin—who can totally be forgiven for eating in the caf because a guy can't be expected to figure out everything on his first day.

15

"There he is! There!" I whispered to Hayley, trying to point with one pinky. "He's wearing a blue T-shirt."

Hayley's brows leapt when her eyes found him, suggesting that up until then she hadn't completely bought the whole Brad-Pitt's-brother thing.

"Wow. What's *his* talent?" she asked.

I smiled. "Still under scrutiny. I suspect that it's being ridiculously photogenic."

"That's a talent?"

"Models think so."

"Yeah, why do models get so much credit for looking good, anyway?" she asked. "It's not like they did anything to deserve it—it's simply an accident of birth."

Hayley *says* she understands the theory, but sometimes I have to wonder.

"That's what talent is," I said as Kevin disappeared. "In fact, that's kind of its definition. Come on, let's eat in the cafeteria."

"In the cafeteria? You *are* in love," she said, shaking her head. "Not to rain on your parade, but what do you actually know about this guy? Besides how his jeans fit, I mean."

And that's when I made my first big mistake.

"I know he's going to take me to the Snow Ball," I said, naming our school's annual winter formal.

"In your dreams!" the world's most obnoxious, sociest voice said behind me. "Like *he'd* ever go out with *you*!"

I turned to find myself face to face with Fourteen-Karat. I hadn't even heard her walk up.

"Why don't you mind your own business?" I said. As you

can see, my retorts remain sterling when it comes to F.K. "I suppose you think he'll take *you*."

My second mistake, and this one was huge. The moment those words came out of my mouth, I knew just how big I'd messed up. It was as if Fourteen-Karat and I were musketeers and I'd just whacked her across the chops with my glove.

F.K. sucked in her breath. Her eyes went all squinty. And then this really creepy smile curled the corners of her mouth.

"Yes," she said. "That's exactly what I think."

Can You Believe Her?

I spent the rest of lunch and all fifth period obsessing about my encounter with Fourteen-Karat. I mean, it's not like I seek the girl out. She just attaches herself to me. Like a remora. Or one of those burrs you get stuck in your socks. No, worse—she's like when you sneak out of the movie to use the bathroom only you've got a half-chewed black Jujyfruit stuck to your shoe and you end up dragging a big old streamer of toilet paper right back out through the lobby. *That's* what Sterling Carter is—toilet paper on the shoe of my life.

Let me just assure you I have no idea why she singled me out. By now you're probably thinking I must have done *something* to make her hate me, but that's simply not the case. Like I said before, it started with my hair and just never stopped. The girl tormented me every chance she got all through freshman year.

"The thrift shop must *love* you," she said one night, in front of about a million people packing our bleachers for a football game. "You keep that place in business single-handed."

Her best friend, Rosalind Pierce, almost killed herself laughing, the way she always does. If that girl ever had an original thought, time would stop and the earth would spin backward on its axis. It's a mystery to me what Fourteen-Karat sees in her, but I suspect it has to do with the fact that the Pierces are loaded. Everyone F.K. associates with is like that—beautiful, rich, or extremely popular in some other obvious way, like Tamara Owens, the cheerleading captain. F.K.'s group is the pinnacle of the elite, and they never let anyone forget it.

Not that I care. Much. I mean, my friends are all pretty cool, with the added bonus that there's still oxygen in the atmosphere at our social level. I could totally ignore Fourteen-Karat's clique if she would only let me. But a few weeks after the football incident she passed me in the quad and shouted, "Hey, Cassie! Elvis called—he wants his shirt back."

I admit it, all right? I love retro and long skirts and anything with frilly cuffs. So sue me. Why should Fourteen-Karat care? Honestly, if it were some other girl picking on me, I might think she was jealous. Why else go to so much trouble just to bring me down? But if you spent even one day at my high school, you'd know how ridiculous that is. Fourteen-Karat Carter is an undisputed social *queen*.

We all know what I'm the queen of.

So if I was going to convince Kevin to ask me to the formal instead of her, I'd need the best plan of my life. To have any chance against Fourteen-Karat, I'd have to pull out all the stops.

Hayley and I strategized during PE, which we both take sixth period to avoid the whole showering-and-dressing-for-school-twice thing.

"I'd love to know what her deal is," I said as we trotted out to the courts with our tennis racquets. Ms. Yamamoto is very big on having everyone dressed and outside on time; after that we can pretty much stand around looking athletic. "If that girl *has* a talent, I swear it's ruining my life."

"I thought ruining your life was Trevor's special gift," Hayley said.

Trevor is my younger brother. Don't get me started.

"Yes, it's amazing how many people share that skill," I said impatiently. "The question is, what am I going to do about it? How am I going to get Kevin to like me?"

Hayley fooled around, twirling her racquet on top of her tennis shoe. Finally she looked up. "You're doing it again."

"Doing what?"

"That thing you do. It's pathological."

In the first place, I didn't know what she was talking about. In the second, *pathological* isn't something you want to be called by your best friend.

"Spell it out for me," I said.

"Technically, you haven't even met this guy, and you're already turning it into a whole big deal."

"Who said I want to get technical?"

"That's my point: you never do. And you wind up getting hurt."

"Hayley! This is different!" For some reason, I needed her to believe me. "*Kevin's* different."

"How do you know?"

"I just do. Besides, there are other factors now."

"Like the way you're going to feel if Kevin takes Fourteen-Karat to the dance?"

I told you Hayley was smart.

"It's just . . . I saw him first! And Sterling Carter has everything. She'll probably already be elected Snow Queen, so why should she get Kevin too? I put up with her crap all last year, but this time she's gone too far."

Which, now that I'm looking back, might give you the wrong idea, so let's just be clear on one thing: this wasn't about the dance. It was *never* about the dance. Going to that formal simply popped out of my mouth. If F.K. hadn't been eavesdropping, I'd have forgotten it ten minutes later. Probably.

But now Fourteen-Karat had me. If Kevin didn't ask me to the formal, I was going to look like the world's biggest loser. Worse, if he asked her, I was going to *be* the world's biggest loser. I'm pretty much used to coming in second, but coming in second to Sterling Carter is more than any human being should be asked to bear.

I promised myself by the end of PE that I wouldn't let that happen.

A girl has to draw the line somewhere.

Meanwhile, Back at the Ranch House . . .

When I got home that afternoon, I was bent on a total makeover. The problem is, when your hair's already short, there are only so many things you can do with it. I thought about extensions, but only for a second. Where I live, that kind of thing's not really cool. Everything's supposed to look natural. Don't get me wrong, it doesn't have to *be* natural, but it shouldn't stick out like a big neon sign flashing FAKE, FAKE, FAKE.

At least it's growing out, I thought, dropping my backpack on the entryway floor and checking my still-short do in the big beveled mirror over the bench.

A couple of weeks after I met Fourteen-Karat, I had my hair completely whacked off. The roots from that summer's disaster were an inch or two long, and even though my hair was all the way down my back, I couldn't deal with that brassy bleach job anymore. I told the stylist to cut it off, but make it cute.

She only heard the first part.

I was hoping for pixie-punk. What I ended up with gave F.K. a field day.

"Hey! GI Carrottop!" she taunted me. "When does boot camp start?"

I wish I could say she was wrong, but when that stylist

got done wrecking me, there were places my hair stood straight up. The top part still only reaches my ears.

Maybe I could wear clips now, I thought, trying to twist a section near the front into something interesting. I was beginning to make progress when Trevor strolled out from the kitchen and stopped to bother me.

"Ah, but you are bee-*you*-tee-ful," he said, with a bad Pepé Le Pew accent and this really annoying sneer. "*Mon Dieu!* You must want to kiss yourself all over."

Trev's in eighth grade now, so he thinks he's a god. I can hardly wait until he starts high school and finds out just how ungodlike freshman boys are. I'd be looking forward to it more, though, if we weren't going to be at the *same* high school—that's just too heinous to dwell on. My only consolation is we're two grades apart, so even though technically we'll be in the same place, it'll be like living on different planets.

Nothing new there.

"Don't you have an important video game in progress?" I asked, dropping my hair like I hadn't really been looking. He had a pizza bagel in one hand and a splat of sauce on his T-shirt, like the utter slob he is. "Doesn't that fantasy world of yours collapse when you're not there to play with yourself?"

"Funny, Cassie."

Trevor *hates* it when I joke about him playing with himself. Which is why I do it, of course. The thing is, it's just so easy to make fun of something so pathetic. Trev's juvenile obsession with video games, I mean. Not . . . eew.

"Don't dish it out if you can't take it," I said.

He stood there a few more seconds, groping for something to say. His jaw worked up and down, giving me ample time to notice the sheen of pizza grease on his chin.

"Your hair still looks stupid," he said. Then he stomped off to his room.

Ouch.

Sometimes I might not give him enough credit.

The big baby was still sulking later that night when Mom and Dad got home from work. He made this whole issue out of not looking at me when we all sat down to dinner. Like that's some sort of punishment. Mom didn't notice. She was too busy passing around Chinese takeout and complaining about her new secretary at the law firm. Dad probably *did* notice, but the chance of him mentioning anything that might turn into an argument is somewhere between zero and none.

You see, my mother's talent is arguing. There's absolutely no doubt on this point. Mom is ready to argue any subject, with anyone, at any time—which makes her so good at her job it's scary. My dad's talent? Avoiding conflict. He's an absolute genius at it.

What you need to understand is, avoiding conflict is not the same thing as making peace. You could send my dad to Ireland and he'd know exactly what to say to get the Catholics and Protestants all drinking in the same pub, playing darts, and having a great time. It wouldn't be until ten minutes after he left that everyone suddenly realized they hadn't solved a single thing and, in fact, they were still pretty mad at each other. If you ask me, avoiding conflict is one of those talents that's only a gift to the person who has it.

On the other hand, it probably has a lot to do with how long he's stayed with Mom.

"Anton is the third secretary I've had this year!" Mom griped, skewering a chunk of sweet-and-sour pork with her chop stick. "Don't universities have standards anymore? Do they simply pass out diplomas to whoever pays tuition?"

"Mmm," Dad said, nodding sagely.

"I mean, I'm not unreasonable, am I?" Mom asked.

The way my eyebrows jumped, it's a good thing she wasn't looking at me.

"You? Never," Dad said. "This kung pao is incredible, honey. Where did you get it?"

"That new place over on Laurel. You like it?"

"Delicious. How do you always know exactly what I want?"

I know what you're thinking. Blatant, right? But somehow my dad can say stuff like that without sounding like he's kissing up. Mom was so pleased she actually forgot about her secretary for the rest of dinner, which was a welcome break, believe me.

Later, when I was throwing away the take-out cartons and loading the dishwasher, Mom wandered into the kitchen and put some water on to boil.

"How was school today?" she asked.

Can somebody please tell me why parents bother with that question? What are we supposed to say? "Well, since you asked, it's numbing my brain, stunting my soul, and I've been counting the days to graduation since I was nine years old." I mean, they went to school once too. Don't they already *know* that?

"Fine," I said.

"How is that nice Ms. Conway?" Mom asked.

Nice? Obviously I could only stare with my mouth hanging open.

"What?" Mom said.

"Well, first of all, I dare you to call her Ms. Conway to her face. It's *Mrs*. Conway, and pity the fool who forgets it."

Mom poured hot water into a mug and dunked a tea bag up and down. "Interesting."

"Yeah, sure. Conway is all kinds of interesting. Except when she's talking, of course."

"You just don't like her because she makes you work. Your other teachers are too easy on you."

"Right. That's it," I said, real sarcastic, which is a good way to save face when someone forces you into a compromising admission. "The fact that she's the crankiest woman on the face of the earth has nothing to do with it."

"What do you mean, cranky?"

"She's into these major mood swings. Some days she starts out all right. We'll maybe have a discussion about the reading or something, and for five or ten minutes, class will be almost bearable. Then someone says the wrong thing and *bam!* The next thing we know, we're writing these excruciatingly detailed essays on the difference between metaphor and simile. It's like it comes out of nowhere."

Mom nodded in rhythm with her tea bag. "Interesting," she said again.

I closed the dishwasher. "Yeah. We're all on the edges of our seats."

And then, I don't know why, I blurted out the last thing I intended to say. "One good thing happened today, though. This cute guy named Kevin transferred in from Orange County."

She just stood there, staring. And the worst part was, I knew why: I could totally feel myself blushing.

"He *must* be cute," Mom said at last. "Does this Kevin have a last name?"

"Matthews," I spat out immediately. I could at least have *pretended* to think about it.

Mom took a sip of her tea, then gave me this funny smile. "So are you going to learn from your past, or just jump in like you always do?"

"I don't know what you're talking about."

"Really? How about Will Malone? Jeffrey Avila? And what was the name of that lifeguard over the sum—"

"All *right*, Mom."

Like I said, scary good at argument.

"All I'm saying is, consider getting to know the guy this time. *Before* you fall in love."

"Who said I'm in love? I never said that."

"No? I'm glad to hear it, because love at first sight is the biggest myth there is. Well, that and the existence of soul mates. I don't know which one makes me laugh harder."

"You don't believe in soul mates?" Love at first sight is something you either believe in or you don't—like ghosts— but I thought everyone believed in soul mates. "What about you and Dad?"

My mother laughed. "Your dad and I are a good match. We have most of the same values. Aspects of our personalities mesh well. If you want to call that soul mates, fine. But that's not what people mean. The myth is that there's this one perfect person out there, and if you can only find him he'll make everything easy. Perfect. Right. And not just in love but in your whole life. *That's* the part that cracks me up. It doesn't work that way."

"How does it work?" I probably should have dropped it, but she had me kind of fascinated.

"It's up to you to fix your own life, and the sooner you let go of 'perfect,' the better off you'll be. Marriage is work. *Love* is work."

"Wow. You make it sound so thrilling."

Mom smiled again. "I didn't say it wasn't, I only said it wasn't easy. When you meet the right man, it's worth it."

"You just said there *is* no right man."

"No, I said there's no such thing as soul mates. Your best bet is to find a nice guy, get to really know him, and then decide if he's someone you want to fall in love with."

She made a good case—she always does. But do people ever *decide* to fall in love? Besides, I couldn't say this to her, but sometimes I look at her and Dad and wonder if there's any passion there. Not that I generally like to think of my parents and passion in the same sentence. In fact, my gag reflex is pretty much working overtime right now.

That's what I get for trying to have a personal conversation with my mother.

Detention Essay #8
Mrs. Conway

What People Should Know About Me
by Cassie Howard

People should know that I'm basically a nice person. Maybe it doesn't seem that way, considering everything that happened, but I am.

I hardly ever get in trouble. I mean, yes, I'm grounded and in detention right now, but this is the first time that's happened. Well, it's my first stint in detention. Besides, let's face it: you and I both know people at this school who get up to much worse things than I did. I've never been arrested, for example. I'm not violent. I would never <u>intentionally</u> steal anything. I've never even been caught smoking in the bathroom. Of course, smoking is so stupid I wouldn't be caught doing it anywhere. But still.

I like animals. And little kids, most of the time. I would never pick on someone smaller than I am, or on someone bigger who didn't really deserve it.

I'm usually honest, and that's the truth. If you don't

want to know what I think, then don't ask my opinion. I can sugarcoat a little, if it's going to spare hurt feelings, but I don't like beating around the bush and I hate it when people do that to me. Life's too short, you know? Just spit it out and let's move on.

I'm a good friend. Once I decide I like someone, I'm totally, completely loyal. My best friend, Hayley Johnson, and I have been together since fourth grade. Sometimes I think about what my life would be like without her and I literally shudder.

I have good intentions. It's not like I messed up on purpose. Obviously it would be better if things had gone the way I planned, but nobody's perfect. (Except for a certain nauseating soc who's the reason I'm here in the first place.) My mother says the road to hell is paved with good intentions, and I'm sitting here, so she must be on to something, but I have no clue why that's the case. Good intentions ought to equal good results, don't you think? It would certainly make life easier.

In conclusion, people should know I'm not that bad. If they gave me a chance, they would probably like me. Or at least not hate me.

P.S.—Dear Mrs. Conway: I realize the title you gave me was "What People <u>Don't</u> Know About Me," but I obviously had to change it. You couldn't seriously have expected me to spill anything personal in a mandatory essay?

P.P.S.—Can I get a copy of this for my parents?

Operation Soul Mate

I gave some thought to what my mom said, but in the end I decided to ignore her. For one thing, being a great arguer is not the same as always being right. Besides, if love doesn't change everything, a whole lot of songs are wrong. Not to mention movies, books, and practically every show on TV. I still believe in soul mates, and I *definitely* still believe in love at first sight.

I ought to. I have enough practice.

It's just that so far it hasn't been mutual.

Maybe I aim too high. The sad truth is, I'm far from the best-looking girl at school. Strictly B league—maybe B-plus when everything's really working (which isn't nearly as often as things start sliding toward C). Unfortunately, I tend to fall for A-plus guys.

In any event, I was painfully aware that there was no good reason to believe a guy like Kevin Matthews would be interested in me. No good reason except that I wanted him to be. Needed him to be. I don't know why—that's just how it was. So when I went back to school the next day, getting Kevin to like me was the only thing on my mind.

That and getting Conway to change my seat.

"Mrs. Conway?" I called, waving my arm in the air after roll call. "Can I move to that empty desk in back? This chair is broken or something."

"What's wrong with it?" she asked suspiciously.

"Something's loose." The classrooms at my school all have those individual desk-and-chair combo units. I rocked mine back and forth to demonstrate the problem.

"You mean that same wobbly leg you've been entertaining yourself with all month?" Conway said. "Suddenly it bothers you?"

"No, it just . . . I don't think . . ."

I swear that woman notices *everything*.

"If you're tired of rocking yourself to sleep during class, I suggest you fold up a sheet of paper and stick it under the leg on that side."

A couple of people snickered.

"But—"

"I believe we were completing the exercises on page ninety-three," she said, holding up her copy of *Modern English Grammar*. Everyone started flipping through their books, knowing better than to wait for her to ask twice.

Round one: Conway.

I'll admit it was embarrassing. But since I was positive no one had guessed the real reason I'd asked to move, and since Kevin actually smiled at me in the hallway after class, I was over it by lunchtime. I couldn't wait to fill Hayley in, but when I found her outside in the quad she was talking to Quentin and Fitz.

"There you are!" she said. "We're going to get in line for pizza, but we were waiting for you."

"Oh. Okay." Those guys eat with us sometimes. "Which line is shorter, Fitz?"

"Are you yanking me?" he whined, letting his head loll back on his neck. "Why do you make me do this?"

"Just choose one," Quentin told him. "Come on."

Fitz considered the lines at both of the open-air kiosks and finally pointed to one.

"What do you want?" Quentin asked him.

Fitz gave Quentin his lunch order and some money, then went to stand in the "short" line. The rest of us walked across the quad and got in the other one.

"Poor Fitz. I don't understand why he has to stand over there by himself," Hayley said, as we breezed through the "long" line at hyperspeed. "Why can't we just let him choose the bad line and then get in the good one with us?"

"Because simply by *being* in the good line he would make it the bad line," I explained, grabbing a Diet Coke. "As long as he stays over there, this continues to be the good line and we all get to eat a lot faster."

In fact, Quentin was already balancing two giant slices of pizza and looking for an empty pocket to stash napkins in. Hayley and I helped by picking up his change and carrying an extra soda each. Loaded down with lunch, we walked back across the quad to Fitz, whose line had moved maybe five feet. When we arrived, the cash register was spewing an uncoiled receipt tape all the way down to the concrete.

"Good job," said Quentin, handing over Fitz's pizza. "Cassie's right, man—you have a gift."

"My parents will be so proud," Fitz said sarcastically. He stepped out of line, and the broken register immediately chugged back to life.

"My folks are going away Halloween weekend," Quentin said when the four of us had found a bench and started eating. "I'm having a party and you're all invited. Be careful who you tell, though. I don't want the whole school showing up."

At our school, this is not an idle fear. Most big parties are open, which means if you're cool enough, and brave enough, you can show up wherever you want to. The way it really works, of course, is that the cool people only go to parties thrown by other cool people and the less cool people are afraid to go anywhere they aren't specifically invited. But every now and then, if a party falls on just the right night, and the host is popular enough to attract the cool people but not so high up the food chain as to scare off everyone else, *everybody* comes—including the police. Halloween was the only bright spot in a month of dead October evenings, and Quentin was exactly the type of guy this could actually happen to.

"Don't worry. My lips are sealed," I promised.

"Do your parents know about this?" Hayley asked.

Quentin's sly grin made it clear that Hayley had hit on a key element of his plan. "They said I could have some friends over that night. So long as everyone who comes to my party is a friend . . ."

"Got 'em on a technicality," Fitz said, taking another bite of pizza. "Gotta love that."

"What are you going to dress up as, Fitz?" Hayley asked.

"I'm not dressing up."

"Yes, you are," Quentin told him. "It's a *Halloween* party, dude."

"Great," Fitz said with a sigh. "That ought to help me with the girls."

"It will if you wear a mask," Quentin said, slapping Fitz on the back.

Poor Fitz is always putting up with cracks like that. He's a really great guy, but Quentin's by far the better-looking of the two. He never lets Fitz forget it either, which is not his most endearing trait.

"And if you wear a muzzle, Quentin, you guys'll be a couple of babe magnets," Hayley told him, smiling sweetly.

Fitz almost choked on his soda. He gave Hayley this very appreciative look, and I knew from personal experience exactly what he was thinking:

Who cares what Quentin says when you have a friend like Hayley?

Contact

After sixth period, I was headed for my locker when I jogged around a corner and almost ran right into Kevin. The main hallway had mostly cleared out by then. That was the good news. The bad news was that I'd just gotten out of PE, and—as I might have mentioned—I always take PE last period to avoid showering at school. At least I'd changed back into normal clothes.

"Kevin!" I said, backing up to a safe distance. "Hey! How's it going?"

Embarrassing? Yes. But even then I realized it was the best thing that could have happened. If I hadn't practically knocked him down it could have been weeks before I worked up the courage to talk to him.

"Hi, Cassie," he said.

I almost fainted. Kevin Matthews knew my name!

"You're here late," he added.

"I . . . um . . . homework! I nearly forgot all those sentences we're supposed to diagram for Conway."

Kevin shook his head, a bemused smile on his perfect lips. "What's her damage, anyway? Who diagrams sentences?"

"Yeah. I mean, I don't know. She's just . . . Conway. So far as I know, the other English teachers here are normal."

"And yet I got her. Lucky me."

No, I thought. *Lucky me*.

"Are you going to do them?" he asked.

"Do what?"

"Those sentences."

"Oh, yeah, you've *got* to do them. Geez. You do *not* want to show up in Conway's class without your homework."

His smile widened until my knees felt weak. I mean, maybe it was those two laps I pretended to jog around the track, but I don't think so. Have I mentioned his teeth?

"All right, Cassie," he said.

My heart stopped beating. "All right?"

"I guess I'll do them, then."

"Oh. Right. Good."

"See you tomorrow," he said, walking off.

I waited until he turned the corner before I slumped into the nearest locker.

Kevin Matthews had said my name. Twice!

Not only that, but he'd said he'd see me. I mean, obviously he'd see me, but he made it sound like he'd be looking. Hope flooded my heart. Kevin was exactly as nice as I thought he'd be, even cuter up close, and he'd actually noticed me.

Take *that*, Fourteen-Karat!

Round Two — The Second Round

I let a few days go by before I sprang my next move on Conway. My new plan relied heavily on timing, and I didn't want to mess it up by risking a premature launch. In the meantime, I lived for those brief, seemingly random encounters with Kevin. I say seemingly because I put a lot of effort into making them seem random. I learned where his locker was, scanned the quad incessantly during lunch, and courted both tardy slips and my algebra teacher's accompanying sarcasm by staking out the hallway after English. Twice I worked up the courage to say hi as Kevin walked past, but the day he spotted me first and nodded in my direction, I got so completely tongue-tied my "hi" came out more like "huuunuuh." He'd been in our class a whole week before I kicked off phase two of my Move-Cassie plan.

According to my calculations, I needed to get to English after Kevin arrived but before the tardy bell. This would give me the opportunity to drop into the empty desk next to his and pretend I wanted to compare homework. The key was to make the whole thing look impulsive, as if I'd just walked in, noticed him sitting there, and decided to ask him a question. The genius part, though—and the part that made me nervous just thinking about it—was that when Conway started the roll, I intended to stay where I was. She'd notice, of course—but would she care enough to stop class and move me back to my regular seat? I had a feeling maybe she wouldn't.

On Tuesday, I found out.

I sprinted out of first-period biology, getting to Conway's room so early that the only students in there were the ones still leaving from the previous class. I had to walk past the open door and lurk by the drinking fountain for ages before I let myself saunter back, praying the whole way. When I returned, Kevin had miraculously appeared in his seat and Mrs. Conway was nowhere in sight.

Heart in my throat, I began the long walk to Kevin's desk. His head was bent over something he was writing, and I was so completely nervous that all of a sudden I couldn't feel my feet. The last bit of aisle between us stretched out like a tunnel. . . .

And then Kevin looked up and smiled, and the next thing I knew I was sitting in the chair next to his. I don't even remember how I got there. It's possible I floated.

"Hey, Cassie," he said, still scribbling away. "What are you doing back here in the cheap seats?"

"Huh? Oh!" I dug through my backpack, pulled out a crumpled sheet of homework, and waved it like a backstage pass. "I was wondering what you got for the last one. Number ten. Wasn't it hard?"

"I'll let you know when I get there. Right now, I'm having some trouble with number four."

I looked at the paper in front of him. He wasn't even halfway through the assignment we were supposed to turn in at the bell. "You're doing your homework *now?*"

"These sentence trees are a waste of time. I could probably learn to do them, but why?"

Here's the truth, and it's not something I'm proud of, so let's keep it between us: thanks to Conway, I can diagram sentences in my sleep. I'll probably be eighty and drooling in my rocking chair and my grandchildren will be whispering about whether or not I've snuffed it, when all of a sudden I'll lean forward and blurt out, "Use dashed lines when connecting subordinate clauses!" or, "Put the modifiers *under* their objects!"

Which'll probably buy me a trip straight to the rest home.

"No. No, that's a dependent clause," I told Kevin, pointing. "You have to move that down. Here. Wait. No. Give me your pencil."

In under sixty seconds I'd gone from barely able to speak to him to completely bossing him around. "I can't believe you're starting this three minutes before the bell rings," I scolded, grabbing his paper and taking over.

"And yet you're going to finish with seconds to spare," he said, watching passively. "Oh, look. You've even solved that pesky number ten."

I froze, caught in the act. A blush burned up my cheeks. Had he guessed I'd been faking my ignorance?

"Well—I—uh—" I stammered just as the tardy bell rang and Conway barreled into the room.

"You're a pressure player," he said knowingly. "That's a gift, coming through under stress."

I managed a relieved smile. That *is* a gift—it's just not *my* gift.

Then Conway started the roll call and I had to focus on looking like I belonged where I was sitting. By the time she worked her way up to "Howard?" my throat had gone completely dry.

"Here!" I called back, trying for nonchalance. The thing is, you really need moist vocal cords to pull off nonchalance—I sounded like a cross between a foghorn and a squeaky hinge.

Conway peered at me over her roll book. "Is something wrong, Miss Howard? Do you have a cold?"

"No. All good here." *Pounding heart, purple cheeks, upper lip breaking into a sweat . . . Yep, Mrs. Conway, everything's one hundred percent normal in Cassieland.*

"Why are you sitting back there?"

A hush fell over the class as thirty-four students waited to hear my answer. Even Kevin looked interested.

"Well, I, uh," I faltered. "That is, Kevin and I . . . we were finishing—I mean *discussing*—the homework. And then the bell rang. So."

Mrs. Conway shook her head.

"And I hate that wiggly chair," I added, sounding totally weak.

Cyn Martin snickered, and she wasn't the only one. People around the room cast mocking looks my way.

"Fine," Mrs. Conway said in a very frosty tone. "I would ask you to move that desk to your old position, but I'm assigning partners for a collaborative project today. Since you and Kevin are such good *discussers*, you may as well stay where you are and work with him."

That nipped a few snickers in the bud, let me tell you. I was so shocked, I nearly fell out of my new chair.

"For the next three weeks," Mrs. Conway continued, addressing the class, "we will be writing one-act plays. You will each be assigned a writing partner, who will become your acting partner at the end of this unit, when you read your plays before the class."

Groans circled the room, completely destroying any residual interest in me.

"I expect you to work diligently on this assignment during all the class periods between now and then. If you'd like a passing grade, you should also plan to meet with your partner outside of class."

She picked up a sheet of paper and made some changes with her pencil, then started reading off partners, beginning with me and Kevin.

I could barely hide my excitement at hearing our names paired together. My plan had worked better than I'd ever dreamed! To make my joy less obvious, I gave Kevin this very sincere I'm-sorry-you're-stuck-with-me-if-that's-a-problem look, but he just smiled and shrugged it off.

Who says crime doesn't pay?

Two Days Later . . .

One-act plays.

What I know about one-act plays would fit in a tooth-paste cap with plenty of room left over. Obviously, however, I was hoping to keep that information from Kevin. In fact, since he didn't exactly ask to have me as a partner, I thought it best to wow him with my writing and acting talents.

Except those aren't my talents.

Nevertheless, I was completely determined to fake them.

So the very same Tuesday that Conway gave us our play assignment, I went to the library during lunch. I only stopped in the quad long enough to tell Hayley my big news and eat one of her cookies; then I was off to the library, brimming with good intentions. I had dragged down a couple of huge, dusty drama anthologies and was attempting to read them at a back table when a sudden giggle caught my ear.

Before I go on, you should know that our library isn't exactly crowded during lunchtime. I hate to admit this, considering how I've already said I was there, but cool people do not spend their lunchtimes in the library. If they do, they sure aren't giggling.

So of course I had to know what was funny, which meant I had to stand up and crane my neck around a row of bookshelves. To my complete and utter amazement, Kevin Matthews was slouched by himself at a corner table. And standing directly in front of him, her miniskirt level with his green eyes, was Fourteen-Karat Carter.

Giggling.

And tossing her silky hair.

And just generally making me want to kill her.

But the worst part was, Kevin was eating it up. I mean, he may be a perfect guy, but he's still a guy. If life has taught me anything, it's that the male ability to penetrate female phoniness is pathetically inadequate. They're all born genetically deficient when it comes to seeing through girls like Fourteen-Karat.

I crept a little closer, peeking out from between shelved books.

"I'm so glad I *met* you!" Fourteen-Karat said. (Hair toss. Giggle.) "It's so cool to run into someone from my hometown."

Huh?

I squinted to read the strained print on the T-shirt stretched over her ample chest: NEWPORT BEACH SURF SHOP.

"Yeah," said Kevin. "Cool."

"I'll bet you miss surfing the Wedge," she said.

"I've sponge-surfed there a few times. Otherwise . . ." He shrugged. "I don't like snapping boards that much."

"I know!" Fourteen-Karat's eyes were as round as if a board had just snapped right in front of her. "That place is so killer!"

"When's the last time you were in Newport?" he asked.

"My family drives through now and then, but I was just little when we lived there. I wouldn't know anyone now."

How convenient, I thought, clenching my teeth. I was pretty sure she was lying, but I didn't know how to prove it.

Or even how to bring it up without looking like an eaves-dropping dweeb.

Kevin nodded, just soaking her in.

"So, have you met a lot of people here?" Fourteen-Karat asked. "Is everyone pretty nice?"

"Not bad."

She leaned forward slightly, using her palms to ease her skirt lower on her tan thighs. The only effect this had was to call attention to how short it was in the first place. A quarter-inch doesn't make a heck of a lot of difference at those latitudes.

"Good," she said, gazing directly into his eyes.

I won't claim I didn't know that pushing a book off the shelf would be noisy—that was the whole idea. But I honestly didn't realize the one I chose was holding up half the row. It hit the linoleum with a sound like a bomb going off. The books that had been beside it fell over like dominoes, then began sliding off as well.

Boom! Thud. Thuddle, thuddle, thuddle . . . Thwack!

Our librarian, Mr. McKay, showed up on the run.

"What's going on here?" he demanded, out of breath.

Kevin and Fourteen-Karat had both turned to stare in my direction. There wasn't much I could do except step out of the shadows and pretend I didn't see them.

"I, uh . . . leaned on the wrong thing, I guess," I told Mr. McKay. "Sorry."

I bent to start picking up books, but not before I caught the smirk on Fourteen-Karat's face.

Smirk away, I thought. *No one's looking at your thighs anymore.*

She suddenly seemed to realize the same thing.

"Do you want to go outside?" she asked Kevin. "With all the noise in here, you aren't going to get any work done anyway."

"Okay, just a minute," he said.

I heard footsteps coming my way.

Do not look up, I told myself. *As long as you keep pretending you don't see him, you can pretend this never happened. Whatever you do, do not look up.*

I looked up.

"Hey, Cassie," he said, smiling. "I thought that was you."

What gave me away? The flaming red hair or the royal purple cheeks?

"Hey, Kevin." It's hard to look casual when you're blushing like a preacher at a peep show, but I gave it my best effort. "What are you doing here?"

I could see Fourteen-Karat at the table behind him, actually piling up his papers in her hurry to get him out of there.

"Not much. You?"

"I just stopped by to pick up some library books."

He caught my joke and laughed, which made me feel a little better. Mr. McKay gave us both a dirty look as he hefted my first pile of books back onto the shelf.

"Kevin? Are we leaving?" Fourteen-Karat cooed.

"Yeah, all right. I guess I'm out of here," he told me.

"I didn't know you knew Four—er, Sterling."

"I just met her. She seems nice."

"Mmm," I replied, not sure what else to say. For one

thing, the seemingly nice piranha in question was very much within earshot. Besides, I didn't want him to know I was jealous.

"See you tomorrow," he said, walking off.

"Should we go get a Coke?" Fourteen-Karat asked, handing him his stuff. "If we hurry, there's still time before the bell."

"Okay. If you want to."

"Let's," she said, shooting me a triumphant look. "Nobody cool ever hangs out in here."

Pure Fourteen-Karat

"She totally paraded him through the quad!" Hayley reported in the locker room before PE. "Introducing him to her girlfriends . . . If she'd had a leash and collar, I swear she'd have made him heel."

"Well, that's *good*," I said, pulling on those heinous blue shorts they make us wear. "I mean, he couldn't have liked that. Right?"

The smile Hayley gave me wasn't the encouraging look of total agreement I'd hoped for.

"Right?" I repeated.

"He's a guy," Hayley said, developing a sudden interest in her shoelace.

"He *liked* it?" I exclaimed, outraged.

"He'll see through her," she said loyally. "I mean, eventually. Unless he's really stupid."

"I don't *have* eventually, Hayley! He could be asking her to that formal right now." A terrible thought hit me. "Maybe she's already asked him!"

Hayley shook her head. "I doubt it. Even Fourteen-Karat isn't brave enough to ask a guy out the first day she meets him. How *did* she meet him, anyway?"

"I'm not sure. It had something to do with a tight T-shirt."

Have I mentioned how much I hate that girl?

Just So You Know . . .

I feel like I should say something here: I know it's wrong to hate people. I *hate* that I hate Fourteen-Karat, if that makes any sense. Before I met her, I wouldn't have thought I had it in me. I guess you just never know—I mean *really* know—until you meet the right person.

Kind of like falling in love, only evil.

The Cybergeek Relents

That afternoon I had two simple goals: put Fourteen-Karat out of my mind, and do my homework in peace. Unfortunately, before I could use the computer, I had to kick my brother off it.

"I've got homework, Trevor," I told him.

"Goody for you. I'm online," he said.

"I believe that's my point."

"Are you sure? Because I've got plenty of time if you want to call Hayley and check."

"Very funny. I've got an English assignment I need to research. Why can't you play with yourself in your bedroom?"

The second I saw his surly look, I realized that insulting him might not be the best strategy for gaining his cooperation.

"Get bent, Cassie," he said. "Just for that, I'll be here till dinnertime."

If you can believe it, my family has only one computer. Worse, it's in the den, a location whose only virtue is its proximity to the refrigerator. There's no privacy there at all, so instead of Web surfing and instant messaging my friends, I only use the computer for tasks of no real value, like homework. I rarely even send e-mail, because when it comes to computers, my little bro's absurdly smart. I don't know if it's from all those video games he plays or if he was born with the geek gene or what, but he can make a computer sit up and beg. If I do *anything* personal on that hard drive, he finds it. You may think I'm paranoid, given passwords and the Delete key. If so, I've got two words for you: Monica Lewinsky. Old files never die—they simply sit around waiting for someone with way too much time on his hands.

"Look, I'm sorry," I told Trevor. "I had a bad day. Actually, it started out pretty good, but now . . . I really need to use the computer, and if you're only playing games . . . can't you use your PlayStation?"

"I'm playing interactive Stealth with a guy in Japan," Trevor informed me snottily. "I can't do that on a PlayStation."

"What time is it in Japan?"

"When is your assignment due?" he countered.

"In three weeks."

"Three weeks is a lifetime from now! If you were a fruit fly, it would be like four lifetimes. Or eight."

"Please, Trev. It's a big assignment," I said desperately.

He gave me this long, scornful look. Then, amazingly: "I'll let you have it at four."

"Deal!"

All things considered, his solution was surprisingly human. Especially since I didn't *have* to do English research that day. I could have started brainstorming ideas for my Western civ paper, or written up that morning's biology experiment, or even nodded off over my algebra homework.

But none of those things was going to make me look like a one-act-play genius. And if I wanted Kevin's attention, I wasn't going to get it with a tight T-shirt.

Unfortunately.

I mean, not that I would. But . . . you know. I wouldn't mind having the *option*.

If nothing else, it would make using my brain seem a lot more noble.

Making a Play

"You don't have any ideas at all?" Kevin asked me a couple days later.

Of course I had ideas. I had *plenty* of ideas. Unfortunately, none of them had to do with our stupid one-act play.

"It might help to define our structure," I said, pen hovering above my notebook like I might actually write something. All around the room, pairs of our fellow students labored under Conway's watchful eye. Some of them even seemed to be making progress.

"What structure?" Kevin asked. "It's a one-act play. That *is* the structure."

His obvious impatience didn't do much for my self-confidence. *I don't have to ask him today,* I thought. *There's still time to wait for the right moment.*

It hadn't been hard getting Quentin's permission to invite Kevin to his Halloween party—as Quentin's girl+friend, I simply called and asked. But working up the nerve to ask Kevin was looking a lot harder.

"Right," I said nervously. "That's the *overall* structure. But how many scenes should we have? How many characters?"

"Shouldn't that depend on what our play's about? Forget about structure, we need a *subject*, Cassie."

As usual, the sound of my name in his mouth totally melted me. That and the way his shirt hiked over his navel when he leaned back in his chair.

"Okay," I said, inspired. "Okay, what if it's as simple as this? Two characters—a girl and a guy—and they're just sitting around talking."

"About what?"

I racked my brain . . . and ended up ripping something from the headlines of my life.

"Well, what if they're talking about this other girl they know who's trying to steal the guy from the first girl. Yeah, that'll work. See, our characters are a couple, and someone is plotting to break them up."

"Plotting?" Kevin raised one brow. "Is this a love story or a murder mystery?"

"At this point, it could go either way."

He laughed and I felt redeemed, completely, wholly alive just because I'd made him smile. If that's not love, I don't know what is.

"Do you want to go to a Halloween party?" I blurted out. "This guy I know, Quentin, is having one."

Kevin shrugged. "I guess I could."

"It's going to be really fun."

"Yeah? Okay, I'll go."

I was glowing, absolutely thrilled. . . .

Then: "Who's driving?" he asked.

Talk about bursting my bubble.

"I, uh . . . I'll take care of that," I said vaguely. "No problem."

But it was, because I won't be sixteen until February. I have my permit and I've fulfilled all the legal requirements except the last fifteen hours of driving practice, but my birthday is an eternity away—even assuming my parents still let me take the test then. I'd been so busy worrying about whether Kevin would go to the party with me that I'd just that moment realized someone would have to drive us. And that someone could *not* be one of my parents. And it could not be me with one of my parents in the car. In short, it could not involve my parents in any way.

I mean, that's just obvious, right?

Quentin and Fitz already have their licenses because they're juniors, but Quentin wasn't going to want to leave his own party and Fitz doesn't own a car. Besides, I wanted to be alone with Kevin.

Maybe a taxi? I thought. *Or would that be lame?*

I decided to worry about transportation later.

"Do you want to meet me after school today?" I asked hopefully. "We could go to the library and work on our play."

"I have . . . a thing. Besides, we don't have a play to work on yet."

"We have an idea," I reminded him.

"Yeah, but . . . You were serious about that?"

"It could work. If you want, I'll start writing something tonight. Then, if you like what I did, we can add more tomorrow."

"That would be great," he said, with obvious relief. "I'm still trying to catch up from transferring here, and to tell you the truth, this isn't my favorite class."

"There's a shocker," I said.

Kevin laughed again. "Nothing personal. At least, not against you."

We both glanced at Conway, who had so many pencils

piercing her bun that morning she looked like a voodoo doll.

"I don't hear writing!" she called on cue.

Let me ask you something: what does writing sound like?

"I understand completely," I told Kevin.

Sophomore Honors English
Mrs. Conway
Second Period

The Third Wheel
A one-act play by
Cassie Howard and Kevin Matthews

<u>Scene One</u>

[Kenneth, a handsome young executive, and Clarissa, his stylish fiancée, sit at a corner booth in a New York City diner, their untouched dinners in front of them.]

Clarissa: So what do we do now?

Kenneth: What do you want to do?

Clarissa: For starters, you can't see Goldie again. Not anywhere. Not ever.

Kenneth: That's going to be a problem, since we work in the same building.

Clarissa: You'll have to fire her.

Kenneth: I'm not her boss. Be reasonable, Clarissa.

Clarissa: Don't put this on me! You're the one who
            was cheating, trotting at that woman's heels
            like a trained dog on a leash.

Kenneth: Cheating? You're crazy! I don't even like her.

Clarissa: People saw you, Kenneth. That evil,
            scheming tramp is tearing us apart.

Kenneth: No one could ever split us up. You're the one
            I want, Clarissa—the only one I'll ever want.

Clarissa: I'd like to believe you. I just don't know if I
            can.

Kenneth: I'll do anything you say. Just give me
            another chance.

Clarissa: What about Goldie?

Kenneth: I told you—she's nothing to me. You're
            blowing this out of proportion.

Clarissa: I know her type, and I know what she's
            capable of.

Kenneth: I won't see her again. If that's what it takes to
            convince you, then that's what I'm going to do.

Clarissa: What about your job?

Kenneth: I'll quit my job. I can always work
            somewhere else.

Clarissa: Or . . .

Kenneth: Or what? What are you thinking?

Clarissa: Maybe there's another way . . . a way to make Goldie quit.

Kenneth: How?

Clarissa: You can't be naive enough to think you're the first man in her life. A woman like that has enemies—and they aren't *all* female.

Kenneth: Are you talking about . . . ?

Clarissa: Exes. Lots of them. And doesn't your company have a policy against employees dating each other?

Kenneth: You can't be suggesting . . .

Clarissa: There has to be some poor fool she's dumped who'd love to get revenge.

Kenneth: And what's to keep her from getting revenge right back? If she's going to be fired anyway, why not take everyone she's ever dated down with her?

Clarissa: Ha! So you admit it!

Kenneth: I'm just saying, a lot of people could get hurt.

Clarissa: A lot of people have *already* been hurt,

Kenneth, starting with me. It's time Goldie got what's coming to her.

Kenneth: You're right, I guess. You're always right.

Clarissa: You'll do it, then?

Kenneth: Of course.

Clarissa: And after she's gone, you'll forget you ever met her?

Kenneth: Met who?

Clarissa: That's better. I think I'm already starting to forgive you.

Kenneth: You think? How can I make you sure?

Clarissa: Well . . . maybe if you kiss me . . .

I Wish!

Okay, no. I didn't actually bring that play to class. I might have risked it if my paper had been going straight to Conway, but I had to rehearse it with Kevin, don't forget. I've known guys oblivious enough to let something that obvious sail over their heads. (Quentin, for example—not to be cruel, but that guy can't buy a clue.) But Kevin was still enough of a mystery that I was afraid to take the chance. Not to mention the little matter of reading the stupid thing in front of the whole class. I'm pretty outgoing, but please— anyone would draw the line at inviting her crush to kiss her in front of thirty-three fellow students.

With the possible exception of Fourteen-Karat.

So I couldn't turn in that play. Which meant I would have had to go to school the next day with nothing to show Kevin. Which would have made me look like a slacker. Or a liar. Or an incompetent. Or all three. So to avoid that triple disaster, I came up with a plan.

Just remember this: I didn't say it was a *good* plan.

Detention Essay #4
Mrs. Conway

Why Plagiarism Is Reprehensible, Morally Wrong, and Deeply Un-American
by Cassie Howard

<u>Reprehensible</u> isn't a word I've ever used. I had to look it up, and quite honestly, the dictionary didn't help that much. My best guess is that a reprehensible act is one deserving criticism and disapproval. If I've got that right, then plagiarism is definitely reprehensible. It is reprehensible because everyone knows you are not supposed to copy someone else's work and pretend it is your own. That's so obvious I don't know why the school even needs a rule about it. Isn't the never-ending criticism of disapproving parents more than enough punishment?

Plagiarism is morally wrong because it breaks down into stealing and lying. A plagiarist steals someone else's work, then lies about who wrote it. Stealing and lying are more than just wrong, they're like Ten-Commandments wrong. Which, again, makes me wonder why the school needs to be so involved. Aren't we dealing with a higher power than Principal Ito here?

Plagiarism is un-American because this country was built on hard work and initiative. If everyone went around stealing other people's work instead of doing their own, we would end up recycling the same ideas over and over, and no one would ever invent anything new. We would never find the cure for cancer, or the key to world peace, or a safe and effective way to naturally lighten red hair. Instead of being a world leader, America would become dependent on other countries, which could be a real nightmare, since so few of them seem to like us. Therefore, in the interests of peace on earth and keeping America strong, plagiarists have to be punished.

But is detention really the answer? Once a person learns her lesson, there must be a better way for her to show her remorse than hanging around after school writing endless assigned essays. Especially after that person has apologized a million times and offered a very clear explanation as to how the entire incident was really a simple mix-up. Unless you're thinking all this extra writing is making up for the play I should have written. If that's the case, then I'd just like to point out, very respectfully, that you also made me turn in a new play, so by now I ought to be way ahead of the game.

Right?

Please just give it some thought. Even prisoners get paroled.

A Simple(minded) Plan

The first thing you ought to know is that I never intended to turn that play in. The second play, I mean—the one I took to class the next day so I'd have something to show Kevin.

My plan was extremely simple:

1. Arrive at school early and go straight to the library.
2. Copy a few pages out of one of those big drama anthologies.
3. Flash them in front of Kevin to pretend I wrote something, but convince him that I can do better.
4. Rush directly home after school and write something we can actually turn in.

Sounds easy, right? And it was—at first. In fact, everything went like clockwork right up to step 3½. That was when Kevin insisted on actually *reading* my counterfeit play.

"This is great!" he said, scanning the pages. "Wow, Cassie. You're a good writer."

"Not really," I said nervously. Conway was pacing the room, as usual. The last thing I needed was for her to overhear and ask to see my masterpiece.

"Don't be modest. We could get an A with this."

"With that? No."

I tried to grab the pages back, but Kevin held on to

them. "I really like this, especially the part where Sam tracks John into the woods. It's totally different from that boyfriend/girlfriend thing you were talking about yesterday. What happens next?"

"What do you mean?"

"What does John do?"

"Oh, in the play? I don't know. Yeah, that's the problem," I said, seeing a way out. "I have no clue. I'll have to write something else."

"No way!" he said. "We can figure this out."

"Sorry, but it's hopeless. I'm totally blocked. I'll just do it over."

"Cassie!" Kevin's eyes bored into mine, making it seriously hard to concentrate on improving my argument. "You're not listening. I *like* this. I want to use it."

"But . . . well . . . if I don't know what's going to happen . . ."

I could not have sounded more lame. It had simply never occurred to me that he might be stubborn about keeping those pages. I mean, *I* was the one who had written them.

Supposedly.

"Let's just see what we can come up with," he said. "There's forty minutes of class left. We ought to be able to think of something."

"That's not enough time!" I protested, getting panicky.

"Well, if not, I can meet you in the library after school today. I can only stay an hour, though, because I've got something else later on."

"You . . . want to meet me after school?"

"Sure, if we don't get finished this morning."

You don't have to say it: I should have confessed right there. I just wasn't thinking clearly. For example, the word *plagiarism* never crossed my mind. Somehow I even managed to overlook the fact that I was lying to Kevin. I hadn't *intended* to lie—I had just failed to fully consider the effect he had on me. I still wasn't used to the way my brain went all fuzzy every time our eyes connected. So instead of doing the right thing, I nodded like a fool.

"After school is good," I said. "I mean, if we don't get finished this morning."

Like I was going to let that happen.

Second Thoughts

For the next few days I bounced back and forth between a sweet dream and my worst nightmare. The longer I delayed fixing our play, the more time I got to spend with Kevin. But every minute I bought that way I paid for three times over in lost sleep and self-loathing.

I loved being with Kevin, especially when we got so busy talking we forgot to do any work. I loved that he always smiled when he saw me, and the way he laughed at my jokes. I loved the glint of his green eyes and each highlight in his spiky hair. I loved how the air squeezed out of my lungs every time I caught sight of him. I loved it all—all except the enormous mess I was making of both our lives.

I wanted to fix it, honestly. Every night of tossing and

turning ended in a firm resolution to set things right the next day. Then I'd see Kevin, and the thought of disappointing him in any way was so horrifying that I'd completely wuss out. Besides, it's not as if all this were happening in a vacuum. Fourteen-Karat was everywhere I looked, circling me and Kevin like a great white eyeing an injured seal.

Somehow she found out every time we met in the library, and just happened to show up needing a book. If we stopped to talk in the hall after class, her uncanny sense of timing led her by at that very instant. She had nothing but smiles for Kevin and smirks for me—and even if he didn't notice, I knew exactly what she was up to. Her mere presence was a threat requiring my complete and unwavering attention.

Unfortunately, a few other problems were taking up major space in my brain:

1. We could never turn in the play we were working on.
2. Kevin still didn't want to hear any of my other, original ideas.
3. It might have been possible to alter the published play enough to make it our own—or at least to make it unrecognizable—but Kevin wouldn't let me change a word.

I knew I had to tell him what I'd done. I *absolutely* had to tell him. But I wanted us to be solid first. Kevin+Cassie solid. Fourteen-Karat-proof.

Foot-in-Mouth Disease

"Are you crazy?" Hayley demanded over lunch a few days later. "You still haven't told him?"

"Could you maybe scream a little louder?" I asked, flinching. "I don't think the *entire* quad heard you."

"This isn't like you, Cassie. What good can come of it?"

"It's just a mistake, all right? I'll get it straightened out."

"It's going to turn around and bite you in the butt. You know I'm right."

I did, too, but I was still clinging to the childish belief that I could outrun whatever butt biting I had coming. After all, the due date for our play was a week and a half away.

"I'm going to tell him after Quentin's party," I said, making a sudden decision. "By then we'll be so tight he'll probably just laugh it off."

Hayley didn't look convinced. "That's your plan?"

"What's wrong with it?"

"You don't really want me to answer that."

"Not really."

We ate silently a minute before the sight of Fitz and Quentin cutting through the crowded quad caught Hayley's attention.

"Fitz came up with the best idea for costumes!" she told me, waving to them. "He's going to be a magician and I'll be the rabbit he pulls from his hat."

"Seriously?" I said, taken aback.

"You don't think that's cute?"

"No, it's just . . . isn't that kind of a couple's costume?"

Hayley blushed. Remember that rosy glow I told you about? This time her cheeks looked like she'd gone crazy at the Clinique counter. I could not believe my eyes.

"You and Fitz?" I exclaimed. "No way!"

"No, *not* me and Fitz," she said, gesturing frantically for me to keep my voice down. "Not yet, anyway."

"But . . . but . . . he's Fitz!" I finally got out. "That would be like dating your brother. I mean, if you *had* a brother and he was really smart and not very cute." A horrible thought struck me. "Eew! It would be like dating Trevor!"

The moment those words left my mouth I knew I shouldn't have said them out loud. For one thing, Fitz deserved better. For another, it made me sound really shallow. Worst of all, it made Hayley incredibly mad.

"You're unbelievable," she said, jumping up. "Who do you think you are?"

"No, Hayley. I didn't mean—"

"Just because Kevin got assigned to you for a stupid class project doesn't make you the catch of the school. It's not like he had a choice!"

"I didn't say—"

"Ever since you laid eyes on that guy you've been a colossal pain. Everything's Kevin this and Kevin that. And in the precious few moments you're not drooling over him, you're moaning about Sterling. Did it ever occur to you that I have a life too?"

"Hayley, I—"

"Just forget it. I was obviously insane to hope for any support from my best friend."

She stormed off before I could say any more, leaving me there with my mouth hanging open. She left in such a hurry that she forgot her backpack. You might think that would spoil her whole exit, but you don't know Hayley. She just marched back and picked it up like I wasn't even there.

I tried again. "Hayley—"

She flashed me the international talk-to-the-hand signal, wheeled around, and strode off into the quad. It didn't even occur to me to follow. I just sat there by myself, thinking what an insensitive jerk I'd been.

All of a sudden, a long, piercing whistle cut through the quad. Heads turned and conversations stopped as people tried to spot the source of that blast. But I already knew who'd done it—no one can whistle that way except Hayley. When she's happy, she'll chirp along to the radio, but when she's angry, that whistle's all business. With a beacon like that to home in on, I had no trouble spotting her again just in time to see her flag down Fitz and Quentin, running up to join them.

"Great," I said with a sigh.

I hate fighting with Hayley. She never just lets me apologize. I can say I'm sorry for hours, but she still makes me do penance.

And this time there was the added fear that she'd repeat what I'd just said to Fitz. I can be such a moron sometimes. I *love* Fitz. I mean, not in a romantic way. But it would kill me to hurt his feelings.

It would kill Hayley to hurt them, too, I realized.

So I was probably safe on that score. Not that it made me feel a whole lot better about myself.

I'll make it up to her, I vowed. *I'll call her tonight and apologize. Maybe she'll give in and let me come over to help with her costume or something.*

Except that then I remembered I still had to come up with my own costume.

And a ride to the party.

And a one-act play.

Not to mention my other homework.

I'll apologize tomorrow, I decided. *Knowing Hayley, she's not going to let me off the hook that easily anyway.*

So since it couldn't be helped, I decided to make the best of our time-out—to take advantage of it, even.

It wasn't as if I didn't have a few other things to do.

Serf's Up

Do you believe in karma? I didn't use to, but now I'm not so sure. Based on my recent experiences, I can confirm that one bad act attracts another. And they don't just come in threes, either. They come in this whole metaphorical blizzard that blankets the ground, getting thicker and thicker until *whoosh!* One false move and you set off the avalanche.

So it only figured that that afternoon, while I was *not* writing my play, *not* telling Kevin the truth, and *not* calling Hayley to apologize, Trevor decided to bother me.

I was working on my Halloween costume when he

showed up, leaning against my bedroom doorframe and acting for all the world as if we're in the habit of having something to do with each other instead of nurturing our normal sibling relationship of distance and mutual mistrust.

"What are you doing?" he asked.

"Gee, let's see. I'm standing here in a gold plastic crown and a red velvet robe, so I must be choosing my school clothes for tomorrow."

"You're a queen every Halloween."

"No, I'm a queen every other Halloween. And only since sixth grade."

That was the year I discovered I have the same name as an actual queen of England. Oh, yeah. Did I forget to tell you that Cassie's a nickname? My real name is Catherine. Catherine Howard.

Granted, if you were going to *choose* a queen for a namesake, you could pick one who had a better run. Poor Catherine was married to Henry VIII, so that ought to tell you something. She wasn't Henry's second queen, but she was his second to last, and she was the second of three Catherines. There probably would have been more, but mercifully for the Catherines of England, Henry finally kicked the bucket. He was a pig when it came to women, but he actually executed only two of his six wives. Catherine Howard was the second one.

Seeing any pattern? Now that I'm embracing karma, maybe I'll look into past lives too.

Anyway, the important thing here is that Trevor was wrong.

"Why are you bothering me?" I asked. "Sprain your game thumb?"

"You think you're so smart, Cassie. You're not."

This was not the type of world-class insult a person lies awake at night thinking up, but something about the way he said it made my insides freeze.

"Smarter than you," I retorted nervously.

Trevor rearranged himself in my doorway, assuming this very casual position. Too casual. "At least I do my own homework."

I gulped, waiting for it.

"Interesting play you're writing, Cass. Funny thing is, I already read it. In a book. Last summer."

"You were snooping in my computer files?" I shouted, mustering as much righteous indignation as I could. "I *knew* I shouldn't have left anything on that hard drive! You're such a weasel, Trevor!"

"A weasel who does his own homework," he said, grinning. "Why don't you tell Mom I was looking at your precious files? Go ahead. I dare you."

We both knew that would never happen. And, unfortunately, we both knew why.

"What do you want, Trevor?"

"The thing is," he said slowly, taking his time, "I'm getting too old for trick-or-treating. No one even cares if you have a good costume, and I made a great one this year. Batman. It has the cape, the cowl, and everything."

"And this is my problem because . . . ?"

"I want to go to Quentin's party."

I don't know how he found out about Quentin's party, and I have no idea why a mere eighth grader thought he'd have any business attending. All I knew for certain was there was no way I could bring my geeky kid brother to a high school party. Even if Kevin *weren't* going.

"You're tripping," I said. "No way."

"No way?" He cocked one eyebrow at me like a juvenile James Bond. "You must know I copied that file and hid the disc where you'll never find it."

"You'd better hope you're right, because if I do, I'll stick it someplace the sun won't find it."

"I don't think you understand—"

"No, Trevor, *you* don't understand. That file you have? I never turned that play in and I'm not going to. I was just practicing my typing."

For a moment he looked stunned. Then his beady eyes got suspicious.

"I don't believe you."

"I don't care."

If he ratted me out, my mother would still have more questions than I cared to answer, but he had made it a question of principle—the principle of never being seen in public with Trevor.

"This isn't over," he said. "I'm watching you, Cassie."

"Which is pretty darn annoying, since I'm trying to get dressed. So if you don't mind . . ." I picked up my gold-painted plastic scepter and waved him away like a queen dismissing a serf. "Off you go!"

He glared at me, frustrated. Then, finally, he retreated down the hall.

Oh, I'm sorry. Did I promise you an avalanche?

Just wait.

A Driving Consideration

Halloween should be a holiday—a *real* holiday, involving time off from school. Nobody learns anything that day anyway. Not that the other days are such an educational bonanza. But still . . . why insist on something that's never going to happen?

Unfortunately, insisting on the impossible is how people like Conway earn their livings. She expected us to work on our one-act plays like nothing else was going on.

"Are you ready for the party tonight?" I asked Kevin as soon as she was busy snooping elsewhere. "Got your costume finished?"

"Costume? I wasn't planning to wear a costume," he said.

"But—but—it's a Halloween party! Costumes are the whole point!"

"What are you wearing?"

I opened my mouth to tell him, then abruptly changed my mind. Announcing that I was going as royalty might have sounded conceited.

"I'll throw something together," I said. "You'll see it tonight when I pick you up."

"So you got us a ride?"

"Not exactly. But don't worry. I'll definitely have one by tonight."

I could always ask my parents to drive us, but I was still holding out for a miracle. If Hayley and I made up at lunchtime and Fitz borrowed his dad's car, maybe they'd swing by for us.

Although I had to admit that didn't seem likely. I'd said some exceptionally stupid things this time.

"If you want, I could meet you there," Kevin offered.

"Really?"

It wasn't how I'd have chosen to arrive at our first major function, but right then it looked better than my other options.

"It's no problem. I mean, if it makes things easier."

"Yes. All right," I agreed, relieved. The ride home was more crucial anyway, and I was sure I'd be able to get us one from somebody at the party. "I'll meet you in front of Quentin's house. That way we can walk in together and I can introduce you to whoever you don't know."

"Introductions won't be much help if everyone's in costume. I'll probably see the same people on Monday and not even recognize them."

"Don't wear a mask," I said, thinking fast. "Then even if you don't recognize them, they'll still recognize you."

At the very least, I wanted people to see who I was there with.

"I don't think I'm even going to wear—"

"How are things progressing here?" Mrs. Conway interrupted, sneaking up so silently she nearly gave me a heart attack. "I don't see much happening in this corner."

I slammed my notebook shut to keep her from reading my counterfeit play.

"Fine," I said. "Everything's fine."

"What are you working on?" she asked.

"Our play."

Kevin leaned back in his chair, just smiling and letting me handle it.

"Funny," Conway said. "I could have sworn I heard you talking about a Halloween party. Is your play about a Halloween party?"

"No." Although that wasn't such a bad idea, especially since I still needed a subject. "But today *is* Halloween. You can't expect us to ignore that."

"That would be my preference, yes." Conway adjusted one of the pencils that skewered her graying bun. "Please ignore the completely irrelevant fact that it's Halloween."

I rolled my eyes as she walked away. Kevin's smile stretched wider.

"I don't hear writing, Miss Howard," Conway said without turning around.

Let me just say this: I hope I never get so old that Halloween becomes irrelevant.

Hallo-wienie

Hayley wouldn't even look at me when I spotted her in the quad at lunchtime. She must have seen me, though, because how else would she have known where not to look? I thought about trying to make up, but she was eating with Fitz, which created obvious apology problems. So instead I went looking for Quentin, to ask about a ride home after his party.

I checked our school's big front lawn on the theory that if Quentin wasn't with Fitz, he was probably at the cheerleaders' Halloween bake sale. Sure enough, I found him at the edge of the crowd, trying to blend with the basketball players. Call me psychic, but some guys just can't resist brownies with candy corn on top.

(You can't see me, but right now I'm rolling my eyes in this very ironic way.)

Anyway, the cheerleaders had put two tables on the grass and taped paper banners around them. There were plates of cupcakes and cookies, but the fact that the customers were ninety percent male made it clear that the big draw wasn't baked goods. The only girls I recognized were the cheerleaders themselves, plus Fourteen-Karat and Ros Pierce, who had attached themselves to their buddy Tamara, the cheerleading captain, like they were on the squad too. I was glad that Kevin was nowhere in sight, because the amount of hair-tossing going on behind the bake-sale tables was having an intoxicating effect on the guys. Quentin's eyes were positively glazed over.

"Hey, Quentin," I said, tapping him on the shoulder. "Listen, about your party tonight—"

"It's going to be huge!" he exclaimed. "Everybody's coming! Sterling says it's going to be the party of the year!"

"Excuse me?" I rocked back in my clogs. *"Sterling?"*

"And not only is *she* coming, she invited the rest of the cheerleaders. So every guy who hears about it will show, and so will their girlfriends, to keep them in line, and—"

"Sterling Carter is *not* a cheerleader." Talk about focusing on trivia. "Besides, last I heard, this party was supposed to stay small. Weren't you the one who wanted to keep it quiet?"

He shrugged. "That was before. I mean, I didn't want a bunch of *losers* showing up."

"Too late now."

Quentin looked confused. "What's your problem?"

Have I mentioned how incredibly dense he can be?

"I thought you didn't want your house to get trashed," I said.

Quentin shrugged again. Then he actually smiled. "At least I'm going down in a blaze of glory." He lowered his voice and leaned in closer. "You know what else? I think Sterling likes me."

"You're such a wienie!" I exclaimed, unable to hold back any longer. F.K. was obviously only going to his party because she'd found out Kevin would be there. I didn't know *how* she'd found out, but you'd have to be thick to believe she'd just spontaneously fallen in love with Quentin, a guy who'd been available for the past year.

So of course that was *exactly* what Quentin believed. In fact, he was feeling so cocky that, instead of getting mad, he found my outburst funny.

"*Some*-body's *jeal*-ous," he sang, with this infuriatingly smug expression. "All those months we were hanging out, you never even saw what a good thing you had. But now that someone else wants me . . ."

I'd like to believe he was kidding, but no. Like I said before—completely dense.

Even Cowgirls Cause the Blues

That night, I made my dad drop me off a block from Quentin's party. The sky was dark by then, and tons of kids were out trick-or-treating, so I figured no one would notice me walking.

"Are you *sure* you don't want me to take you to the driveway?" Dad asked as I struggled to untangle my red velvet robe from my seat belt.

"No, this is good," I said, giving the robe a yank. I heard some stitches pop, but it was worth it to make my escape. When your father has to drive you to what could be the event of the year, it's best not to be seen arriving. Dad drove off shaking his head, but he drove off, and that was the main thing.

Quentin's long driveway was clogged with cars. Someone had strung orange lights and paper skeletons along the front porch, and I could hear the stereo blaring from way out on the sidewalk. Sheer curtains revealed the crowd already packing the living room, but I was determined to wait outside until Kevin arrived so we could make our entrance together.

It's not easy to look casual in a crown. You'd think that on Halloween a crown wouldn't be hard to carry off, but something about that headgear simply commands attention. Now that I'm thinking about it, that's probably why queens started wearing them in the first place. Anyway, all kinds of people were walking by on their way in to the party, and it was getting hard to pretend I wasn't standing out on the sidewalk alone, wearing a thrift-store white satin formal, a red velvet robe, a gold plastic crown, and about two pounds of costume jewelry. And tennis shoes. I always wear sneakers on Halloween—that's just common sense.

A bunch of cheerleaders showed up in an SUV, every one of them dressed as a cat—you know, if cats wore leotards and tights. A leopard, a tiger, a cheetah, a jaguar . . . I did a double take on the blond lion, suspecting Fourteen-Karat, but that one turned out to be Ros. F.K. wasn't even in the group, and I breathed a little deeper, daring to hope that she'd suffered a sudden case of measles—or leprosy.

It felt like I'd been standing outside for an hour when it suddenly occurred to me that Kevin might already be in the house. Maybe he'd forgotten I said I'd meet him in front. I paced the sidewalk, torn, afraid that if I ran in to check I'd miss his arrival—not to mention our chance at a royal entrance. I'd just about made up my mind to risk a quick look anyway when a red convertible pulled up and stopped behind the other cars in the driveway. One of the Blues Brothers was driving, and a cowboy and an NFL cheerleader were riding in the backseat. If it hadn't been for the hot car—and the fact that the cheerleader was flashing an extraordinary amount of cleavage—I probably wouldn't have been distracted for more than a second. But the cheerleader made me look, and the cowboy made my jaw drop.

Kevin had just shown up with Fourteen-Karat Carter.

"Thanks, Elwood," F.K. told the driver, climbing out and slamming the door. The guy tugged on the brim of his black hat, pulling it lower over his shades. I don't know who he was; all I know is he was way too cool to be a parent. Kevin got out on the other side and the car backed up and drove away. Without stopping to think, I ran right up to him.

"Hey!" I said. "What's going on?"

"What do you mean?" He was wearing his usual jeans; the "costume" part of his outfit consisted of a cowboy hat, boots, and a bandana tied around his neck. Not too original, but at least he'd tried.

"I just thought . . . I mean . . . well . . . I was standing here waiting for you. Did you get held up?"

What I *wanted* to ask, of course, was what he was doing with Fourteen-Karat and whether I'd been unclear about the fact that I had asked him there as my date. But what if I *had* been unclear? I would never survive the humiliation—especially not with F.K. hanging on every word.

"Why? Am I late?" he asked, looking confused.

Before I could answer, Fourteen-Karat jumped in.

"No," she said scornfully. "Everyone knows you're not supposed to show up at a party on time."

The full impact of her costume suddenly hit me. Like Kevin, Fourteen-Karat was wearing boots—but hers were white go-go boots. Her top consisted of a tiny white vest over a long-sleeved blue blouse, which was tied in a knot immediately under the previously mentioned cleavage. Her low-cut white hot pants looked like they'd been spray-painted over her rear and beneath her tan midriff. The appliquéd stars on her outfit were blue and silver, and so were the pom-poms she carried.

F.K. wasn't just any cheerleader—she was a Dallas *Cowboys* cheerleader.

Coincidence?

I don't think so.

"You'll want to hurry inside," I told her. "Quentin's waiting for you, and the real cheerleaders are already here."

The way she was sticking to Kevin, I wasn't sure if she'd go. But she just gave me a haughty look.

"I wasn't planning to stay out here on the sidewalk," she said, with a toss of her glitter-streaked hair. "See you inside, Kevin."

And spinning on one cheesy boot heel, she headed for the door, working those shorts overtime.

"Let's go in too," Kevin said, following her every twitch. "It's not that hot out here."

"Yeah, but wait," I said, grabbing his elbow.

He seemed surprised I was touching him. I was kind of surprised myself, but I had to get his attention somehow.

"Why did you come with *her?*" I asked, just blurting it out. "I'm the one who invited you!"

Kevin blinked a few times. "You couldn't find us a ride. You seemed glad when I said I'd find my own."

"Yes, but . . ." But what? He totally had me. "I didn't know you'd be riding with Sterling," I admitted.

"Is that a problem?" He seemed genuinely puzzled.

Of course it's a problem! I wanted to scream.

"It's only . . . well . . . you're not here *with* her, are you?"

"What? We just ran into each other at school today, and she offered me a ride."

"This was her idea?" Leave it to Fourteen-Karat to grab

her first good chance to get between us. On the other hand, if she was the instigator, that meant Kevin was truly only along for the ride. I took a deep, calming breath. "I just thought . . . well, it looked like maybe she wanted it to be more."

"Really?" He glanced in the direction Sterling had gone, then shook his head. "She knew I was meeting you here."

I just stood there without a clue how to respond. F.K. was obviously working some new angle I hadn't figured out yet, but the good news was that Kevin seemed in the dark too. Meanwhile, she'd gone off and left us together. . . .

"I like your crown," he said.

"You do?"

I touched it with one hand—as if he might have been talking about some *other* crown—and hoped my hair was holding up. The thing about queens is, they don't usually have short hair. I'd ended up curling mine and forcing as much as I could up inside the circlet of gold paint and plastic jewels. It did make my hair look longer, except on my neck, where even a truckload of bobby pins could only do so much.

"I do," he said, taking my hand. "Come on. Let's go inside."

Trick, or Treat?

You might think I should have been satisfied. You might be right.

After all, I'd just walked into a huge party with Kevin Matthews. The fact that he'd let go of my hand before we cleared the doorway was a technicality, really. No one cool was going to show up holding hands, and my skin was still all tingly where he'd touched me. If Fourteen-Karat hadn't been there, I'd have been just about in heaven.

But Fourteen-Karat was there. And she was driving me up a wall.

From the moment Kevin and I walked in, the girl was everywhere. When we were in the living room, meeting people and checking out costumes, Fourteen-Karat was messing with the CD player. When we went to the kitchen to get a drink, she was fooling with the dry ice, making the punch spill fog to the floor. But the worst part was when she followed us to the backyard and started hanging all over Quentin.

There were probably close to a hundred people out on the back patio. Quentin had strung lights on the fence and dragged a couple of speakers outside, eliminating any last hope of having the neighbors forget to rat him out to his parents. When Kevin and I found him, he was standing with Fitz and Hayley, who looked unexpectedly cute together. Instead of the standard black tux and white rabbit, Fitz had dressed in white tails and Hayley was a furry black bunny. I had no sooner spotted them than Fourteen-Karat crept up behind Quentin and slipped her fingers over his eyes.

"Guess who," she cooed.

"Sterling?" he asked hopefully. He was sporting this whole Goth look: black leather pants, skintight black T-shirt, a spiked leather collar, and dripping black makeup around his eyes. I realize it sounds questionable, but Quentin's the kind of guy who can totally carry that off.

"Smart boy," Fourteen-Karat said, dropping her hands and draping herself around his neck. "Are you always so smart?"

Obviously not, I thought.

"Cool party, but why isn't anyone dancing?" she asked him.

"Maybe they're waiting for you and me to get things started."

"Maybe they are," she said, pressing up against his back. "I'm good at getting things started."

"Oh, please!" I blurted out, too provoked to keep quiet. Everyone turned to stare at me. "I mean, if people want to dance, they'll dance," I added lamely.

"It never hurts to help things along," Quentin said. Taking Fourteen-Karat's hand, he started pulling her toward the middle of the patio, but she dug in her go-go boots.

"No, maybe Cassie's right," she said, looking at Kevin. "Besides, I'll bet the six of us can have more fun sticking together."

I was the only one who saw Hayley roll her eyes, which made me seriously want to hug her. Even when Hayley's mad, she stays loyal.

"I'll tell you what let's do," F.K. said, an evil glint in her eyes. "Let's play truth or dare."

I swear, she looked right at me.

"Or not," Hayley countered. "This is a Halloween party."

"Then we ought to have a costume contest." F.K. let go of Quentin long enough to pose in her skimpy outfit. "How do you think I'd do, Quentin?"

"It wouldn't even be a contest. You'd slaughter everyone."

"Thanks a lot!" Hayley and I protested.

"You both look good too," he covered unconvincingly.

Fitz whispered something in Hayley's ear that made her turn all glowy. I looked hopefully at Kevin, but his eyes were still on that showoff Sterling.

"You have no idea how many places I had to go to find size-four hot pants," she complained, running her hands over her hips to smooth out that scrap of white Lycra. "It's like nobody carries size four anymore."

Which shouldn't be an issue, since you haven't worn size four since middle school, I thought.

"Well, lucky for us, you found some," poor, dumb Quentin replied.

Just so you know, I'm not one of those girls who thinks we all need to be anorexic. I don't *care* what size Fourteen-Karat wears. But isn't it enough to look the way she does? Does she have to lie about it too?

"Come on, let's dance," I said, grabbing Kevin's hand and dragging him off. "I love this song."

" 'The Monster Mash'?" he said uncertainly, trailing along behind me.

"It's a graveyard smash," I assured him, throwing myself into the music.

One thing I can do is move. I can dance to pretty much anything. It took me a few seconds to convince Kevin I was serious, but eventually he started dancing too.

And then it spread like wildfire. Everyone who'd been hanging around waiting for something to do found a partner and found the beat. And I'll tell you something I didn't know: on Halloween, when everyone's into it, "The Monster Mash" is a good dance song. Not only that, but it turns out a fake plastic scepter has a lot of dance-floor potential. I started out using it to salute other dancers, but pretty soon I was tapping girls on the head like their fairy godmother and knighting the guys on their shoulders. It sounds silly, but people actually started dancing up to me to get bopped with that thing. Kevin was laughing and I was laughing. And the best part of all was Fourteen-Karat on the sidelines, looking like she'd love to do me serious bodily harm.

We kept that up for three or four songs. Then Quentin and Fourteen-Karat came over, and the next thing I knew F.K. was dancing with Kevin and I'd been pawned off on Quentin. He didn't even realize he'd been ditched.

"Isn't she great?" he shouted over the music.

There was nothing I could say back that I wanted to shout at a party. Besides, I'd already tried to warn him. I gritted my teeth for the rest of that song, but when the next one started and Fourteen-Karat kept her claws in Kevin, it was time to take drastic action. Kevin was either too polite to shake her off, or he just didn't realize what she was up to.

"Limbo!" I shouted to Quentin. "Let's have a limbo contest!"

Uprooting an unlit bamboo tiki torch from the edge of the grass, I finally convinced him to hold its other end.

"Limbo!" he yelled, catching on at last. "Come on, everybody, limbo!"

Okay, yes. Limbo *is* kind of corny, but it's more fun on Halloween. It's hard enough dancing forward while you're bent over backward, but try doing it with a crown on. Or a mask, or cape, or gorilla suit. The whole level of difficulty goes way up. After we'd lowered the bar twice, Jeannie Patrick gave up—do French maids *really* wear spike heels?—and took my end of the stick.

I ran toward the back of the line, looking for Kevin, but instead I found Hayley trying to convince Fitz to limbo with her.

"Do it with Cassie," he begged, spotting me. "I'm no good at this."

But Hayley insisted until somehow the three of us ended up in line together. More or less together, anyway, because Hayley still wasn't cutting me much slack.

"Fun party," I ventured as we danced our way forward.

"Mmm," Hayley said.

"You and Fitz look cute in your costumes."

"Yes, we do." She nearly smiled when she said it, though, which meant I was making *some* progress.

I had to keep both hands on my crown when my turn came to limbo, but my sneakers helped. I cleared the bar and spun around to watch Hayley come through behind me. That was when disaster struck. One of her bunny ears touched the ground and Fitz stepped on it hard. The cap the ears were attached to choked up under her chin and yanked her backward off her feet. Hayley grabbed the limbo pole to catch her balance, but the bamboo snapped, landing her splat on her cottontail, laughing hysterically.

"I can't believe it," she gasped between peals. "Fitz, you stopped another line!"

Sure enough, people were backing up—and some of them weren't too happy about the delay.

"What's going on?" a werewolf yelled, craning his neck to see. "Let's move it!"

Hayley continued laughing as an embarrassed Fitz hauled her to her feet and dusted her fur with both hands.

"I'll get a broomstick from the kitchen," I told Quentin, dashing off.

The kitchen was packed and someone had turned down the lights until it was darker inside than out. I slipped in a puddle of punch, slid halfway across the room, and slammed into Tate the Great. Bryce Tate is the biggest guy in our school and he's on the football team, so the guys all worship him. The girls are less impressed, and that's about all I know. That, and that sliding into his back feels like hitting a wall.

"Hey, whatcha doing?" he grunted, turning around as I struggled to push myself off him. His costume involved a red muscle shirt and two horns stuck to his forehead. "Why, hello, princess!" he said, suddenly turning all Don Juan. "Looking for a handsome prince?"

"I am a *queen*," I informed him with as much dignity as I could muster. "Why would I marry and lose all that power?"

I grabbed the broom before he could recover and was on my way back out when a sneering voice stopped me cold.

"Planning to do a little flying, Cassie?"

I wheeled around, horrified to spot Fourteen-Karat in a dark corner with Kevin. I swear, she *wanted* me to see them.

"Limbo pole," I explained, pretending I hadn't caught her crack. If anyone flies a broomstick around Hilltop, we all know who it is. "Come on, Kevin," I said, reaching across her and grabbing his arm. "I need you to hold the other end."

I pulled him out of the kitchen, across the patio, and straight to the front of the limbo line. People cheered when they saw the new pole, and somebody cranked up the music. Kevin held his end of the broom even with mine and the dancing started again, but it was impossible not to notice him glancing back toward the kitchen.

"Are you having fun?" I shouted.

"Yeah." He flashed me a brief, unconvincing smile.

I was getting a bad feeling. Again.

"Someone else hold this," I shouted, motioning to the bystanders on the sidelines. Jeannie and a guy in camouflage took over at the broomstick.

"Come on," I told Kevin. "Let's dance. It'll be fun."

He seemed reluctant as he followed me to the back of the line.

"Is something the matter?" I made myself ask.

"No. It's just . . . I don't know how to limbo."

"Is *that* why you were hiding in the kitchen?"

"I guess so. Yeah."

"There's nothing to it," I assured him, relieved. "Come on, just copy me!"

(Limbo)²

I came in second in the limbo contest. Of course. The only person who danced lower than I did was Vinnie Chee, and he was wearing a Spider-Man costume. I'd have won if I hadn't been wearing that robe.

It's always something.

The thing was, I couldn't have cared less about a stupid dance contest. There weren't even any prizes. What I cared about was placing second with Kevin.

The entire rest of the party I couldn't stop wondering if I'd blown it with him somehow. It wasn't like English class, where we'd get so busy talking that the rest of the room disappeared. Kevin stayed by me the rest of the night, answering my questions and smiling when I said something funny, but he wasn't really there.

And I had a scary feeling I knew why.

At midnight, Quentin gave us a ride home. There were plenty of people still hanging around, but I had a curfew and it wasn't a long drive so I managed to convince him. He left Fitz and Hayley in charge, and the three of us piled into the beat-up old minivan Quentin had inherited when his mother bought a new one.

The sidewalks were deserted except for scraps of candy wrappers and the occasional smashed egg. The jack-o'-lanterns had all burned out. But when we turned onto

Kevin's street, there were so many people outside it looked like a street fair.

"Those college guys at the end must be having another party," Kevin said. "I'll bet my mom's having fits. She thought living on a cul-de-sac would be quiet."

Cars were double- and triple-parked everywhere, blocking all the driveways. Without a second's hesitation, Quentin pulled up and parked at an empty stretch of curb directly in front of Kevin's house—the only available spot on the entire street.

"Someone must have just left," Kevin said as we climbed out of the van. "My mom probably told them she'd call the cops."

Quentin smiled, taking it for granted. "If not, it would have been something else," he said out the driver's window.

"What's he talking about?" Kevin asked me as I walked him to his door.

"Quentin? He's good at finding parking spots, that's all."

"Whoopee."

"Yeah. Well. We all have to go with our strengths."

We reached his doorstep and hesitated, just kind of looking at each other. Even with Quentin nearby in the van, it was the closest I'd come all night to getting Kevin alone. Maybe he realized the same thing, because with no warning whatsoever, the connection between us blazed back to life—I could tell by the way his gaze locked with mine. My heart started racing like crazy.

"So . . . I, uh, guess I'll see you Monday," I said.

"Yeah."

He didn't move to leave. Neither did I.

"It was fun," he said. "Tonight, I mean."

He glanced toward the van, then took a step closer.

Is he going to kiss me? I wondered, my heart pounding harder. *Now? Here?* Because Quentin was totally going to see us if he did. We were standing right under the porch light. . . .

And I didn't care, I realized. I didn't care one bit.

Kevin put his hands on my shoulders and pulled me close. For one amazing second, his lips seemed headed for mine. Then his face jogged past me and he wrapped me into a hug. I could feel his heartbeat against my chest. I could feel his heat through our clothing. His cheek bumped into my crown. And then—and I'm not one hundred percent sure about this—his lips brushed the top of my head. Like a little kiss dropped into my curls.

"Good night, Cassie," he said, turning me loose. "You have the coolest hair."

I could not believe my ears. "It's red!"

Kevin smiled. "It sure is."

Maybe that doesn't sound like a compliment to you, but it had me floating on air. I could hardly believe we were standing there together, that someone had finally chosen me.

So much for Fourteen-Karat, I thought, gazing into his green eyes. *Because this is how it ends: me and Kevin together, and not a blonde in sight. . . .*

Okay, I'm a moron, but I was in love.

Second Try

That weekend was a blur. Every time I thought about seeing Kevin again, I got so excited I nearly went crazy. Granted, a kiss on the head—assuming that was what had happened—didn't *necessarily* mean the same as a kiss on the lips. But the fact that Kevin had left the party with me meant it was more than Fourteen-Karat got. Besides, his eyes had said more than his mouth. I could hardly wait for school on Monday so we could pick up where we'd left off. I was actually yearning for Conway's class.

Unfortunately, I had two whole days to kill before then. So I used my excess hours to do what I should have done long before: I holed up in my room and wrote a one-act play. My new idea still revolved around a couple, but this time there wasn't a whiff of a third person between them. This couple was tight. Supertight.

Except that the girl was dying of a horrible disease. And the guy couldn't bear to say good-bye. The whole play was about her trying to convince him that his life would go on without her. Which it won't, I don't think, because when she finally dies and he walks off the stage, you pretty much know he's on his way to do something stupid and tragic and really romantic.

You wouldn't believe how sad it was. I was crying when I finished, and I'm the one who wrote it. I thought about calling Hayley, partly because I wanted her opinion but mostly because it would have been a good excuse to see if she was speaking to me again. It was awfully late, though, and in the end I fell asleep with crumpled pages on my bed and a pen sticking me in the side.

Sunday morning I woke up more excited than ever about seeing Kevin and showing him our new play. We didn't even have to turn it in until Friday, which gave us an entire week to sit around doing nothing together. I got dressed and headed down the hall, planning to type my handwritten pages and make them look perfect for Monday.

The instant I reached the den, things started to go wrong.

"Hey, Cassie!" said my dad, looking up from the Sunday comics. "You're just in time!"

"For what?" I asked cautiously.

My mom was in the den too. And on the other side of the breakfast bar, Trevor was crashing around our kitchen like Julia Child in drag. He was actually wearing an apron, while a baseball cap turned backward served as his version of a chef's hat.

"Your brother is cooking us brunch!" Mom said.

"You're kidding."

"Nope," Trevor said proudly, straightening up with oven mitts on both hands. "I'm practicing my signature dish for our home ec test next week."

"Your *signature* dish?" I echoed sarcastically. "I thought that was Froot Loops."

Mom gave me a warning look, but Chef Boyardee was completely unfazed.

If anyone cares about my opinion, this whole home ec thing has spun out of control. Trev and his friends only took the class to meet girls. Meanwhile, my mother is fully behind it, calling it feminism's ultimate flip side. If you want to know what that means, you'll have to ask her. All I know is, so long as Trevor and I are at separate schools, I don't care what he does. So long as we're at separate schools *and* I don't have to eat anything he cooks, I mean.

"I'm making omelettes," Trev announced proudly. "And a hash-brown casserole."

"Yeah. Not that hungry," I said, heading for the computer.

"You're going to eat," my mother informed me. I knew just by her tone that I wasn't going to win, but I appealed to Dad anyway.

"Dad, don't you always say that homework comes first? I have a ton of English to do for Monday, and I want to get started now, before Trevor hogs the computer. I'll make myself a sandwich later."

My father looked up from his newspaper to find the whole family staring at him, waiting for his reply. Right away he got that deer-in-the-headlights expression.

"Did you say Monday?" he asked, dropping the paper and standing up. "Thanks for reminding me! I need to put a quart of oil in my car before work, and I'll just do it now, while I'm thinking about it."

He headed for the garage.

"Do it fast," Mom told him.

"Mmm," he said, still walking.

Fifteen minutes later we were all seated around the dining table facing plates of Trevor's signature dish, which turned out to be omelettes—making the casserole was just showing off.

"Looks good," Dad said, digging into his eggs. "Yum! Ham!" he added with his mouth full.

"Ham?" my mother said. "Oh, Trevor, you know ham makes me retain water."

"Relax," he said, looking ridiculously pleased with himself. "Yours has spinach and mushrooms."

"Ooh!" Mom said, lighting up and reaching for her fork.

"I *hate* mushrooms," I burst out. "I always *have* hated them, I always *will* hate them, and Trevor *knows* that. There's no way on—"

"That's why yours has baby shrimp," he said, stopping me midrant.

"What?"

"All the omelettes are different," Trevor explained, gesturing around the table. "That's my signature!"

"Oh."

Between the absence of mushrooms and the way my mother was looking at me, there was nothing left to do but pick up my fork and start eating. And here's something I wouldn't have guessed: Trevor can make an omelette. The eggs were fluffy, the shrimp pink and delicious—he'd even garnished our plates with twisty orange slices.

"This is excellent, Trevor," Mom said. "You are quite the cook."

"Chef," he corrected. "Guys are chefs."

So much for feminism.

"Yes, quite the talent," said my dad. "Girls love a man who can cook. I mean, um . . . a chef."

Talent! I scoffed to myself. I'd have been willing to concede some minor cooking skill, but Trev's ability to make eggs is nothing compared to his ability to make me crazy. *That's* a gift.

By the time the plates were cleared away, my parents had complimented Trevor so many times he was wriggling like a puppy. Mom made *me* wash the dishes—which was not remotely fair, since Trev had made an epic mess—but it was worth it just to get back to my play.

I spent the next seven hours on the computer, making what I'd written the day before even better. The words flowed as if they were coming from somewhere else and just passing through my brain on their way to my fingers. Except that this time they *weren't* coming from somewhere else. This time they were all mine.

When I had triple-checked every comma, I printed two copies and stapled them into these fancy maroon covers my mother's law firm uses. I imagined Kevin's thrilled face as he thanked me for finishing such a boring assignment and my insides squirmed with joy.

I was happy. I was *relieved.*

I was in for the shock of my life.

Take My Brother. Please.

I woke up at midnight with a pain like a spear through my gut and this very queasy feeling that someone had sucked all the air from the room. I lay there gasping, a cold sweat rising on my face, waiting for it to pass. But a few seconds later I realized things were only getting worse. Pulling on my robe, I fumbled my way down the hall and switched on the bathroom light.

The first thing I noticed was that I looked awful. I mean really, truly bad. My face was fish-belly white, my eyes were glassy, and I was panting like a dog. I had to hold on to the edge of the sink just to keep from falling down. I wondered if I should take some aspirin or Pepto-Bismol or something, but I'd barely opened the medicine cabinet when my mom showed up wanting to know what I was doing.

"I don't feel so hot," I said.

"Funny. You *look* hot," she replied, touching her wrist to my forehead. "You might be running a fever."

She found the thermometer and made me put it under my tongue, but not being able to open my mouth caused an immediate problem.

"I cam breeb," I told her, my words distorted by my closed lips. "I knee dair!"

"Stop talking," she ordered. "Just keep still until—"

But that was as far as she got. Whipping the thermometer out of my mouth, I pressed it into her hands with my eyes bulging out of my head. The floor lurched under my feet.

"Cassie!" she cried. "Are you going to throw up?"

I was already down on my knees with my head in the bowl, heaving for all I was worth.

"Ninety-nine point two," my mother read over my shoulder. "Although I'm not sure you left this under your tongue long enough."

"It's not going back in now," I grunted just before I hurled again.

"Of course not," she said, still hovering.

"Mom, I know you're trying to help, but I can puke by myself."

"I don't mind staying."

"I *want* to puke by myself."

That's really not the type of thing you need an audience for. Besides, the way my gut was cramping, it was only a matter of seconds before I'd have my other end over the bowl.

"I don't understand this," she said, not leaving. "If you hadn't been home all day, I'd ask what you'd been eating."

She had barely uttered the words when another massive heave filled the bowl. And that's when I got my first clue. I've probably already grossed you out as much as humanly possible, so I'm just going to say this: little pink shrimp.

"Trevor!" I shouted, the mere name bringing up another half gallon.

"Ooh. Shrimp." Mom hit the flusher handle. "The thing about shellfish is it never tastes that bad, but when it goes off, it's deadly."

"I'm going to kill him!"

"This isn't your brother's fault."

"Of course it is! He did this on purpose! No one ate that shrimp but me!"

"Because all of our omelettes were different," Mom said. "That's Trevor's signature."

"Signature my— Uh-oh, Mom, get out. I'm not kidding."

I barely managed to push her out and shut the door before I had to drop my pajama bottoms.

"Throw up into the tub!" she called through the door. "If you have to sit on the toilet, lean over the bathtub."

I know. Excruciating, right? I can't believe I'm even

telling you this, except it turned out to be important. And not just as another example of Trevor's idiocy. This food poisoning had *consequences*.

You'll see.

Besides, you might as well know. Everyone else does.

Dear Traumarama:

There's a place called Too Much Information, and my mom is a frequent visitor.

Maybe it's her personality, or it could come from being a lawyer and working with so much evidence. All I know is "Cassie was sick" would get me off for anything from a hangnail to tuberculosis, but my mother's absence notes always look like the one I had to take to school Tuesday morning:

> *Please excuse Catherine Howard for her absence yesterday. She woke up Sunday night with a painful stomachache and a temperature of 99.2 degrees. Shortly thereafter she began vomiting and was soon suffering from such severe diarrhea that she was unable to leave the bathroom until three in the morning. A twenty-four-hour bug of some sort can't be ruled out; however, the problem was more likely the result of minor food poisoning. Cassie was feeling better late Monday morning, but I thought it best to keep her home to replenish all those*

fluids. Please feel free to call me at work if you have any
further questions.
Sincerely,
Andrea Smythe-Howard

Could anyone *possibly* have further questions? I had to
wear dark glasses just to turn that thing in. And while I'm
on the subject, should *minor* and *poisoning* ever be used in the
same sentence?

But wait. It gets worse.

Ros Pierce came into the office while Ms. Masters, our
school secretary, was filling out my absence pass for home-
room. Ms. Masters is nice, but she likes to talk, so I nearly
died when Ros got in line right behind me. What if Ms.
Masters *did* have a question? Plus my mom's note was still
on the counter in plain sight. If such embarrassing personal
information ever got back to Fourteen-Karat, I was obviously doomed.

I shifted my backpack, trying to keep Ros from reading
over my shoulder. She immediately leaned the other way
and I shifted back again in a hurry. I was practically hyperventilating by the time Ms. Masters finally picked up the
note and dropped it in a box beneath the counter. She
handed me my pass and I grabbed it like a life preserver. I
was reasonably certain I'd managed to block Ros's view, but
I still couldn't wait to get out of there.

"Cassie?" Ms. Masters called just as I reached the door.

"Yes?" It took a superhuman effort to make myself stop
and turn around.

"If you need to use the bathroom during class today, you just run right out. I'll clear it with your teachers."

I stood frozen, horrified by her lack of discretion.

"No point taking chances," she added sympathetically.

"Right. Thanks," I forced out somehow. Then, before she could deliver a commentary on the unpredictable nature of diarrhea, I turned and bolted for the main hall.

Just breathe, I told myself as I stumbled through the office door into the hall. *Breathe normally, I mean.*

There was no question Fourteen-Karat was about to get some embarrassing intel from Ros. And there was no denying that was bad. But they didn't have the details, so how much damage could they do? Besides, who'd really care besides me?

My breathing slowed to normal and some of the blood left my face. Removing my sunglasses, I attempted to blend in with hallway traffic. First period was about to begin and the hall was packed. Normally I'd have looked for Hayley, but that morning I had my eyes peeled for someone else.

After three whole days of reliving it, I was now ninety-five percent certain that Kevin had kissed my hair on Halloween—and I was nearly positive that when I saw him again I'd just know. If he felt about me like I felt about him, I'd read it in his face.

That's what I hoped, anyway. Before I could test my theory, I hit a little snag.

The Best-Laid Schemes of Mice and Queens . . .

I couldn't find Kevin before first period, so the instant biology was over I ran to Conway's room. I wanted to catch him alone before class—and not just to fill him in on our new play.

If there's an upside to food poisoning, it's being able to fit into jeans you couldn't have worn the week before. Not only that, but with all the free time I'd had once I'd quit puking Monday, I'd discovered a new way to fix my hair that was actually kind of cute. I was hoping Kevin would think so too, but when I finally spotted him walking toward me in the hall, I completely forgot about pants and hair and even Trevor's murderous intentions. All I could see was Kevin.

"Hey, Cassie!" he said, spotting me. "You're back!"

"Did you miss me?" I asked hopefully.

"Well, yeah. You weren't in class. Were you sick?"

"Nothing serious," I said quickly. "And I worked on our assignment over the weekend. I have a surprise for you."

"I have a surprise for you, too."

"Me first." Unzipping my backpack, I whipped out Kevin's copy of our new play and waved it under his nose. "Ta-da!"

"What's that?"

"I wrote a new play! And it's all finished, too, so if you like it, we'll just turn it in and we're done."

"You did what?" he said, looking at me strangely.

"I wrote another play."

Kevin took his copy reluctantly, barely glancing at the fancy cover. "I hope you didn't spend a lot of time on it."

"Listen, Kevin," I said, trying to head off the obvious objection. "I know you liked the other one, but if you give this one a chance—"

"That's not it," he said.

"Then what?"

I could tell just by his expression that I wasn't going to like whatever he was about to say. But I never, ever imagined the next words out of his mouth.

Detention Essay #11
Mrs. Conway

If I Ruled the World for a Day
by Cassie Howard

Honestly, I don't know how much anyone could fix in just one day. It sounds like a good deal, absolute power and all, but twenty-four hours would fly right by. Besides, everything would probably get wrecked again as soon as my time was up. But if I had the chance, I'd at least try to do some good. Here are my ideas:

1. Establish World Peace.
This one's just obvious, but since no one's done it yet, it might also be impossible. We are talking <u>absolute</u> power, right?
2. Wipe out World Hunger, Cancer, and AIDS.
Three complete no-brainers.
3. Lower the Driving Age.
Or at least get rid of all those stupid restrictions. How are people ever supposed to grow up

and have a life if they can't even drive a car? You probably think I'm only saying this because of what happened to me, but if driving laws were reasonable, that entire incident would have been a nonevent. I mean, it's not like I crashed.

4. Make Gossip Illegal.

People who gossip have no idea how much misery they cause. Or maybe they do, in which case they ought to serve double sentences. Does it really help anyone to have their personal business spread all over school? No! The sad thing is, it doesn't even help the people who do it. There's absolutely nothing to be gained by gossip—it's pure maliciousness. And I <u>am</u> saying that because of what happened to me. There are girls at this school who live for the chance to tear you down. If I ruled the world for a day, they'd all be picking up trash in orange jumpsuits.

You know what? Even if I only accomplished #4, my time as ruler of the world would be well spent.

Excuse Me?!

"You did *what?*"

"I turned in our play yesterday," Kevin repeated.

"But—but—that's not possible!" I stammered. "It wasn't even finished!"

"I finished it over the weekend. You know, to surprise you."

He'd surprised me, all right. Just not the way he'd intended. I leaned against a nearby locker, in need of the support.

"It's not due till Friday!"

"Yeah, but we haven't been making much progress, so I figured I'd just get it done. I would have shown it to you yesterday, but you weren't here. And then, during class, other people had finished too, so Conway said whoever wanted to turn in their play early could spend the rest of the week doing independent study in the library."

He grinned triumphantly. My answering expression must have tipped him off that I was less than thrilled.

"You couldn't seriously expect me to turn down an offer like that?" he asked disbelievingly.

"But—but—I didn't even see it!" I protested.

He gave me an incredulous look. "What do you mean? You *wrote* it."

"Right. I meant I didn't see what *you* did."

"I added maybe a page and a half, to end it, and a couple of words here and there. Why? Don't you trust me?"

"Of course I *trust* you. But—"

"Look, let's just go in before Conway takes roll. I'll give you your copy at the library so you can make sure I didn't wreck anything." His tone made it pretty clear he'd expected more appreciation.

"Right," I said, gulping. "Okay."

I couldn't even look at Conway as we walked past her to take our seats. Had she read our play yet? If so, had she recognized it? With any other teacher, I'd have had a chance of slipping through the cracks, but that woman doesn't know what a crack is. I honestly felt like I might pass out.

Right before the bell rang, I reached across Kevin's desk and snatched my new play, hastily stuffing it into my backpack.

"Hey! Why'd you do that?" he asked.

I just nodded toward the front of the room, like I couldn't talk with class about to start. Honestly, I wasn't sure why I'd done it. I was totally panicking. The last thing I needed was for Conway to wander down the aisle, spot that second play, and start asking incriminating questions. No, what I *needed* was to get back our first play somehow and swap it for the new one. If Conway hadn't looked at ours yet, she'd never know the difference.

But Kevin would.

I sat petrified all through roll call. I'd never been in trouble at school before, but if Conway recognized that play, I was dead. I hadn't intended to plagiarize—but I had. I hadn't wanted to lie to Kevin—but I had. If this story ever came out, people wouldn't understand how it had all been one big accident; they'd think I was a terrible person. Dread squeezed my heart into a pebble.

And I still had no clue what to do.

How could I tell Kevin what I'd done? Not to mention explain it to Conway?

But I couldn't leave things the way they were. Even if I didn't get caught, my conscience was killing me. Besides, I'd done the work! I had it right in my backpack.

"All right," Mrs. Conway said. "Those of you who've completed your plays may leave for the library now. Sign in and out with Mr. McKay—and don't think I won't check."

I got my legs beneath me somehow and stumbled toward the door, my backpack over one shoulder. Just as I passed her desk, Conway's eyes met mine. My heart dropped to my stomach, and my stomach dropped to my feet.

Did she know?

Just tell her! a voice in my head screamed. *Tell her you want to switch plays.*

I glanced from her to the doorway, not sure whether to fess up or run. And that's when I spotted Kevin in the hall, gesturing for me to hurry.

You've probably already guessed what I did.

It's not something I'm proud of, okay?

EX-CUSE ME?!!!

At lunchtime, I ran straight out to find Hayley. It didn't matter if she was still sort of mad at me. I didn't even care if she was already eating with Fitz. I needed my best friend, and I needed her desperately.

To my amazement, she was standing beside our old bench, one hundred percent Fitz-free. I ran through the crowd in a frenzy to tell her what had happened.

"I am dead!" I exclaimed, the words just tumbling out. "Oh, Hayley, I'm in big, big trouble."

Hayley's face was all sympathy. "I know. I heard."

"If I don't— What? You *what*?"

I can't describe the way my heart started slamming around in my chest. Was my life already over, then? Had Conway reported me? And how had Hayley found out when I was still in the dark?

"*What* did you hear, Hayley?"

"It's not that bad," she said soothingly, but she was obviously pretty embarrassed for me. "I mean, it isn't *good*, but—"

"Hayley!" I dropped my backpack and gripped her by the shoulders. "Tell me what you heard!"

Hayley made a face. "Sterling Carter is a pig. The way she was laughing in Spanish today . . . She's the one who started it."

"Started *what*?" By then I was practically screaming, but if

Sterling already knew I figured things couldn't get any worse. "Tell me *exactly*."

"You don't want me to repeat it," Hayley said, shocked.

"Yes! Repeat it! And do it now, before I have a complete nervous breakdown."

Hayley looked astonished. She peered into my eyes, and suddenly the light switched on in hers.

"I can't believe it," she said. "You really have no idea."

"Hayley!"

"Well . . ." It obviously killed her, but she finally spit it out. "There's a rumor going around that you're spending a lot of time in the bathroom."

"You're kidding!" I said, almost fainting with relief. "Is that all?"

I actually had to hold back a laugh. Sure, it was bad, but—

"With morning sickness," she added.

Don't Even Go There!

And don't expect me to either, because you and I would need to know each other a lot better before I wanted to discuss that. Let's just say certain . . . *acts* would have to occur before morning sickness was even possible. And they haven't occurred. Ever.

Hayley, of course, knows this. The rest of the school may or may not know this, but it isn't exactly the kind of thing a person can run around clarifying.

My knees gave out. I sank onto the bench.

"This time next week, I'll probably be in Catholic school," I moaned, hiding my face in my hands. "Or reform school. Is there a reform school in Hilltop?"

Hayley sat and put a reassuring arm around my shoulders. "No one's going to believe it," she said. "Well, a few people probably will. But when you don't have a baby, it'll all blow over."

"So I'm only ruined for the next nine months, then," I said bitterly.

"Less than that. Let's see, if you're already feeling sick . . ." Hayley started counting on her fingers.

"It was food poisoning!" I yelled.

And then I started to cry. I couldn't help it. If you've ever had rumors spread about you, you know how it feels. People tell you not to worry; they say lies can't hurt you. Are they *insane*? Besides, if I was going down, I at least wanted it to be for something I'd actually done.

Hayley tightened her arm to pull me closer. "Are you *crying*? Cassie, this'll blow over, I swear."

I shook my head without lifting my face from my hands. "You don't understand. I'm having a really bad day."

"I know what we should do. Let's start a rumor about Sterling. You want to?"

"Not really."

"It is kind of stooping to her level. But she deserves it."

I forced my head up to see a familiar fierce expression hardening Hayley's face.

"No, don't say anything," I begged. "I don't want to give her a reason to look for more ammunition."

"Let her look! What's she going to find?"

So I finally spilled the whole ugly story, right down to the depressing fact that I hadn't even enjoyed my time in the library with Kevin that morning. After three long days of fantasizing about seeing him again and imagining how great things would be when I did, the reality was that we'd barely spoken. I'd glanced at "our" finished play, then spent the rest of the hour hiding my guilty conscience by pretending to read Western civ.

"Wow," Hayley said when I'd finished. The obvious awe in her voice didn't do much to lift my spirits. "What are you going to do?"

"I was hoping you'd have an idea."

"Me!"

"Just tell me what *you'd* do," I begged.

"Well . . . if it were me . . ." Hayley's eyelids fluttered as she weighed the possibilities, hatching new ideas and then discarding them one by one. "I don't know," she said at last. "It sucks every way you turn. If you tell Conway the truth, Kevin'll probably never speak to you again. And if you don't . . ."

"Yeah. Thanks for spelling it out."

"Don't jump on *me*," she said, taking her arm off my shoulders. "You asked!"

"You're right. I'm sorry."

"So what *are* you going to do?"

"No clue," I said miserably.

We sat there awhile in silence. I think Hayley was trying to be sensitive. I was too depressed to speak.

"Are you going to eat lunch?" she ventured at last.

"Not hungry. Go ahead."

She took some pretzels out of her backpack while I stared into space, consumed by my impending doom. Every now and then, someone would walk past and flash me a mocking smile—a not-so-subtle reminder of my supposed pregnancy—but you'd be amazed how little I cared just then. Crazy escape plans swirled through my head. A mysterious fire, a run to Mexico . . .

But I kept coming back to two key questions: 1) When was Conway going to read those plays? and 2) What were the actual chances she'd recognize mine?

Because I was starting to consider a new possibility: maybe I wouldn't get caught.

No, that didn't make what I'd done right. And yes, it did seem unlikely. But it occurred to me sitting on that bench that even Conway couldn't have memorized every one-act play in the world.

Besides, it wasn't my fault, I thought, daring to breathe a little. Granted, I'd run up to the edge of that cliff, but Kevin had pushed me over. If worse came to worst and I did get caught, I had an excellent explanation. I even had another play already written. The best thing to do was stay cool. So long as I didn't panic—

"Hey, girls." A voice two feet away nearly gave me a heart attack. "What are you doing?"

I looked up to see Fitz grinning down at Hayley.

"I *told* you," she said, with a significant sideways glance at me.

"Oh, yeah. Right," he said uncomfortably.

I squeezed my eyes shut with humiliation. Even Fitz had heard.

"All right, then. I just wanted to say hi," he said. "I'll, uh . . . catch you later."

I opened my eyes in time to see his left leg stretch into a deep, awkward lunge, the fingertips of his right hand sweeping forward across the pavement. From there he jumped onto his toes, waving his arms overhead in the universal crowd-goes-crazy gesture. He winked at Hayley and then he was gone, strutting off across the quad.

"What was that?" I asked.

Hayley's dimples puckered. "I think it was a strike."

"A . . . what?"

"A strike. He's warming up for Memory Lanes this Saturday."

Memory Lanes is this very big school-sponsored party at the Hilltop Bowl-o-Rama. They rent the place for the whole night, and at nine o'clock they lock the doors and no one gets in or out until morning.

I don't know about where you live, but in California bowling is not a must-play sport. In fact, you can go your whole life without bowling and no one will think less of you. So I can assure you that the reason Memory Lanes sells out every year has nothing to do with bowling. It's the all-night aspect, the fact that you can spend those off-limits hours with the person you love and not get grounded the next day. Next to prom, which is only for seniors, and the winter formal, of course, Memory Lanes is the most mandatory couples event at our school.

I'd never been. Obviously. Until that moment, I hadn't even realized that was the week it was taking place.

And now Hayley was going with Fitz. It was like making an announcement to the entire school that they were serious about each other.

Hayley+Fitz. The real deal.

For a couple of minutes, I actually forgot my plagiarism problems, forgot my alleged morning sickness, forgot everything except wanting to be half of a couple so badly it ached up under my ribs.

I wanted to go to Memory Lanes.

And I wanted Kevin to take me.

Another Strike. Out.

Waiting for Conway's class on Wednesday was the most stressful experience of my entire life. I'd barely slept the night before, wondering if she was still awake, grading plays. I could picture her bent over some enormous desk in her living room, making an electric sharpener smoke with all the red pencils she pulled from her bun.

For her, marking papers is probably more fun than watching *The Late Show*.

But then I realized, still lying there wide awake, that given Conway's insistence on being called Mrs., I needed to put a husband in my mental picture somewhere. And I tried, I swear. I eventually added a desk lamp, a microwaveable dinner, and—I'm sorry to report—a couple of cats, but

I couldn't imagine her living with another human being. Who could put up with her 24/7? The guy would have to be a saint. Saint Conway.

Anyway, I hardly slept Tuesday night, so by Wednesday morning you'd think I'd have been too tired to care. No such luck. When the bell rang at the end of first period, I nearly passed out. I actually had to psych myself up to leave biology, which *proves* how scared I was. My heart thudded as I dragged my feet down the hall to Conway's room. I was in the final stretch when Jeannie Patrick grabbed my arm, spinning me around.

"Do you know what people are saying about you?" she demanded.

I nodded unhappily.

"I hope it's not true, because I'm telling everyone it's a lie. It *is* a lie, right?"

My supposed pregnancy should have been the last thing I wanted to discuss just then, but I was touched by Jeannie's support.

"It's a lie," I reassured her. "I had food poisoning, that's all."

Jeannie shook her head. "Sterling Carter's out to get you. You should have heard the stuff she was saying at Quentin's Halloween party."

"About *me*?" I shouldn't have been surprised, but I was.

"Oh, not directly. You know how she is, pretending to whisper to Ros and making sure the whole room can hear her."

I nodded. "I know how she is."

"While you were dancing with that guy—What's his

name? Kevin?—Sterling called you pushy, desperate, and completely without shame," Jeannie reported.

"She *what?*"

"Then she cut in and got him to dance with her instead."

"Oh, that's it!" I said, furious. "If she wants a war, she's going to get one!"

"Just thought you should know. Gotta go."

Jeannie dashed away down the hallway, which I suddenly noticed was nearly empty. My swelling anger at Fourteen-Karat shriveled as I realized I was now in danger of being tardy on top of everything else. Running at full speed, I skidded through Conway's doorway in unison with the ringing bell.

I almost died when she looked up from her roll book and locked eyes with me instead.

"Why shouldn't I mark you tardy?" she asked, pencil hovering over her book.

"Um . . . because . . . ," I forced out, fighting for breath. "Because a tie goes to the runner?"

A couple of people laughed.

"Go sit down," she said irritably, but she didn't mark the page.

Somehow I walked to the back of the room, trying to pretend my cheeks weren't flaming as I took the seat beside Kevin.

"Nice," he teased in a whisper while Conway read the roll. "Real smooth."

I sank lower in my chair, still just trying to breathe.

"Those of you who have already turned in your plays can leave for the library now," Mrs. Conway announced.

"And don't let me hear another negative word from Mr. McKay or this will be your last day there."

Ten of us got up to leave. Cyn Martin and Mike Peters led the rush, followed by six more people, then Kevin, then me. That meant five plays had been turned in early. Surely Conway would have already graded five measly one-act plays? I slouched out the door at the back of the group wondering if I might actually be in the clear.

"I've got a load of math to finish before fifth period," Kevin told me in the hall. "I won't be much fun in the library today."

"That's okay." Not talking was probably safer anyway.

"Do you have any homework?" he asked.

"I could do some biology."

We turned the corner, and that's when I saw it—a giant Memory Lanes banner strung across the hallway up ahead. Fat, heart-shaped bowling balls scattered pins at both ends, and between the pins were painted these words:

MEMORY LANES THIS SATURDAY. TICKETS ON SALE NOW.
BE THERE OR BE SPARE!

"Wow, Memory Lanes already," I said, grabbing the unexpected opportunity to raise the subject. "They sprang that on us early this year."

"Yeah?"

He didn't sound too interested. I injected my voice with extra enthusiasm.

"I don't remember exactly when it was last year, but I'm pretty sure it was later."

"Did you go?"

"No. Well, I was *going* to. . . ." Which is true, because I'd have gone in a New York second if anyone had asked me. "But . . . you know what it is, right?"

"Bowling?" He raised an eyebrow. "I've heard of it."

"Not just bowling!" I hurried to correct him. "I mean, all right—it's basically bowling. But bowling's not the *point*."

"No?"

"No! It's just a fun time. To hang out. With a person you might want to—"

"How stupid!" he exclaimed, stopping dead in the middle of the hall. "I just remembered I put my geometry book in my locker before first period. Now I'll have to go get it."

"Now? You're going to your locker *now*?" He'd get detention if a teacher caught him wandering the halls. More importantly, his timing couldn't be worse.

"I'll see you at the library."

He was gone before I could argue, loping off the way we'd just come. I crossed my fingers for him as he dodged around the corner, but I couldn't help being annoyed.

How big a hint does a girl have to drop?

Ticket to Slide

"Just stand in line with me," I begged Hayley at lunchtime. "I don't want to look pathetic."

"Right. Better if we both look pathetic," she said.

I knew what her problem was: she was mad because I

didn't want Fitz to wait in line with us. Who could blame me for *that*?

"Please, Hayley?" I pleaded. "How's it hurting you?"

After all, she was already invited to Memory Lanes—if anyone asked her, she could tell them who she was going with. I, on the other hand, had decided to take the drastic step of buying two tickets myself, just in case Kevin asked me. If anyone got nosy, I wanted to be able to pretend I was only waiting in line with Hayley.

"Let me get this straight," she said. "You're going to pay for tickets you don't even know if you're using?"

"They'll sell out! They always sell out, and Kevin's new here, so he doesn't know that. What if he asks me at the last minute and there aren't any tickets left?"

"Won't it look weird when you just magically make some appear?"

"I'll say I got them off a friend who decided not to go."

Hayley gave me a piercing look. "Have you noticed how good you're getting at lying?"

That wasn't a subject I wanted to consider. "Hayley, this is love. *And* war. Everyone knows that makes everything fair."

"Whatever," she sighed, finally allowing me to pull her to the back of the line.

The ASB (that's Associated Student Body, in case your student government is called something different) had set up tables along one edge of the quad, topped by reams of tickets and metal boxes for collecting money. The line to buy circled most of the quad, and even with eight people selling, it was moving at a crawl.

"Here's an idea," said Hayley. "Before we waste our entire lunchtime, why don't you ask Kevin if he *wants* to go with you?"

"Hayley!" I said, shushing her frantically. "Be serious. *He* has to ask *me*."

"Why? You invited him to Quentin's party."

"That was different!" Halloween is a major holiday, but no one could call it romantic. "Besides, I can't ask him to two things in a row. It'll look pushy . . . and desperate . . . and completely shameless."

Hayley's mouth twitched at the corners. "I see you've been talking to Jeannie Patrick."

"Yes." And then it hit me. "Hey, wait! You already knew about that?"

Hayley shrugged. "She told me at the party. I didn't think it was worth repeating."

"If people are talking about me, I've got a right to know!" I said indignantly. "How am I supposed to defend myself if I don't even know what they're saying?"

"How are you going to defend yourself if you do?" she countered.

"At least I'll know how embarrassed I should be."

"Fine. I was only trying to protect you. But if you think you need to know everything . . ."

"There's *more*?"

"Sterling was out of control that night. I overheard her telling Quentin she pitied him for ever being seen with you, and that he ought to aim higher next time if he doesn't want the whole school to think he's a loser."

"I'll bet Quentin let her have it," I said, steaming.

Hayley grimaced. "I suspect he would have loved to—but not the way you mean."

"He's so stupid!" I cried, betrayed. "Can't he see what she's up to?"

"Apparently not. Except, Cassie? What if she really does like him?"

"She doesn't! But as long as she's got Quentin panting after her, she can make him take her anywhere Kevin and I go." I gasped. "He might already have asked her to Memory Lanes!"

"I don't think so. Fitz would have mentioned it."

"We have to find out and tell him not to take her—no matter what."

The look Hayley gave me was not reassuring. "Like she can't get another date? I hate to say this, Cassie, but maybe if you stopped worrying so much about Sterling, things would go better for you."

"You're taking her side now?"

"Don't be ridiculous. It's just . . . you've changed. Ever since you met Kevin, you've been acting . . . I don't know. Not yourself."

"Right! *Not* myself," I flung back. "Not the sad little girl who stands on the sidelines while other girls get what they want. I'm *sick* of second place, Hayley. This time I'm going to win."

"If you don't get suspended first," she said darkly.

"Yeah. Thanks." I'd managed to forget about Conway for fifteen whole minutes.

"All I'm saying is, maybe you ought to back off a bit. Let him come to you."

I don't want to sound like a bad friend—especially not since Hayley was standing in that nightmare line with me—but I hate it when she acts like she's smarter than I am. Which she is. But does that mean she knows everything?

"Maybe you haven't heard," I told her, "but girls don't have to sit home waiting for guys to call anymore. We can ask out whoever we want."

"Right," Hayley said without batting an eye. "Like, for instance, *you* could ask *Kevin* if he wants to go bowling."

Let me just say this: if Hayley and my mother ever join forces, the world's in a lot of trouble.

Can You Hear Me Now?

I called Hayley that afternoon, after my homework was done but before my parents got home. Imagine me and Hayley on the phone, speaking in the assumed privacy of our respective bedrooms.

Me: Hi. Finish your homework?

Hayley: Except for pre-calculus. I'll probably be up until midnight with that.

Me: Nice. How many more weeks before summer?

Hayley: Too many. Then again, if we skipped

straight to June, you'd miss Memory Lanes. Did you call him yet?

Me: No! I told you, I'm not going to.

Hayley: Yeah, well. You say a lot of things.

(Imagine a pensive silence here, while I try to figure out if that's a crack.)

Me: At least I have tickets now. Plus, you saved Fitz from standing in line for yours, which is like a service to the whole school.

Hayley: I guess. But *he's* getting our tickets for the Snow Ball.

Me: That's over a month away.

Hayley: What's your point? You think we won't still be together?

Me: No! I mean . . . It's just . . . Doesn't he have to ask you first?

Hayley: He already did. Today.

(Imagine Hayley sounding totally smug. Imagine me feeling left out. Again.)

Hayley: I'm going shopping for a dress
            tomorrow after school. Want to
            come?

Me: Okay, now that's *definitely* early.

Hayley: Yeah, but I want to start looking before
            everything gets picked over.

Me: Maybe I should start looking too. You
            know, just in case.

Hayley: So you'll come?

Me: Assuming Conway doesn't bust me
            tomorrow. I really wish I knew whether
            she'd read those plays.

Hayley: You could still tell her what happened.
            Give her your other play. If you wait until
            she catches you, that door is closed
            forever.

Me: It's probably closed right now. I mean, I
            already waited this long.

Hayley: True.

Me: If only Kevin weren't mixed up in this!
            Then I might take a chance and tell

Conway the truth. But what's he going
to say if he finds out I copied our play
from a book? Right now he thinks I'm
smart.

Hayley: You are smart. Besides, if Kevin weren't
           involved, none of this would have
           happened.

Me: I'm just going to cross my fingers and
           ride it out. Do you think he'll ask me to
           Memory Lanes?

Hayley: I don't know. Maybe.

(My face itches. I scratch it, only to be reminded of another
problem.)

Me: I'm getting a zit on my nose. What if I
           wake up tomorrow and I have this giant
           red pustule right in the middle of my face?

Hayley: Sounds attractive.

Me: Hayley, this is serious! He's not going to
           ask me if I have a big zit!

Hayley: So he's all about the inner you.

Me: He won't be able to *see* the inner me if
          he has to look past a giant red honker.

Hayley: If he's that shallow, why do you like
          him?

*(Imagine a long discussion here where I remind Hayley that
Kevin is only flesh and blood, whereas Fourteen-Karat is
flesh in all the right places, not to mention perfectly smooth
tan skin. Imagine Hayley trying to pretend this doesn't
matter. Imagine my frustration with someone who's only
had a boyfriend one week and already forgot the whole
system.)*

Me: I'd better get off the phone. My mom's
          going to be home any minute, and if I
          haven't done my chores she goes ballistic.

Hayley: Yeah, okay. I've got stuff too. See you
          tomorrow.

*(Imagine the sound of a phone hanging up. Imagine my
brows bunching quizzically when the line still sounds open.
Imagine my heart nearly stopping when I hear snickering on
the other end.)*

Me: Trevor!

Trevor: That's my name. Don't wear it out.

Me: What are you doing on the phone, you
           little creep?

(*Imagine me hyperventilating as I try to figure out when he
picked up.*)

Trevor: Let me break it down for you, Cass.
           There are two things a person can do
           on a phone: talk and listen. If you'll
           notice, I wasn't talking.

Me: I'm going to *kill* you! Wait till I tell Mom
           you were eavesdropping!

Trevor: Mom, Cassie? Oh, no. I don't think you'll
           be talking to Mom.

Me: Listen, Trevor, whatever you think you
           heard—

My voice on tape:

           If only Kevin weren't mixed up in this!
           Then I might take a chance and tell
           Conway the truth. But what's he going
           to say if he finds out I copied our play
           from a book?

Me: (*Shrieking in horror*) You *recorded* me?
           Trevor, you sneaky little sh—

Trevor: If I were you, I'd watch my mouth, Cass.
            You wouldn't want to upset me, would
            you?

Me: I'm coming to your room to get that
            tape and then I'm going to—

(Imagine me, listening to a dead line.)

Zits, Lies, and Audiotape

Remember that discussion we had about karma? Here's how it works: you break a couple of rules, you zig where you should have zagged, and the next thing you know your pestilent younger brother has a tape of the most incriminating conversation of your entire life and your nose is leading you around school like Rudolph's on Christmas Eve. When I woke up and saw myself in the mirror the next morning, I could only *pray* for fog.

Or an eclipse.

Any natural disaster would have worked.

But nothing bad ever happens when I *want* it to, so sixty minutes and four layers of concealer later I was walking down the hall to biology, stuffing my hands into my pockets to avoid inadvertently wrecking an already iffy makeup job.

In biology, Mr. Rich was dissecting a pigeon, but all I could think about was the way my nose was throbbing. And Trevor. And that horrible tape. And where he could have hidden it in the seconds it had taken me to storm his bed-room. And—most frightening of all—what he might do with it next.

Because there were no two ways about it: my brother owned me now. Owned me like a dog. I was totally at his mercy.

And the little psycho knew it. He was *reveling* in it. He'd already promised to have some "very special assignments" for me soon, and believe me when I tell you I didn't want to know what they'd be. We both knew I'd have to do any-thing he said.

It felt like waiting for a bomb to go off. And not just the one on the end of my nose.

"Cassie?" said Mr. Rich.

"Huh?" I said, jerking to attention.

The whole class started laughing.

"I *said*," Mr. Rich repeated, pointing to the mess he was making of that poor dead bird, "what is this vein called?"

Everyone was smirking at me. I put a hand over my face, pretending I needed to scratch my forehead but really kind of hiding my nose. "Which vein?" I asked, stalling. "Can you point to it again?"

Mr. Rich pointed.

"The, uh . . . the chest vein?"

"Very nice," Mr. Rich said, in a voice that implied just the opposite. "How about paying attention now?"

Teresa Harvey identified the vena cava, and I tried to focus after that, but you can imagine how well I succeeded. As soon as the bell rang, I took off for the bathroom, des-perate to touch up my makeup before Kevin saw me.

I nearly cried when I saw my reflection. My nose looked like a mutant cherry tomato. I piled on more concealer, but that only made things worse. In the end I had to bolt, rushing through Conway's doorway just seconds before the bell rang.

"Cutting it close again, Cassie." Her eyes met mine with uncomfortable intensity.

"Sorry," I mumbled, dropping my gaze and hurrying to my seat. But at least one thing was finally going my way: Conway was still clueless. If she'd recognized my play, her outrage would have been obvious.

And she has to have read it by now, I thought. Putting my elbows on my desk, I slumped down until my hands hovered around the middle of my face. I gave Kevin a quick smile from between my fingers, then pretended to be very interested in the roll call.

There ought to be sick days for zits like that. I'm completely serious.

I can just see my absence note:

> *Please excuse Catherine Howard. She had a pimple the size of a watermelon. After hours of mental torment, it finally gushed pus last night, but I felt it best to keep her home, to replenish all those fluids.*

Never mind. Bad idea.

Mrs. Conway reminded the class that the plays were due the next day. Then she dismissed us for the library. I walked out beside Kevin, still using one hand for camouflage and painfully aware that if he didn't ask me to Memory Lanes soon we probably weren't going. We were under the banner in the hallway, trailing the rest of our group again, when I finally brought it up.

"Are you doing anything fun this weekend?" I ventured.

"Maybe," he said. "Are you?"

"I *could* be," I hinted. "I'm not *entirely* booked up yet."

He smiled, forcing me to drop my hand to smile back. I waited for the look of revulsion to enter his eyes, but he didn't seem to notice my gross disfigurement.

"You will be," he said. "If that's what you want."

My heart raced. Was that code for an impending invitation?

"You think so?" I asked hopefully. "Maybe you know something I don't?"

He shrugged. "I can just tell you're the sort of girl who always gets what she wants."

"No!" I protested. "Oh, that's so not true. I *almost* always get what I want."

Kevin laughed. "I see."

He obviously didn't.

"No, listen. I didn't mean I almost *always* get it. I meant I always *almost* get it. There's a huge difference."

He just shook his head, still grinning. "You ought to go into politics."

Butt Weight, There's More. . . .

"I can't figure it out," I complained to Hayley as we climbed off the city bus at the mall that afternoon. "I really thought he was going to ask me. He made it sound like he was hinting. . . ."

"There's always tomorrow," Hayley said.

"The tickets are sold out. I checked."

"But by a strange stroke of luck, you've got that cov-ered." Hayley stopped to stare at a mannequin in Visions's front window. "Let's go in here."

Visions is a local store, kind of a cross between a fancy boutique and The Gap. They carry it all, from prom dresses to jeans. There's even a section of vintage clothing.

"I want a white dress," Hayley announced. "Or pink."

"Pink? Really?" I'm the one who likes pink.

"Well, maybe peach," she said, reconsidering. "Or lavender. I don't know yet."

She started examining a long rack of formals, where the selection for the upcoming holidays ran more to black and wine than pastels. I flipped through a few dresses, but it was hard to get excited about a dance that was still a month away.

Especially since I didn't have a date.

"Who do you think will be Snow Queen this year?" I asked. Our winter formal's Snow Queen is kind of like homecoming queen, only bigger, because it's not restricted to seniors. Anyone can run.

Hayley shrugged. "One of the usual suspects."

Anyone can run, but only the superelite ever win. Being Snow Queen is a soc's dream.

"Here's a pink one," I said, pulling out a dress to show Hayley.

"That's not pink, it's fuchsia."

"Just checking."

A little farther along I found a cream-colored satin number, very sexy, with a beaded bodice and a long, fitted skirt. I started to show it to Hayley, then held it against my body instead, smoothing it to my limited curves. Glancing around, I spotted a mirror and walked over to see how I looked.

"Why?" I groaned, appalled. If that dress was a scoop of vanilla, my nose was the cherry on top.

"What?" Hayley asked, turning toward me.

"My nose! No wonder he didn't ask me!"

"It's not that bad. I wouldn't even notice if you didn't keep bringing it up."

I gave her a skeptical look.

"Well, I wouldn't notice *constantly*," she said, taking the dress from my hand. "Now this has potential. I'm trying it on."

I sat on the floor beneath the rack, putting on fresh concealer while Hayley considered more dresses. When she'd narrowed her choices to three, I put my compact away and stood up to follow her to the dressing rooms.

That's when I spotted Fourteen-Karat.

She and Ros were over by the jeans. They had their backs to us, but there was no mistaking that perfect blond mane or the tight tan thighs beneath the micromini.

"She's not really going to buy *pants*?" I hissed to Hayley. "I thought her bare legs were part of the permanent exhibit."

Hayley followed my gaze, tensing when she spotted Fourteen-Karat. Grabbing my arm, she pulled me off to the dressing rooms.

"Stay here until she goes away," Hayley instructed, shutting me into a big booth with her. "Every time you two get near each other, something bad happens."

"And that's *my* fault?" I asked, outraged.

Hayley slipped an emerald green dress over her head. "No. But why do you want to play her game?"

"I don't *want* to," I said sullenly, sinking onto the dressing room bench.

I sulked while Hayley fussed with the dress, tweaking it this way and that, trying to make it fit better. All of a sudden, a loud, incredibly obnoxious voice broke our self-imposed silence. Fourteen-Karat Carter had entered the dressing rooms.

"I'll try these jeans on," she announced, "but I'm still not sure I like them."

"You will. Everything looks cute on *you*," Ros simpered.

I pretended to stick my finger down my throat, miming gagging. Hayley clapped a hand over her mouth to keep from laughing and giving us away.

"Take the booth next to mine," F.K. said.

"We can both use this big one," Ros offered.

"Why? It's not like people are waiting."

"True," Ros said, sounding embarrassed.

I heard a couple of doors shut, then nothing but zippers and banging around. Meanwhile, Hayley had put on the cream-colored dress, which looked absolutely gorgeous on her. Envy stabbed my insides, but I pasted on a smile and flashed her a thumbs-up.

"These pants are cut small," Ros complained. "Do yours fit?"

"Mine are too loose," Fourteen-Karat bragged.

"Size four is too *loose?*"

"Yeah, I knew I liked that other style better. I'm going back out to get those."

"Give me a second and I'll go with you."

"No. Wait here," Fourteen-Karat instructed. "I'll just run out wearing these, and I'll bring you a bigger size. What do you need? An eight?"

"I guess so," Ros said unhappily.

"I'll bring the tens, too, just in case."

"How does Ros *stand* her?" I whispered to Hayley when I was sure Fourteen-Karat had gone. "She makes wearing a normal size sound like a crime."

"Ros is no prize herself," Hayley whispered back.

Which is true, but I almost felt sorry for her, bumping around that big dressing room by herself, waiting on Fourteen-Karat . . .

And then I had a brilliant idea.

"Stay here," I hissed to Hayley. "I'll be right back."

"Where are you going?" she whispered. "Promise you're not going after her!"

"I'm not. I swear."

Opening our dressing room door, I peered out cautiously. I could see Ros's feet beneath a closed door across the way, and the door of the stall next to hers standing open. Darting out of our dressing room, I hurried across the empty aisle and into Fourteen-Karat's. Her discarded skirt was on the floor; I snatched it up and turned the waistband inside out, intent on only one thing. . . .

But where the size tag should have been, only a frayed edge remained. I grabbed her denim jacket off a hook—same drill. Both tags had been cut out.

"Sterling?" Ros said from the other side of the cheesy wall.

Replacing the jacket, I ran back to Hayley and silently shut our door.

"What are you *doing*?" she demanded.

"Tell you later," I whispered back.

Fourteen-Karat returned, keeping up a running commentary as she threw some pants over Ros's door and began trying on more herself. The two of them finally emerged, Ros having decided that nothing fit right and F.K. having selected a pair of size fours she claimed fit perfectly.

"What were you doing out there?" Hayley asked me the second they left.

"Sterling's such a liar. I went and checked her clothes, to see what size she *really* wears."

Hayley's eyebrows rose. "Sneaky. Potentially mean. And yet I'm strangely impressed."

Unfortunately, then I had to admit that I hadn't learned anything. But Hayley had a plan.

"It's simple," she said. "Check the tags on the pants she's buying now."

My eyes widened. "She's probably already at the register."

Hayley gave me an impish smile. "Let's go."

We rushed out of the dressing room. Sure enough,

Fourteen-Karat was at the front of the store paying for her jeans, while Ros lingered twenty feet away, looking at the sweaters. Charging through the racks, Hayley and I ran up behind Fourteen-Karat. Her new pants were on the counter, their tags conveniently tucked out of sight. In another second, the cashier would put them in a bag.

Which is why I basically skipped up and grabbed them.

"Buying these?" I asked, holding them tauntingly out of reach.

"What are you doing? Give those back!" F.K. lunged, but she wasn't fast enough to keep me from reading the tags.

"Size eight!" I crowed triumphantly. "That's so odd, Sterling, because don't you tell *everyone* you're a size four?"

"Those pants are cut small," she said, yanking them away from me.

Behind her, I saw a small, disbelieving smile flit onto Ros's lips.

"Two whole *sizes* small?" I mocked.

Sterling's blue eyes narrowed. "You think you're so smart. Just wait."

"For what?" I asked recklessly. "Your next stupid rumor? Try to make it good next time. Pregnancy is so unimaginative."

Fourteen-Karat drew herself up like she was going to explode. Then, somehow, she reined it back in. Stuffing her pants into a shopping bag, she gave me this infuriatingly condescending look.

"Just wait," she repeated. "The rental shoe's about to be on the other foot."

That was a hint, but I lost it in the sucker punch of Fourteen-Karat's final zinger: "See you later, *Bozo*. Does that nose honk like a horn or just squirt water at the other clowns?"

Then she strutted out Visions's front door, her miniskirt twitching over her too-perfect-to-lie-about size-eight butt.

See, that's the thing with Fourteen-Karat: even when you win, you lose.

. . . <u>Now</u> How Would You Pay?

By Friday morning I'd quit expecting Conway to bust me any second. Furthermore, as long as Trevor wanted to keep power over me—and believe me, he *lives* for that—I could pretty much forget about his tape. Best of all, my zit was on a downhill slide. There was only one thing left to stress about: the fact that if Kevin didn't ask me to Memory Lanes in the next fifty minutes, we probably weren't going to go.

All through Conway's announcements, I cast meaning-ful looks his way, willing him to read my mind. By the time we were trailing the others to the library, I was getting wor-ried. If he was going to ask me, he ought to do it in the hall-way, while we still had some privacy. The Memory Lanes banner was just ahead. This was his big chance.

The banner was closer, closer, closer . . . directly overhead . . . farther, farther, farther . . . receding into the distance . . .

"So! Memory Lanes tomorrow," I blurted desperately. "Are you . . . uh, are you going?"

"Yeah," he said. "Looks like it."

My heart stopped. If he was going with me, wouldn't I know about it?

"You, uh . . . you have tickets? Because I heard they sold out."

"They did. I would have missed the whole thing, but luckily Sterling knew that would happen and she'd already bought some."

"You're going with *Sterling*?" It screeched out of my mouth before I could stop it.

Kevin looked amazed. "Yeah. So?"

"It's, uh . . . it's just that I . . . I thought . . ." I fumbled, struggling for air. "I mean, I was *hoping* . . . well . . . maybe you and I . . ."

The expression on his face only made it worse.

"We had fun on Halloween," I finished lamely.

"We did." His eyes studied mine, which I'm embarrassed to say were filling with tears. "Cassie, you're not upset with me, are you?"

"I—I—I—"

"Because I heard this was a couples event, like some romantic type of thing. If it was only for friends, I definitely would have asked you."

"Because we're friends," I said dully, the full weight of my birthright crushing my heart to dust. "You and I . . . we're friends."

"Aren't we? You're probably the best girl friend I've ever had. Hanging out with you is almost like having a sister."

Girl+friend.

Sister!

I'm such an idiot.

Morning Sickness

Saturday was the first day of the worst three days of my life. I cried myself to sleep Friday night and woke up feeling like I'd been dragged beneath a truck. And that was only a taste of the horrors to come.

Trevor, for example.

"I might have a job for you tomorrow," he announced, poking his head into my room before I'd even climbed out of bed. "I'll let you know."

"Oh, please. Do that," I said sarcastically. "And by all means, be as mysterious as possible."

"That's my plan," he said gleefully. "You'd better learn to like it, because if you don't do what I say . . ."

"Get out of my room, you little toad," I said, forcing myself out from beneath the covers to push him into the hall. "Even SWAT teams knock."

Which probably isn't true, but I was in no mood for Trevor that morning.

"Cassie, Cassie, Cassie," he said like an eighth-grade Godfather. "Someday I'll come to you for a favor—"

"Get *out!*" I said, pushing harder.

He went, sniggering all the way, leaving me to fantasize about kicking his scrawny butt through a wall. As always, I resisted. Unfortunately, the resulting adrenaline left me so wide awake that there was nothing to do but get dressed and ponder the abyss of my life.

Kevin and Fourteen-Karat.

Kevin and Fourteen-Karat at Memory Lanes.

Kevin and Fourteen-Karat, Hilltop High's hot new couple.

The mere idea made me feel like drowning myself in a bucket of vomit.

Second Sight

"What are you so mopey about?" my mother asked when I shuffled into the kitchen. She was sitting at the breakfast bar with a cup of tea, not a care in the world.

"Nothing," I said, banging cabinet doors as I searched for something edible. Trevor had polished off all the good cereals, leaving only my parents' fiber pellets.

"Why is there no food in this house?" I complained. "Why can't you buy groceries more often?"

Mom raised an eyebrow at me. If I'd been in a better mood, I'd have backpedaled in a hurry. About the most dangerous thing anyone can suggest is that my mother is falling down in the household duties department.

"Well, let's see," she drawled sarcastically. "Maybe if I wasn't so busy being a *lawyer*, I'd have more time to run out for Cocoa Critters. Sorry to inconvenience you by paying for the house and your clothes and whatnot."

Here's what I'd like to know: why do parents act like it's *our* fault they have to take care of us? I mean, bringing me into this world sure as heck wasn't my idea, and when you consider all the aggravation it's cost me, a bowl of cereal doesn't seem like a lot to ask for.

"If my chores aren't getting done to your satisfaction," Mom continued, "perhaps you'd like to do them yourself."

"Perhaps I would, if I could drive," I flung back. "But I can't carry all our groceries home on my bicycle."

An evil glint entered Mom's eyes. "You could if you shopped every day."

"No way! I am *not* going to the store every day!"

"And neither am I," she said, returning to her tea. "Deal with it."

A triumphant smile played at the corners of her mouth. I could only stand there steaming as I realized I'd just been tricked into shouting her argument for her.

"Great. Fine," I said sullenly. "I won't eat breakfast, then."

"Suit yourself. But I'll be happy to make a shopping list if you feel like taking a ride."

"Forget it. I don't even know what I was thinking. Of *course* Trevor gets the good cereal and I get the leftovers. You and I could *both* go to the store every day and I'd *still* end up chewing Bran Bullets, because that's the story of my life."

Mom put down her cup. "What are you talking about?"

"Talent. Destiny. It's pointless trying. I give up."

She studied me like an ant that had wandered beneath her magnifying glass. "What happened?" she asked at last.

"Who said anything happened?"

Mom gave me a pitying look. "Please, Cassie. I make my living reading people."

"I thought you made it arguing."

"And how do you think I win?"

I sighed. "If you have to know, Memory Lanes is tonight and nobody asked me."

"Oh." She actually looked sympathetic. "I remember how that feels. But it doesn't have to scar you for life. Why don't you invite Hayley to sleep over? You girls haven't kept me awake all night with your giggling in a while."

"Hayley's going," I said bitterly. "She and Fitz are in love."

"Hayley and Fitz? Honestly?" Which only goes to show how unfair it was of Hayley to get mad at me for the same reaction.

"Well, what about Quentin?" Mom asked, recovering. "Maybe the two of you can go with them. As *friends*," she added in response to my aggrieved look.

"Quentin's going with Ros Pierce."

Because of course I'd thought of Quentin myself, as soon as I'd stopped reeling. If Kevin was going with Sterling, that left me and Quentin both out in the cold. Obviously, taking me was the perfect way for him to keep an eye on things. But for once Quentin was ahead of me: he'd already asked Ros.

"Sterling'll be so jealous!" he'd crowed, forcing me to walk away before I defined *deluded* for him. He never even mentioned that his crush was going with *my* crush. It had apparently never occurred to him that I liked Kevin that way.

Which made two of them.

"That's too bad," my mother said. "But, well . . . if all your friends are going to be there, why don't you just go? It's not like you need a date."

"Yes, it is! It's *exactly* like I need a date. But the guy I like is taking someone else, and even the guy I *don't* like is taking someone else! It doesn't matter what I do, I'm always second best."

"That's not true."

"It's *completely* true!" I cried. "You don't know what it's like, because *you* always win. But this is how it works, Mom: every time you're number one, someone else is getting their heart stomped in second place. And that person is me—that's who I am. The only reason I'm on this planet is to give other people somebody to beat!"

All right, looking back, a wee bit dramatic. But I'd had it. I really had.

My mom took a long time with her response. "You're not a loser, Cassie. And to believe that's your calling in life is just ridiculous."

I started to protest, but she waved me back to silence.

"For purposes of argument, though, let's say you're right, that life *is* stacked against you. Do you know what that would mean?"

"That I'll never win and then I'll die," I muttered sullenly.

"Get over yourself! Simple statistics dictate that if you try a task enough times, eventually you'll be successful. Life is like flipping a coin—you might get a long run of heads, but eventually you'll hit tails. In order for you to never, ever win, the entire universe would have to be structured around you. You'd be a law of nature all to yourself. You would be, quite literally, the most important person on earth."

Mom swirled her tea around her cup, then looked me straight in the eye.

"Let me ask you something," she said. "Do you *feel* important?"

My jaw fell open. It took me a couple of tries before I could even make a sound. "Not that important," I managed.

"Then quit whining and get out there. Flip a coin. Roll the dice. The more you play, the more you win."

I don't know about you, but parental pep talks usually have exactly the opposite effect on me. But this time my mom was right—I could feel it. Something about her argument made such brilliant sense.

"I have to go," I blurted out, running for my bedroom.

The more I play, the more I win, I thought, racing down the hall.

Let the games begin.

Stupid and Tragic and Not So Romantic

I was a nervous wreck by the time I stopped my dad's car outside Hilltop Bowl-o-Rama. My hands shook noticeably as I let myself out the driver's door.

"Talk about your white-knuckle driver!" Dad teased. "With all the driving practice you've had, you shouldn't be so tense."

"I'm not," I said. "Nobody's tense."

Which was a blatant lie, but I felt like if I stopped to explain, I might burst into flames. Besides, I can always count on my dad not to pursue an unpleasant subject. True to form, he moved into the seat I'd just vacated, told me to call when I wanted a ride home, and drove away. That was my cue to go inside, but instead I stood rooted to the sidewalk, taking deep breaths of the cool night air and calming my jittery hands by smoothing imaginary wrinkles from my new miniskirt.

You heard me: miniskirt. And I was wearing it with my highest pair of heels. Not only that but I'd bought a bra that . . . made the most of things, and a blouse that guaranteed people would notice. My hair was mussed up with gel, smoky eye shadow darkened my lids, and I'd even risked red lipstick. Nothing about my appearance was my usual style, but that was exactly the point. My mother's pep talk had fired me up, and the more I'd thought about it, the more hopeful I'd become.

What if I *wasn't* the Queen of Second Place? What if my reign was all in my head, just a run of bad luck, like my mother said?

I'll tell you what: if I wasn't the Queen, then simple statistics were on my side. I was *totally* due to win.

So that night outside the bowling alley I was determined to accomplish two things: (1) crush Fourteen-Karat, and (2) win Kevin's heart. Honestly, just then I couldn't have told you which I wanted worse. My priorities were starting to blur, but I didn't want to think about that, so instead I made a plan. It was simple when you broke it down:

1. Kevin thought of me as a friend because I'd been *acting* like a friend.
2. Fourteen-Karat had been hitting on Kevin from the start.

3. Fourteen-Karat's tactics had obviously worked better than mine.

4. Two could play her game.

Still, even with all that logic behind me, I had to psych myself up before I walked through the Bowl-o-Rama door and handed my Memory Lanes ticket to Principal Ito. He was wearing his usual worried expression, along with a corny 50s-style bowling shirt and multicolored shoes. The alley behind him was packed, but my timing was perfect— no one else was in line.

The principal tore my ticket in half and put both pieces in a bowl. "You're arriving late. It's almost time for lock-down, Ms. . . ." He looked at me expectantly.

"Howard," I supplied. "Cassie Howard."

"Yes, well. Have a good time, Cassie."

"I intend to," I assured him.

Principal Ito couldn't have realized it, but the lateness of my arrival was a key part of my plan. The idea was to let everyone else show up first, let them get good and settled, then crash their party when they least expected it. I wanted to make an entrance. I wanted to shake things up. And I wanted to take Kevin from Fourteen-Karat in the most public way possible.

I wove through the crowd in the direction of the snack bar, just getting a feel for things. The main lights had been dimmed, and rows of tiny blue bulbs illuminated the bowling lane gutters. Masses of helium balloons clustered above the scoring stations and lined the long railing dividing the lanes' lower level from the upper-level snack bar, shoe-rental counter, and video arcade. Overhead speakers blared music at a volume that made the beeps and sirens from the arcade, the cheers and groans of the bowlers, and even the crashing of falling pins fade to background noise. I got in line and bought a soda, mostly to look busy while I scanned the crowd for my target.

I spotted Hayley and Fitz before Kevin, primarily because they were actually bowling. Also, no one could call Fitz's technique graceful. His long arms and legs flailed like the blades of a spastic windmill as he flung himself down the lane, but Hayley didn't seem to mind. She encouraged his every attempt, cheering wildly when he actually got a strike. They were such an obvious couple now; it wrenched my heart to think that if Kevin had asked *me* to be his date, we could be playing against them. Still, wasn't that exactly the situation I'd come to fix? Tearing my attention away from Hayley, I started looking for Kevin.

I knew I was getting warmer when I spotted Quentin and Ros. They were at a scoring station, pretending to enter the scores for their lane, but with all the flirting going on, their accuracy was suspect. Ros kept laughing like crazy, throwing her head back with every peal to make sure she got a good hair toss in.

Here's one thing I know about guys: they love to think they're funny. Every time Ros laughed, Quentin beamed and ventured another witty comment, which made Ros laugh even harder. The whole scene had me wondering who was playing whom, but since I couldn't see any gain for Ros, I decided Quentin was still in the driver's seat. Sort of. Because if the idea was to make Sterling jealous, shouldn't she be around to witness his performance?

And then, huddled in two dark seats against the low wall behind Quentin and Ros, almost lost in the shadows, I spotted Kevin and Fourteen-Karat. And to say that she wasn't concerned about Quentin would be an understatement. She'd practically crawled into Kevin's lap, leaving only enough of one leg on her seat to prevent someone else from sitting there. Her back was draped across Kevin's chest, allowing her to wrap her arms around his neck and gaze up adoringly into his eyes, holding on for all she was worth.

The sight knocked the wind out of me. I'd expected to see them together, but I wasn't prepared for *that*. I squeezed my snack-bar cup so hard the lid popped off and Coke ran down my arm. For a few dizzy seconds, I thought I might faint. And then I started getting mad. How dare she climb him like her own private Everest? Throwing my drink in the trash, I headed straight for the happy couple.

Principal Ito's voice came over the speakers as I passed the shoe-rental counter, announcing lockdown in ten minutes, but I didn't join the people who cheered through the accompanying sirens and disco lights. I marched down the stairs and right past the sign that said BOWLING SHOES ONLY, my high heels clicking on the hardwood floor of the lower level.

I honestly hadn't expected a pair of nonregulation shoes to attract so much attention, but before I covered half the distance, people had stopped bowling to stare at me.

"Hey, Red!" some unimaginative idiot yelled, making more heads turn. "Want a bowling lesson?"

Obviously no one had told him Memory Lanes was a couples' event—his lane was full of leering single guys.

"I'll teach you to handle balls," one of them offered, prompting riotous laughs from his friends.

I raised my chin and kept walking.

"Cassie?" Quentin gasped as I passed him. "What are you doing here? Why are you wearing those shoes?"

I swept past without answering. Part of me realized he'd abandoned scoring to follow, and that Ros was trailing him, but I was so focused on my destination I didn't give those two a second thought. Reaching Kevin's chair at last, I planted my feet shoulder width apart and flashed him my brightest smile.

"Hello," I said flirtatiously, as if Fourteen-Karat weren't even there. "Done any bowling yet?"

I could tell he was surprised to see me, but not as surprised as Fourteen-Karat. She sprang out of his lap like a cat sprayed by a garden hose, positively spitting.

"What are *you* doing here?" she demanded. "Where's your date?"

Kevin hesitated, then stood up too. "Hey, Cassie. I didn't know you were coming tonight."

"I was in the neighborhood, so I thought, why not?" I said, praying I sounded as casual as when I had practiced that line in my bedroom.

"You were in the neighborhood with a *ticket*?" Fourteen-Karat scoffed. "A ticket to a sold-out event?"

"How do you like it so far?" I asked Kevin. "Is it everything you hoped for?" I finally allowed myself a disdainful, split-second glance at Sterling.

"Um, yeah." He seemed a bit dazed. "Wow, Cassie. You look . . . different."

"What? This?" I twisted my shoulders back and forth to make sure he noticed the miracle of engineering beneath my blouse.

"Where's your *date?*" Fourteen-Karat repeated, looking ready to kill me.

"Does a girl need a date to hang out with her friends?" I moved in closer to Kevin and tried to make my voice sultry. "You know what I was thinking? Why don't I rent some of those ridiculous shoes and we can all bowl together?"

"You're going to bowl in a skirt?" Fourteen-Karat asked disbelievingly.

I took in her too-tight new jeans with satisfaction. "What's the matter?" I asked, locking eyes with her at last. "Afraid I'll beat you?"

"In your dreams!" she retorted.

We both knew we weren't talking about bowling.

"So what's wrong with a little competition?"

I heard Ros snort behind me. Then she and Quentin stepped into our circle to buffer the encounter. Fourteen-Karat put her hands on her hips and glared.

"I don't want to bowl," she told me. "And even if I did, it wouldn't be with you. Go hit on someone else's date."

"Is that what I'm doing? That's pretty rich, coming from you."

Kevin looked embarrassed enough to sink through the floor, but I couldn't back down now.

"You'd better be very careful what you say next," Fourteen-Karat warned.

Quentin took me by one elbow and tried to pull me away. "Hey, Cassie," he said nervously. "Come on, we'll bowl with you."

"Quentin!" Ros protested, shooting me a venomous look. "You didn't bring *me* just to hang out with *her*!"

"That's true, Quentin," I said, provoked. "You brought her to make Sterling jealous. By the way, how's that working for you?"

Quentin dropped my elbow like a hot coal.

Ros turned on him hysterically. "Is that true?"

"No. Well . . . yes. But you have to realize . . . ," Quentin mumbled, mortified, "it doesn't mean that I don't like you."

"I *hate* you!" Ros shrieked. I wasn't sure which of us she meant, but before we could get that cleared up, she burst into angry tears. "Stay away from me!" she cried, running off.

We all turned to watch her go, and that's when I saw Fitz and Hayley running toward us from the opposite direction. Hayley gave Ros an amazed look as she passed, then hurried forward to join us.

"What's going on?" she asked. "Cassie, what are you doing here?"

"That's the million-dollar question," Fourteen-Karat said with a sneer.

Kevin put a hand on her shoulder and whispered in her ear. The sight of their faces so close together twisted my stomach into a knot, and when Sterling's lips curled into a smirk, something inside me just died.

"You're right. It's sad," she replied, in a whisper the whole group could hear. "I feel sorry for her, really."

The blood rushed to my face. Did Kevin say I was sad? Or was she putting words in his mouth?

"You take that back," I demanded.

"Take what back?" she asked, all innocence. "I wasn't even talking to you."

The funny thing about can't-win situations is that they're also can't-lose situations. Whether or not Fourteen-Karat understood that, she'd just made it clear to me.

"Take it back," I repeated.

"Or what?" She rolled her eyes for Kevin's benefit, swirling an index finger beside her ear to portray my mental state. "You're going to make me?"

The next part isn't too clear. I remember leaning in to get nearer to her face, and the next thing I knew, I was *right* in her face. She might have leaned in too. Anyway, we bumped into each other. My hands came up and shoved, just to put some air between us, and we both went reeling backward. I'd have landed smack on my butt if I hadn't been caught from behind. I turned to thank my rescuer— and found myself face to face with Principal Ito.

"Exactly what do you think you're doing, Ms. . . . Howard, was it?" he asked.

Behind him, half our school had gathered to witness my humiliation. A sea of faces gawked at me, agog with disbelief.

"I just . . . It was . . ." I hung my head, unable to speak.

"It's nothing," Kevin put in. "A little misunderstanding."

"A little!" Fourteen-Karat snuggled into his side, rubbing one arm as if she'd sustained major damage.

"More like a disturbance," Principal Ito said. "And you, Ms. Howard, appear to be the cause."

"Me?" I protested, rallying a little. "But she—"

"I saw the whole thing," the principal interrupted. "And here's what I observed: Number one, everything was quiet in this corner until you joined it. Number two, you walked right past the BOWLING SHOES ONLY sign with complete disregard for these maple floors. And number three, you pushed Ms. Carter here in flagrant violation of our school's nonaggression policy. You obviously can't follow the rules, so I'm going to ask you to leave."

The crowd gasped. Even I gasped. Everyone knows the school rule against fighting, but my misguided, momentary contact with Sterling was hardly a WWE SmackDown! match.

"You're kicking me out?" I squeaked.

"I'm escorting you to the door," he said—like there's a difference. "Lockdown is in five minutes, and I think it will be better for everyone if you're outside when it happens."

I tried to catch Hayley's eye to see if she was as outraged as I was, but she didn't want to look at me. And that was when I realized that *none* of them wanted to look at me—not Quentin, not Kevin, not even Fitz. I'd embarrassed them all. The only person who would meet my gaze was Sterling, and the look she flashed my way was pure, uncamouflaged joy.

I followed Principal Ito without another word, keeping my eyes on the floor as he marched me through the crowd. But I couldn't block my ears.

"I hope you don't blame *me*," I heard F.K. tell Kevin. "Not after the way she acted . . ."

"I don't blame you," he said.

And that's when I abandoned my last shred of dignity and started to cry.

Sloppy Second

Outside the bowling alley, I headed straight for the Dumpsters in back. Principal Ito had locked the doors behind me, so I knew none of my friends would find me there—not that they'd come looking. I threaded my way into the space behind those big trash cans, squatted down on my haunches, and bawled my eyes out, big sloppy sobs that made my nose run worse than my mascara.

No one would ever speak to me again. Even worse, I *deserved* to be shunned. Every second of my recent insanity played back in my head like scenes from a bad horror movie. I saw myself strut up to Kevin like some wannabe sex bomb, but now I saw it from his perspective. He hadn't been shocked to see me show up; he'd just been shocked, period. I hadn't made him want me; I'd made a complete fool of myself.

And then there was Fourteen-Karat. Her gloating face interrupted my thoughts like a recurring nightmare. Not only hadn't I beaten her, I'd played right into her hands. If anyone who'd seen our altercation in the bowling alley had the job of deciding which of us was the psycho now, they wouldn't have to think twice. It was me.

I was the psycho.

Even Hayley had been embarrassed—and if I'd embarrassed my very best friend, I didn't want to know what the rest of the school thought of me. I'd have to transfer districts. Our family would probably have to move. My reputation would never recover. Even *Trevor* would have to pretend not to know me.

I could never face Kevin again, obviously.

But what was somehow worse was knowing I couldn't face Quentin, either. How could I have been so mean as to rat him out to Ros? He would *never* have done that to me. I even felt sorry for Ros, and that's not a good way to feel.

I stayed on my haunches a good long time, crying until I was drained. When I couldn't squeeze out another tear, I wiped my snotty nose on my slutty blouse and crawled back into the parking lot.

The night hadn't been a total waste. I'd learned three important things:

1. I was immature.
2. I was selfish.
3. I was a horrible, horrible person.

I think it's fair to say that was the worst night of my life.

Back in the Saddle

Considering that I was supposed to be locked down in a bowling alley, I couldn't go home before daybreak without doing some major explaining. I tried to psych myself up for the third degree, but the thought of having my dad come and get me just so my mom could chew me out was too painful to contemplate. Not only would I be in trouble for getting kicked out of Memory Lanes, but also my entire family would know what a pathetic failure I was. I couldn't face them right then. I couldn't face anyone.

Unfortunately, I had nowhere else to go. I contemplated hiking home and trying to sneak into my room after my parents were asleep, but I was afraid to walk so far alone in the dark. Not to mention that my mother has ears like a bat.

And that's when I had a brainstorm. Instead of calling my dad, I went looking for Quentin's old minivan, found his hide-a-key in the wheel well, and let myself in to wait until dawn. Pretty sad, I know, but considering the choices, what else could I do? I felt like a double traitor, using Quentin's car after what I'd just done, so I wrote him a note on a scrounged scrap of paper:

Dear Quentin:

I won't blame you if you hate me. You were always a good friend, even when I wasn't. I wish I could take tonight back and treat you the way you deserve.

Luv,

Cassie

P.S. I'm sorry for sleeping in your van, but I couldn't go home. I promise not to use your hide-a-key again, but move it if you don't trust me.

If you've ever slept by yourself in a huge parking lot, you know it's not much fun. It would have been extremely scary if not for those pole-mounted security lights. I huddled under a smelly beach towel on the van's floor, afraid that if I got comfy on a seat a security guard might spot me and make me leave. And that was the *good* scenario.

I didn't fall asleep for at least four hours. Then, when I did, I jerked awake every few minutes, terrified by the prospect of oversleeping and being caught in the van at seven a.m., when Ito released that mob from the bowling alley. By the time dawn lit the horizon I was more tired than when I'd lain down.

It was a huge relief to finally get up, but one look in Quentin's rearview mirror was all it took to recall the horrors of the night before. Mascara clotted in the corners of my eyes, the van's carpet pattern was embossed on one cheek, and it's better not even to mention my hair. I folded up Quentin's beach towel and wiped my last traces of makeup off on my blouse. Then I put back the hide-a-key, slipped off my useless high heels, and started for home barefoot.

The air was cold and the pavement was freezing, but I was too depressed to care about trivialities like cold, or hunger, or the four-mile walk back to my house. By the time I let myself in our front door, it was just about seven and I was completely numb. I scribbled a note telling my parents I'd found my own way home. Then I staggered down the hall and closed my bedroom door behind me.

Safe, I thought, falling exhausted onto my bed. Kicking off my trashy clothes, I pulled on my crumpled nightgown and snuggled into the flannel sheets, my down comforter settling over me like six welcome feet of soil. I could feel sleep coming fast and there was nothing I wanted more. Complete unconsciousness not only seemed good, it seemed like the only state of mind I'd ever enjoy again.

And just before I fell asleep, one last thought snaked through my brain:

I'm back. I'm here. I never left. I am the Queen of Second Place.

Car-ma

"Up and at 'em, Sleeping Beauty! The early bird gets the worm. Early to bed and early to rise, blah, blah, blah."

I could barely believe my ears.

"Trevor," I moaned, swatting a fold of comforter off my face. "Get out of my bedroom."

"I don't think so."

"For the love of God, Trevor. Get out now if you want to live."

"Actually, it's not remotely early," he nattered on, plopping down in my desk chair. "In fact, Mom and Dad just went out to dinner."

159

"Good for them," I muttered, rolling over to show him my back. I was pretty surprised Mom had let me sleep all day, but she probably figured I needed the rest, what with all that all-night bowling I didn't do.

"We'll need to hurry if you want to get back before they do," Trevor continued, unperturbed. "And I assume you'll want to, since you'll be in big trouble if Mom finds out you were driving Dad's car without him."

"What?" I said, sitting up. "I wasn't driving Dad's car."

"Not yet." The gleam in his eyes was downright scary.

"Not ever! Listen, Trevor, whatever you've cooked up in that evil little brain of yours, you can count me out."

He pulled a miniature cassette from his shirt pocket. "Remember this?"

I was out of bed in a flash, snatching the tape from his hand and smashing it to splinters under my bare heel. "Ha!" I said triumphantly. "That's the end of *that*!"

But no. That would have been too easy.

"Yep," he said, grinning. "You've completely destroyed that blank tape. Did you honestly think I'd be dumb enough to show you the real one?"

I had, actually.

"Maybe I'll go ransack your room until I find it," I threatened. "If Mom and Dad just left, I have plenty of time."

Trevor didn't seem the least bit concerned. "I have a duplicate tape in my locker and friends who know what to do with it if anything happens to me. So unless you want to drive around town in your nightgown, you'd better get dressed. And I've got to tell you, Cass, a shower wouldn't be out of line."

"And just where, exactly, am I supposed to be driving?"

"Sorry, but you're not cleared for that information," he said, smirking. "I've got a couple of quick things to do and then I'll meet you in the garage."

He skipped out my doorway and down the hall, leaving me there by myself. He couldn't be serious!

Could he?

I got dressed, just in case, but I didn't put a lot of effort into it, plucking a dirty sweatshirt and jeans out of a heap on my floor and not even bothering with shoes. Just because Dad had left his car behind and I was fully capable of driving it didn't mean I was going to play taxi for Trevor. I walked to the kitchen, opened the door, and stepped into the adjoining garage to tell him he was crazy.

But Trevor wasn't there yet, leaving me and Dad's old Corolla staring each other down under one dim bulb. Darkness seeped around the edges of the roll-up door to the driveway, and a chilly wind blew through the chinks. Shivering, I opened the Corolla's door and climbed into the driver's seat, just to get my bare feet off the cold floor. I was still there when Trevor burst through the door dressed as Batman, a bulging pillowcase slung over one caped shoulder.

"You have got to be kidding!" I said. "Halloween was over a week ago."

"And what was once a costume is now a disguise," he replied in this goofy deep Batman voice. Climbing into the front seat, he threw his pillowcase in back and handed me Dad's spare car keys. "From the Bat Cave!" he said, pointing at the closed roll-up door.

"It's 'To the Bat Cave,' " I said scornfully. "And we're not moving an inch until you tell me what's going on."

"Wake up, Cassie," he said, peering at me through the eyeholes in his mask. "You're not in charge here."

The entire situation was surreal. It was hard enough to believe that I was up, dressed, and sitting in the garage with my punk little brother. The fact we were sitting in my father's car got kind of lost in the details.

"You didn't make that mask. Or that cape, either," I accused him, distracted. His black vinyl cowl contained a bunch of form-fitted pieces, and the pointy ears on top were exactly like in the movies. There was more black vinyl masquerading as muscles over his chest, and a flowing black cape that tied at his neck. "You told me you made your costume."

"I did!" he said indignantly.

"Like you really sewed all that! Batman's secret identity is Bruce Wayne, not Martha Stewart."

"Are we leaving?" he asked.

If I'd been smarter, or braver, or even less tired, I'd have definitely said no. But right then all I wanted was to get Trevor off my back so I could stop worrying about that stupid tape. I'd known for days I was going to have to buy him off somehow.

"Listen, Trevor, if I drive you where you want to go, then that's it. We're even, right?"

"We'll see," he said, hitting the button on Dad's garage-door opener. The big door rolled up, revealing a dark fall sky, and suddenly I knew I was going to do it. I turned the key in the ignition, wanting only to be free of Trevor's blackmail so I could crawl back under my blankets and hide for the rest of my life.

"Where are we going?" I asked, backing into the street and punching the garage door closed.

"That's a secret," he said, so thrilled with himself he could barely stand it.

"I've got news for you, Captain Underpants. I can't take you anywhere if I don't know where I'm going."

That confused him for half a second. Then he drew himself up to full Bat-height and said, "Turn right. I'll tell you when to turn again."

We went three or four miles on neighborhood streets, and with every yard we traveled, the insanity of my actions became more clear. It wasn't that I doubted my ability to drive—I was totally on top of that—but it hadn't occurred to me until we were already on the road that I was doing something illegal. I'd left the house thinking that if Mom caught me with the car I'd be dead, but no deader than if she caught me plagiarizing an assignment. Now I was thinking in terms of police, and strip searches, and spending my entire life without a driver's license. I was about to turn back and head for home when Trevor piped up again.

"Stop at this corner," he said.

"You mean at the stop sign?" I retorted. "I'm pretty sure I could have figured that out without— Hey!"

The car was still rolling as both its back doors jerked open and two figures in dark clothes and ski masks jumped in. The only things that kept me from screaming were Trevor's delighted grin and the matching flowered pillow-cases over our carjackers' shoulders.

"You made it!" Trevor said excitedly.

"You too, dude!" one of them answered. "I doubted you, man, but you totally came through!"

"Does someone want to tell me why our car is full of juvenile delinquents?" I asked.

"Think of it as a club meeting," Trevor told me.

"Dude!" Ski Mask 2 protested. "We said 'secret society,' not 'club.'"

"Like in Stealth," said Ski Mask 1. "You know, when the Triumvirate steal the death ray from Master Chaos?"

"You're not stealing anything!" I said, alarmed.

"Relax, Cassie," said Trevor. "We're not stealing. In fact, we're about to give someone a nice present."

His cronies in the backseat almost killed themselves laughing, and I finally recognized them by their braying. Bill Ortega, the taller of the two, was Trevor's best friend, and the other guy, Josh, was a close runner-up.

"I'm stuck at a stop sign with three freaks in my car, and if I don't get some answers I'm going home right now!" I snapped.

"Turn left," Trevor said.

I couldn't sit at the stop sign indefinitely, so I turned, still arguing. "I mean it, Trevor. You didn't tell me anyone was coming with us. Either you tell me where we're going or—"

"Dude, just tell her!" Bill interrupted.

"Trevor's in love!" Josh cried, spilling the beans.

"*What?*" My attention was temporarily distracted from the road by the way Trevor was trying to pound Josh over the back of his seat.

"You'll want to go straight at this intersection," Bill told me, his mouth closer to my ear than any eighth-grade boy's had a right to be. "Now veer to the left. Yeah, perfect. Her house is at the end of this street."

"At the end of *this* street?" I said. "Isn't this where Julie Evans lives?"

Bill and Josh started laughing hysterically.

Julie's a freshman at Hilltop, and the main reason I know who she is is that we went to the same middle school. She was in seventh grade when I was in eighth. And, I suddenly realized, in eighth when Trevor was in seventh . . .

"Tell me this is a joke!" I begged Trevor. "You and Julie Evans?"

"Trev and the older woman!" Bill teased.

"Yeah, you dog," Josh added, as if Trevor actually had a chance.

"I hate to break this to you, Trev," I said, annoyed to the edge of reason. "But the chances of a high school girl going out with you are essentially nil. And factoring in the Batsuit, I'd say you have a snowball's chance in hell. Does Julie even know who you are?"

"If she doesn't, she's about to," Trevor said, motioning for me to pull to the curb in front of a huge darkened house.

"I *told* you they weren't back yet!" Josh crowed.

"Sweet!" Bill said, reaching for his pillowcase.

I stopped the car, feeling sick to my stomach. Trevor and his friends were obviously up to no good, and since they were likely to prove totally incompetent at it, the potential for them to drag me down with them was growing by leaps and bounds. But before I could talk them around, three car doors flew open and three dark figures streaked out across the Evanses' front lawn, pillowcases bobbing on their shoulders.

"Trevor!" I whispered out the open passenger door. "Get back here!"

"Five minutes," he called, just as the first roll of toilet paper streaked through the night sky.

The next second, rolls were flying in all directions, big double-quilted comets, their tails unfurling behind them. Paper tangled in the trees and blanketed the lawn, making a bright patchwork against the darkness. And that's when I realized the open car doors had switched on its overhead light, illuminating not only the paper but also my very recognizable and completely unmasked hair.

"Great!" I muttered, leaping out to shut all three doors.

The ground under my bare feet was freezing. Worse, I stepped in a slimy puddle that soaked one leg of my jeans. I wanted to run across the lawn, grab Trevor by the scruff of his Bat-neck, and drag him back into the car. Better yet, I wanted to drive off and leave him there. Instead I hunkered down in the driver's seat, praying those fools would finish before someone drove by and saw us. Julie's house was on a quiet street, but a car could come by any second. The *Evanses'* car could come by any second. I risked a peek out the window. Trevor had drawn a heart on the lawn with shaving cream and was actually taking the time to fill it in.

"Will you idiots hurry up?" I hissed out the passenger window. "I'm a sitting duck out here!"

Trevor continued with his heart while Bill and Josh papered the hedges along the driveway.

"Mom and Dad could be home any minute, Trevor. And if I get busted for this, I'm totally taking you with me."

That snapped him to his senses. Getting *me* in trouble was obviously of no concern. But if it was going to involve him too . . .

"Hey, you guys. Come on!" he called, tossing an empty can of shaving cream into his now drooping pillowcase. "Let's go!"

"There'd better not be shaving cream on your shoes!" I cried as they charged the car. Three doors flew open, making me cringe beneath the light, then slammed loudly enough to wake the dead.

"Brilliant," I said, starting the engine. "You guys are all extremely sly."

Still, it was starting to look as if we might actually get away. My heart pounded as I cruised the dark streets toward home, every nerve stretched for the first sign of trouble. Meanwhile, Trevor and his buddies bounced up and down in their seats, congratulating each other and being as obnoxious as possible.

"This is where you two get out," I announced, stopping at the curb a block from where we'd picked up Bill and Josh.

"No. The next corner," Bill told me.

"No, here. I'm not driving back that way." On the trip to Julie's house, Trevor had sent me weaving all through the neighborhood instead of taking the more direct route down a major road. But now that I knew where I was, I wasn't at the mercy of his lame directions. "Get out!" I insisted when they didn't move.

Bill and Josh climbed reluctantly out of the car,

complaining that they hadn't had time to celebrate their caper. Obviously, I didn't care. As soon as they were clear, I headed for home.

"Take off that ridiculous mask," I told Trevor, turning onto Hilltop Boulevard. "There are other cars out here and you look like a mental patient."

To my amazement, he complied, taking off his cape as well and stuffing them into his pillowcase. "That was so cool!" he said. "Wait until Julie sees!"

"Yes, you're a genius. What girl *wouldn't* love a heart-shaped patch of dead grass in the middle of her lawn?"

"Shaving cream doesn't kill grass!"

"Hel-*lo*! Why do you think people use it?"

He thought for a second. "Because whipped cream melts?"

"I don't know how you get through a day. If it wasn't for the—"

A flash in my rearview mirror cut me off in midsentence, making my heart skip with dread. A police car was hurtling up behind me, and it had just turned on its revolving lights.

"This is it," I whimpered. "We're going to jail."

Trevor twisted around in his seat.

"Don't look!" I cried frantically. "You'll attract his attention."

"Too late," Trevor said, sounding nearly as scared as I was. "Cassie, what are we going to do?"

"I don't know." I checked my mirror again. The patrol car was feet off my bumper, its flashing colored lights filling the whole back window. "I have to pull over."

Trevor's eyes got rounder. "Don't!"

"What do you want me to do, Trevor? Lead a high-speed chase through Hilltop? We're screwed if we stop and dead if we don't!"

Flipping on my turn signal, I steered toward the shoulder, terrified out of my mind. Gravel crunched under the tires as I pressed the brake, but I was still a long way from stopped when the cruiser blew past on my left. Trev and I watched in disbelief as it streaked away down the boulevard, lights blazing.

"It wasn't us!" Trevor exclaimed. "He only wanted you to move over and let him by!"

Already committed, I stopped the car anyway.

"He's after someone else," Trevor insisted, pointing to the disappearing lights. "What a relief!"

Relief? Relief barely scratched the surface. So much adrenaline had just surged through my body, I felt like a rag doll. My hands were limp and clumsy as I pulled back into traffic.

"Okay, here's how it is," I told Trevor. "You and I are even now. Even Steven."

"Well . . . ," he said reluctantly.

"If you tell Mom about my play, I'll tell her you TPed that house."

"And I'll tell her you drove me there."

"And I'll tell her how you blackmailed me and we'll both be locked up till we're thirty. It's your call."

"Okay," he said at last. "We're even. I guess."

"Fine."

"Fine."

I might have enjoyed my victory more if our house hadn't been rolling into view at that moment. If Mom and

Dad had beat us home, any agreement I made with Trevor was completely academic.

"No car in the driveway," Trevor said, reading my mind.

"That doesn't mean it's not in the garage," I told him, trying to remember which of the house lights we'd left on.

"Just hurry up. If it's already in there, we're already in trouble. If not, let's get our butts inside. We're sitting ducks out here."

"Oh, *now* you care about that," I said, hitting the garage-door opener.

We both heaved sighs of relief as the big door rolled up. Mom's car wasn't back. We'd gotten away with it!

"Be sure you park exactly where Dad did," Trevor directed as I pulled in and closed the garage door behind us. "Was this window up or down?"

"Up. They were all up. Climb into the backseat and make sure your stupid friends didn't get anything dirty."

Trevor dove over his seat as I eased the car forward, lining it up perfectly.

"All clear!" he announced from in back.

"Then get out."

"Time to destroy the evidence," he said, exiting the car and removing a can of shaving cream from his pillowcase. "Oh, man! This leaked on my cape!"

"Stop whining and deal with it."

Trevor hid his empty shaving cream cans under some bags in our trash. Then he took off his fake muscles, exposing the black T-shirt underneath. "I'll wash this stuff later," he said, adding his muscles to the pillowcase and tossing the whole bundle behind the washing machine. "I'll do it tomorrow after school."

"Fine. Like I care," I said, walking around Dad's car to double-check my parking job. "Let's just get out of here before they come back."

"Yeah. I want to call Josh and Bill," he said, bounding toward the kitchen door.

He was two feet away when the door opened from inside, bright light from the kitchen flooding the garage. And there in the doorway, silhouetted like an avenging angel, our father stood blocking our path.

"Am I seeing this?" Dad asked, full of disbelief. "Which one of you would like to tell me what's going on?"

Don't Dead People See a Bright Light?

The thing is not to panic, I told myself, nearly passing out. My knees buckled, sending me staggering backward into Dad's front bumper. One of my hands braced against the car's hood, then jerked back off as I realized how hot the metal was.

"Um . . . hi, Dad," my voice said. I wasn't even in my body at that point. "We, uh . . . we . . ."

"Ice cream!" Trevor cut in. "We just went out for ice cream."

"In my car?" My father looked as stunned as we were. "Cassie, tell me you didn't take the car."

"Um . . ." Believe me, there was nothing I wanted to tell him more.

He crossed to the Corolla and laid his hand on its hood. "Good God!" he exclaimed. "Are you insane?"

"Yes," I managed to say. "Very likely."

"Do you know how illegal this is? How dangerous?"

I nodded miserably. "I just kind of forgot."

"We only went down the street," Trevor said, coming to my aid.

"And you!" My father turned on him. "For you to be in the car makes it that much worse! Don't you have more sense than to ride with someone who doesn't have a license?"

"Well, it was . . . you know . . . down the street. Besides, Cassie's been driving for ages. It didn't seem like a big deal."

"It *is* a big deal!" Dad said, as close to yelling as I'd ever heard him. "Just wait till your mother gets home!"

"She's not here?" I gasped, grasping at that straw. Even though her car wasn't in the garage, my muddled brain had still assumed they'd come home together somehow.

"She will be, any minute. She just dropped me off on her way to the store—something about milk and Cocoa Critters."

The irony wasn't lost on me, okay? But I didn't have time to ponder my impending life sentence of Bran Bullets. I had only seconds to act.

"Dad, we don't have to tell Mom, do we?" I begged. "I mean, you can handle this."

He gave me an astonished look.

"Yes! *You* punish me," I insisted desperately. "I was completely in the wrong and I'll do whatever you say. Just . . . why does Mom need to know?"

"She's your mother."

"And she's going to totally freak out!" I said, playing my one good card. "This won't be a five-minute lecture, Dad—it'll be a stress-fest of epic proportions."

I could see in his face that he knew I was right. Not only that, but he wasn't looking forward to it any more than I was. The amount of drama my mom can wring from something that big is exactly the sort of unpleasantness my dad was born to avoid.

"Please, Dad?" I pleaded.

"Well . . . I can't just forget about it. This is serious, Cassie. You have to be punished."

"Absolutely," I said, nodding frantically. "Understood."

"The thing is," he added slowly, "your mother doesn't need any more problems right now. She fired another secretary Friday. Tiffany Something-or-Other."

"Right! She's already dealing with a lot."

I must have sounded too relieved.

"I'm not saying I'm *not* going to tell her. Just that I'll think about it."

I would have liked a little more assurance, but the sound of a car pulling into the driveway whipped all three of our heads around. The garage-door opener whirred to life overhead.

"In the meantime," Dad said, "maybe you two would like to be somewhere else."

"Say no more!" I replied, bolting out of the garage so fast I left Trevor in my dust.

Please, Dad, I thought as I raced to my room. *I'm begging you, say no more!*

Deep Snow

I barely slept that night—partially because I'd already slept all day and partially because I was expecting my mother to break down my door any minute. Sometime around midnight I realized I was probably safe, but I still almost threw up when my alarm clock rang Monday morning. The idea of facing people at school after that disaster at Memory Lanes wasn't a lot less frightening than the thought of facing my mother.

I didn't *think* Dad had ratted me out, because Mom would have let me know if he had. Even so, I yelled that I was up when someone knocked on my door, but I waited to come out of my room until they had both left for work, just in case. By then it was too late to eat breakfast, even if I'd remembered we had Cocoa Critters, and I had to jog to school on an empty stomach.

My face was completely flushed when I hit the main hall. I slunk to my locker with my hair in my eyes, wishing I were back in my room with the covers pulled over my head. When you're already embarrassed, it's easy to imagine that everyone is staring at you. But everyone *was* staring at me—and most of those faces wore mocking grins. People rolled their eyes or shook their heads. One girl elbowed her friend and launched into a frantic, whispered explanation. It was mortifying.

And I deserved it.

I spent Mr. Rich's class wishing the floor would open and swallow me. Lacey Croft and Kelly Darson passed notes the entire hour, and I was positive every word was about what I'd done at Memory Lanes. I pretended to pay attention to Mr. Rich's lecture, but each random glance my way made my cheeks burn even hotter.

And first period was the easy part. I still had to face Kevin.

I walked into Conway's class as late as I dared, my knees almost jelly beneath me. My eyes sought Kevin, freezing wide open as I realized he was already looking right at me. For a second I actually thought maybe things would be okay. If he was willing to look at me, he couldn't be that mad. A tentative smile flicked at one corner of my mouth. . . .

And then he looked away, turning his gaze out the window like I wasn't even there.

Blinking back tears, I stumbled to my original, wobbly chair beside Cyn and hid my face in *Modern English Grammar*.

"Cassie. Hey, Cassie!" Cyn hissed. "What did you move back here for?"

"The plays are finished," I whispered into my book.

"We still have to read them to the class."

Great, I thought. *One more thing to worry about.* I turned a page, praying Cyn would drop the subject. She did, but I could tell by her pitying look that she knew what had happened at the bowling alley. Everybody knew.

Conway took roll, then announced the titles of the four

plays she'd selected to have read that day. Luckily, ours wasn't one of them. I closed my textbook but kept my eyes on its cover as four pairs of students stumbled through their lines.

This is next, I kept thinking. *Kevin and I will to have to read our stupid play, and then it will be obvious to everyone that he's not speaking to me. I'll be an even bigger laughingstock than I am now.*

There are two strange things about being that crazed with anxiety:

1. It's hard to focus on anything besides the contents of your head.
2. Time flies when you're stressing out.

And that's why I was caught by surprise when Conway dismissed the class; I hadn't even realized the fourth play had ended. Lurching to my feet, I snatched up my backpack, frantic to leave the room before Kevin did so I wouldn't have to make eye contact again.

"Cassie?" Conway said before I'd moved an inch. "Can I see you at my desk, please? You too, Kevin."

I stumbled numbly forward, fearing further humiliation. Maybe Conway had heard about Memory Lanes, or had seen the way Kevin looked through me and was going to ask embarrassing questions. She was almost certain to mention the fact that I'd moved my seat again. The other students skipped out the door one by one until only Kevin, Conway, and I were left—and to let you know how bad things were, I was more comfortable looking at Conway.

"We have a problem," she said, slapping a paper faceup on her desk.

I simultaneously recognized our play and registered the big red F inked across it. From the corner of my eye, I saw Kevin's jaw drop. And then I spotted my death sentence scrawled beneath the F:

PLAGIARIZED!!!

Total Blizzard

"It's not Kevin's fault!" I insisted. "This is all a big mix-up." I'd been trying to explain for nearly five minutes, but Conway wasn't listening.

"It's noble of you to take responsibility, Miss Howard," she said. "But for Mr. Matthews to be ignorant of the fact that this play was plagiarized, he would have had to let you write the entire thing yourself."

"Not the *entire* thing."

The withering look Kevin gave me made me realize too late that I wasn't helping. "I mean, he changed lots of words, especially at the end."

"I would have changed them all—if I'd known," he said through gritted teeth.

"And I would be swayed by that argument—if I'd assigned you to edit Miss Howard's work. But since you were supposed to be her cowriter, your excuse doesn't impress me."

"I tried!" Kevin snapped, losing patience. "We can't

both write the same word, can we? I don't know what you want from me!"

Conway's eyebrows ratcheted up a quarter-inch. I know that doesn't sound like much, but believe me, it was scary.

"Then let me tell you," she said. "I want you both here for detention after school today, and every day until I tell you differently."

"But—but—" I stammered. "What if I turn in that other play I told you about?"

"That's a given," she replied. "See you at three o'clock."

Whiteout

I trailed Kevin into the hallway, but he wouldn't stop to talk to me. I was prepared to be told off—and I deserved pretty much anything he could have said—but that's how low I was to him. He didn't even think I was worth yelling at.

"Kevin, I'm really, really sorry," I said, stumbling along behind him. "I never meant for any of this to happen. I just wanted you to think I was smart, and . . . things got out of control."

A muscle jumped in his jaw. His steps got even longer.

"I *hate* that I got you in trouble," I went on. "I *tried* to take the blame."

There weren't a lot of people left in the hall by then, but every passing straggler stared our way. I saw them smile, no doubt imagining that I was apologizing for Memory Lanes.

I wish.

"Kevin, if you'd just let me explain from the beginning, the way things happened, I know I could—"

He finally stopped walking, wheeling around to cut me off.

"Do you even understand what you've done? This isn't some funny little mix-up, Cassie. If this goes on our records, it could ruin us for college."

I hadn't thought of college. And even though he was probably right, I still couldn't worry that far ahead. All I wanted was for him to stop looking at me like something he'd just stepped in. I felt my eyes fill with tears. My throat choked up till it hurt.

"I'm sorry," I croaked, aching to undo my damage. "If you'd just listen—"

"No! I've heard enough from you this week."

The tears spilled over and ran down my cheeks, but Kevin didn't care. With one last disgusted look, he turned his back and walked off down the hall.

"Kevin, I'm sorry!" I called desperately. "I just wanted you to like me!"

My confession echoed off the walls, bouncing from locker to locker and into countless open classrooms. There was no telling how many people heard those humiliating words.

Kevin stopped. He stiffened.

And then he just kept walking.

I didn't go to third period; I spent the entire hour crying in the girls' room, too mortified to show my face. Everything was ruined. Kevin hated me. My friends were ashamed of me. No good college would have me. I didn't even know why I was still breathing, because my life was clearly over.

I forced myself to go to fourth period, but at lunchtime I was back in the bathroom, afraid to brave the quad. The tears flowed like they would never stop, until my eyes were red, my cheeks were blotchy, and my throat was completely raw. All I wanted was to disappear, to vanish as if I had never been born.

Instead I had two more classes to endure, followed by detention with a teacher who couldn't stand me and a guy who wished I were dead.

I honestly didn't think I'd survive it.

Detention Essay #1
Mrs. Conway

The Fragile Nature of Trust
by Cassie Howard

Trust is a fragile thing. It's easy to lose and hard to earn back. When somebody trusts you, you shouldn't take it for granted. You can't be friends with a person who doesn't trust you, and my mother says that a woman who stays with a man she doesn't trust is a fool. I guess that means you can't have love without trust, either.

A lot of good jobs rely on trust. Lawyers and doctors must have the trust of clients and patients or they will go out of business. When politicians get caught in a lie or scandal, they can't get reelected. Usually. Priests, rabbis, and other religious leaders definitely have to be careful, or their followers may lose faith as well as trust. People in all these professions realize that trust is fragile, and they do their best to maintain it.

At school, teachers trust students to do their own work. If we don't, we lose the teachers' trust—in addition to whatever minor respect they might once have had for us. Which is why I really, <u>really</u> need to stress that you can't blame Kevin for this. The whole thing only happened because I was trying to impress him. Which I realize now was incredibly stupid, because he's obviously out of my league. But that's why I <u>needed</u> to impress him.

And once more, for the record, I never intended to turn in that play. The only reason Kevin did was because he didn't know it wasn't original. Which practically <u>proves</u> he's innocent. Why else would he turn in a bogus play when we had a whole week left to write a good one? Anyway, my point is, there's no way Kevin should be accused of plagiarism. And ideally, neither should I. Tomorrow I'll bring in the play I really wrote and hopefully that will convince you my intentions were honorable.

In conclusion, trust is fragile. I never meant to break anyone's trust, and if you knew me better, you'd understand what a huge mistake this all is. I mean, <u>obviously</u> it's a mistake, but it's also an accident. If you'd let yourself believe that for even five minutes, this situation would look completely different.

I guess you'll just have to trust me on that.

The Promised Avalanche

My head was throbbing by the time I got home from detention. Conway had decided that Kevin would be spending his afternoons writing a new one-act play, but since I'd already done that, I'd be writing essays with titles she'd assign. Like "The Fragile Nature of Trust." (You've already read some of the ones I wrote later and probably noticed they're not in order—I just stuck a few in where I hoped they explained things.)

All ninety minutes were hell. Kevin wouldn't even look at me. I had to console myself with the fact that at least he didn't see me crying and wiping my nose on the back of my hand. Conway could have offered me a Kleenex, but I was invisible to her, too. I actually think she was mad at *us* for keeping *her* after school. In any event, I had a pounding headache when I finally let myself in my front door.

And guess who was waiting for me in the kitchen?

"Well! I had an interesting day," my mother said, twisting around on her barstool to paralyze me with one look. "There I was at work, trying to do my job, when my brand-new secretary comes in and says my daughter's principal is on the phone. A little matter of being kicked out of an all-night school function."

Oh, God, I thought, rooted to the spot. *This is it. I'm dead.*

"Yes, an interesting conversation, made more interesting by the fact that you didn't come home that night. I assured Principal Ito I'd be discussing it with you very soon, since I was already planning to come home early. You see, I had lunch with your father today."

He'd ratted me out for driving the car. I should have guessed he'd find a way to do it without being around to face the fallout.

Make it quick, God, I prayed. *Just beam me up right now.*

"So," my mother continued, in a tone a stranger might have mistaken for conversational, "here I am, sitting around waiting, wondering why my daughter is so late getting home from school, when I get *another* phone call. And who do you suppose *that* was?"

I knew the answer. I did. There was just no way I could croak it out.

"What? No guesses?" asked my mother.

I shook my head.

"Strangely enough, it was that nice Mrs. Conway. To tell me you had just left detention. Which you will be attending every afternoon now as the result of plagiarizing an assignment. Really, Cassie, how could you?"

My mom has this habit of seeming quite calm when she's actually about to explode, but now her voice was starting to climb the scale.

"Is this how we raised you?" she asked. "Did we teach you nothing? Did you think we wouldn't find out?"

With her, those aren't really questions. They're just the warm-up, like a pitcher stretching his throwing arm.

"Well?" she said. "Answer me!"

"I didn't think—"

"You didn't think! Exactly!" she cried, and from there she was off to the races.

You've probably been bawled out at least once in your life, so I'll let you imagine how the rest of it went. After an hour-long assessment of my personality flaws, during which she got increasingly louder and more sarcastic, my mother informed me I'd be lucky if she *ever* let me get my driver's license and said I was grounded until further notice—which is exactly how long I have detention for. No leaving the house except for school, no using the phone or the Internet . . . She gave me the impression I was lucky she hadn't called the police.

When she was finally done yelling, she sent me to my room and I did my best to pretend that wasn't where I'd been longing to go all day. I threw myself down on my comforter expecting to cry my eyes out again, but all I felt was empty. I'd thought having my parents know about my mistakes would only make things worse. But strangely enough, that wasn't the case. Their finding out was the last bad thing I couldn't control. And now it had happened. And now it was over.

It was official. Nothing more could happen to me.

If I hadn't been so depressed, I might have been kind of relieved.

Digging Out
(Who knew you could milk a metaphor this long?)

In the locker room after Tuesday PE, Hayley came up and asked where I'd been at lunchtime. I could have pointed out that I'd been missing for *two* lunchtimes or that she'd barely acknowledged my presence since Saturday night.

But I didn't. Who could blame her?

"I had important things to do in the bathroom," I told her, kicking off my gym shorts. "Like hide."

"I heard how you got detention. That whole story is making the rounds. You know, along with the other one, about your brawl in the bowling alley."

"Hence my new favorite lunchtime location." I was trying for sarcasm, but I just sounded beaten.

Hayley shrugged and sat down on the gym bench beside me. She was already dressed to go home and I wished intensely that I could go with her.

"Fourteen-Karat must be like a dog with two bones," I said. "With two stories that juicy, which one does she tell first?"

"It *is* almost too much material. Still, she does her best. And she has Kevin to comfort her now. She's informed our whole Spanish class that he's her new boyfriend. So that I would hear. So that you would hear."

"Like I hadn't already guessed."

I pulled on my jeans, took my hoodie out of my locker,

and stuffed my tennis racket inside. There was no time to shower if I was going to be at detention when the bell rang, but no one wanted to get within ten feet of me anyway. I toyed with the zipper on my sweatshirt, trying to work up the nerve to ask the big question.

"How's Quentin?" I forced out at last. "Pretty mad at me?"

"Yep," Hayley said matter-of-factly.

"And Fitz?"

"Quentin's his best friend."

"Right."

She hesitated, then blurted out *her* big question. "What were you thinking, Cassie?"

"I wasn't thinking. I have that on excellent authority from my mother."

Hayley smiled. "You've got to love a woman with a point."

"I might, if I wasn't grounded for life. Even Trevor's doing a week."

"Trevor? For what?"

"There was this other thing, involving driving Dad's car."

Hayley gaped with disbelief. "Trevor drove your dad's car?"

"Not exactly."

The next thing I knew, I was telling the whole sordid story, from being blackmailed out of my bed through the entire TP incident. "Trevor told my dad we went for ice cream, so he's only in trouble for riding with me. You'd think my parents might realize I wouldn't risk my entire future for a hot-fudge sundae, but apparently not. To hear my mother tell it, I'm capable of anything."

"You didn't tell them what Trevor was really up to?" Hayley asked, surprised.

"What's the point? It wouldn't help me, and he'd be toast."

"Yeah, but . . . You would have enjoyed that once."

"Which doesn't make me particularly proud," I said with a sigh. "I've been such an idiot lately. To everyone, even Trevor. I was a moron to think I could beat Fourteen-Karat—or that it would change anything if I did. And you know what the worst part is? Now that I've screwed everything up, I'd give anything just to have my life back the way it was before."

"You mean when you were stuck in second place?"

"Second place looks like heaven to me right now."

Hayley chuckled. "I'll bet."

"Can you ever forgive me, Hayley? For *all* the stupid things I've done?"

She didn't miss a beat. "Yeah. I think I can."

Have I mentioned how much I love that girl?

"What's more," she volunteered, "I can probably swing Fitz to the dark side. You're on your own with Quentin, though."

"I never should have said what I did about Ros! It was mean, and stupid, and, well . . . Quentin probably has his own adjectives. The only saving grace is that he didn't really like her."

"Here's the thing," said Hayley, shaking her head. "Turns out he does."

"*What?*"

"And since she's still not speaking to him, or looking at him, or acknowledging his existence in any way, he's kind of suffering right now."

"I know how that feels." How Quentin could like Rosalind

Pierce was a mystery to me, but putting myself in his place was depressingly easy.

"I do know he felt bad about you having to sleep in his van," Hayley added.

"He did?" I asked, seeing a glimmer of hope. "Bad enough to forgive me?"

"Maybe. Eventually. Don't push him."

"I won't. Everything's going to be different now, Hayley. You'll see. I'm going to be a better person, a better friend, a better *everything*."

A wry smile twisted Hayley's lips. "You're going to be a better essay writer, that's for sure."

She Said Essays, Not Ads

The next day, this ad showed up in the personals at the back of our school paper:

> Popular, social blonde desperately seeking a clue. I have a sterling reputation, but it's not for my IQ. If you have a brain cell to spare, please find me a shirt that covers my pair.

I immediately suspected Hayley, but I found her in the hallway between classes and she totally denied it. We laughed ourselves sick, of course, the fact that we were blameless only adding to our appreciation.

I should have guessed that Sterling would be less amused. She accosted me at the edge of the quad as I ventured out for lunch, grabbing me by one arm and yanking me into a nook behind a building column.

"I saw your desperate little joke in the paper," she snarled. "If you think you'll get him that way, you're wrong."

"I don't think I'll get him at all," I said, jerking my arm free. "And I didn't run that ad."

"Right," she said sarcastically. "You probably don't even know what I'm talking about."

"Of course I do. That was the best laugh I've had in days."

Her blue eyes narrowed. "I know it was you, and I'm going to prove it."

"Knock yourself out—you'll come up with nothing. Think about it, Sterling: the way you act around here, I can't be the only person who hates you."

The words caught us both by surprise. We just stood there, staring at each other in disbelief. I mean, she must have already known how I felt. I assumed she felt the same way about me. But for me to say it out loud, to say it to her face, was something neither of us had expected.

And all of a sudden, I wanted to take it back.

It was like this light went off in my head, and I couldn't believe how ugly it sounded, how ugly it *was*, to hate somebody. I'd always known hating Sterling was wrong, but that was the moment I realized that hating Sterling had caused every bit of the trouble I was in. If I'd just let it go, everything would have turned out different.

And I could still let it go.

"Listen, Sterling, I shouldn't have said that. I'm sorry. I don't hate you."

I'd clearly surprised her again, but this time she recovered more quickly.

"Like I care," she retorted, tossing her gorgeous hair.

"No, I mean it. And I swear I didn't place that ad."

"Somebody did."

"Well, yeah, but . . ."

And that's when I had my second epiphany: somewhere in our school was another human being who hated Sterling as much as I did. Maybe even more. And Sterling had already figured that out. No wonder she was upset.

". . . it wasn't me," I finished lamely.

"Whatever." She stared me down maybe five more seconds, then abruptly turned and stomped off.

"I really don't hate you!" I called to her back.

Which is to say, I'm trying to quit. It's kind of like smoking, though—you can't stop all at once. If only they made a Sterling patch.

And maybe some type of gum I could chew when she's being extra obnoxious.

SOC

On Thursday morning, on the lawn in front of our school, Tate the Great pinched Tamara Owens's butt and she slapped him upside the face. It was all anyone wanted to talk about—which could not have made me happier. With Tamara and Bryce Tate the headline of the day, the various stories about me slipped right off the front page.

Don't get me wrong; I hadn't fallen out of the Gossip Gazette altogether—and I still had to endure that nightmare of avoided eye contact called honors English—but outside of second period and detention, I felt like I could finally breathe a little. I was still a pariah, but a pariah people had lost interest in. After three days of snickers, stares, and rumors, that type of neglect was a beautiful thing. I wrapped it around me like a cloak of invisibility as I walked out to the quad to meet Hayley. When I spotted her, though, she was on a bench with Fitz and Quentin, and I stopped in my tracks, confused. Was she eating with them instead?

"Cassie! Cassie, over here!" she called, standing up to wave.

I approached cautiously, not sure what to expect. Fitz looked friendly, but Quentin was staring into the space over my left shoulder with this very sulky expression.

"We saved you a place," Hayley said. "Come on, scooch over, Quentin."

He finally met my gaze, grimacing like the sight of me gave him indigestion before he grudgingly moved. I wanted to cry, but I sucked it up and sat down, determined to use the opportunity to apologize.

"Listen, you guys," I waded in. "I'm really sorry about Saturday night. I know I embarrassed you."

"You didn't embarrass *me*," Fitz said.

I wasn't sure if he meant I'd embarrassed Quentin or embarrassed myself. Either way, he was right.

"I don't know what got into me. Temporary insanity. But nothing like that will ever happen again. I promise. I've totally learned my lesson."

Fitz nodded, apparently satisfied. Hayley winked at me. But Quentin hadn't thawed one degree; if Hayley had whistled across him, it would have felt like an arctic wind.

"Quentin?" I ventured timidly. "I'm sorry about Ros."

"Sure you are," he said bitterly.

"I honestly had no idea you liked her. Not that that excuses what I did."

"You're right. It doesn't."

I wasn't making much progress, but at least he was speaking to me.

"You'll get her back," I said. "If you still want her, I mean. She'd be crazy not to see how great you are."

"Yes, every girl wants a guy who asks her on a bogus date and humiliates her in front of her best friend."

Apparently I wasn't the only one who'd been soul searching that week.

"You want to hear something funny?" Hayley cut in, trying to lighten the mood. "You're going to love this, Cassie."

I gave Quentin one last apologetic glance. "What?"

"In Spanish today, we all had to give ourselves Spanish names and Sterling chose Plata Ofilia de Cortéz."

"Huh?" I said, failing to see the humor.

"*Plata* is Spanish for silver and Ofilia was her translation of Ophelia, which—it turns out—is her real middle name."

I rolled my eyes. "That figures. Heaven forbid it should be something normal."

"You're still not getting it! Sterling Ophelia Carter: S.O.C. Soc."

"No way!" I cried, laughing in spite of myself. Even Quentin cracked a smile. "Did anyone say anything?"

Hayley shook her head. "I might be the only one who realized, probably because my mom's always doing that—checking people's initials to see what they spell. It's good for a laugh sometimes, but SOC has to take the cake."

I laughed till the tears rolled down my cheeks, till I had to hold my sides to keep from cracking a rib. And only part of my hysteria was caused by F.K.'s initials. It was just such a relief to have friends again, to know that, despite everything, there were still at least three people willing to stick by me.

"No. No, I have to stop," I gasped. "I don't hate Sterling anymore. It's my midyear's resolution."

Hayley gave me an astonished look. Then, slowly, she nodded her approval.

"*I* hate her," Quentin announced.

The rest of us turned to stare.

"She was just using me to get that Kevin guy!" he exclaimed, like this was some sort of news. "And now she's turning Ros against me."

"With all due respect, dude, you took care of that yourself," said Fitz.

"No, she's saying stuff," Quentin insisted. "Every time I try to talk to Ros, Sterling whispers something and Ros takes off in a huff before I even get there."

Hayley studied Quentin with amazement. "It was *you!* You put that ad in the paper."

"Not me," he said, a furtive smile creeping onto his lips. "I wish I had, though. 'Seeking a clue . . . for my IQ.' Pure poetry, man."

Every Cloud Has a Sterling Lining

The detention essay I turned in Friday, "Actions, Reactions, and Consequences," was hardly tearstained at all. I still avoided Conway's eyes when I handed it over, but after an entire week of detention I was beginning to take being in disgrace in stride.

Conway glanced through what I'd written, then dropped it on her desk. "And you, Mr. Matthews?" she asked. "Are you turning in pages today?"

I risked a glance over my shoulder to where Kevin was scribbling at the bottom of a full sheet of paper. My heart squeezed painfully at the sight of him, all the foolish hopes I'd once had rushing back to taunt me, but I set my jaw, determined to ignore them. If Kevin had been out of my league before, he was in a different universe now. Besides, he still wasn't speaking to me.

"One second," he told Mrs. Conway, still writing.

Conway raised an eyebrow. My gut twisted just on reflex.

"It's late and it's Friday," she said. "I'll have your work *now.*"

"Done!" he said, hitting some final punctuation mark and snatching up his pages. "I'm finished," he said as he gave them to Conway. "With the other pages I've turned in, that makes a whole play."

Mrs. Conway scanned his work, taking more time than she had with mine. "Yes," she said at last. "I'll accept this as your play. Obviously, considering everything that's happened, I'll be deducting some points off your grade, but you're excused from detention. Don't come back on Monday."

"Thank you!" I exclaimed.

"Not so fast, Cassie. Only Kevin is excused—and partly because your essays have convinced me he should be. But you don't need to start making after-school plans anytime soon."

"Oh. Okay."

"That's enough for today, though," she said, shooing me and Kevin toward the exit.

"Is it my imagination, or did she want us gone?" Kevin asked as we emerged into the hall.

I was so stunned he'd actually spoken to me that I could only stare.

"I wonder what Conway does on the weekends?" he added.

"Drag racing," I proposed, recovering my voice. "No, skydiving. No! Naked skydiving!"

A smile curved the corners of his mouth. "Well, one thing hasn't changed: you're still crazy."

"Listen, Kevin," I blurted out, before he could walk away again. "I'm so sorry about that play. And I'm glad you're out of detention. I don't care if I stay there all year now, so long as you're not being punished too."

"It's over," he said with a shrug. "Let's forget about it."

"And about what happened at the bowling alley . . . ," I continued.

He looked pained, but I plowed ahead.

"I want to say how sorry I am for that too. You were with Sterling. And I . . . should have accepted that."

"Yeah?"

"Yeah. I totally get it now."

"Okay."

So maybe "okay" doesn't constitute total forgiveness, but right then it sounded pretty good. I was racking my brain for some clever way to make him smile again when Sterling appeared around a corner and headed directly for us.

"Here comes your girlfriend," I said, praying he'd contradict me.

He didn't.

"Hey, babe," he said happily, turning to greet Sterling. "You didn't have to wait for me!"

"I wanted to," she said with a totally angelic smile. Her blond hair framed her face like a halo, and her outfit was straight off the cover of *Seventeen*. She looked so perfect I had to remind myself that I didn't hate her.

"I missed you," she said with a little-girl pout.

"I missed you too," he said, obviously smitten. "Should we get out of here?"

"Definitely." She gave just the teeniest glance my way.

And all of a sudden he realized the awkwardness of his situation. "Oh! Uh, um . . . ," he said. "We just got out of detention, and we were talking about . . . um . . . Cassie's sorry she pushed you."

Okay, I hadn't said *that*, but I decided not to argue.

"Even though you both kind of pushed at the same time," he added.

My head snapped up. "What?"

"Consider it forgotten," she told me in a ridiculously sweet voice. "That whole situation must have been so hard for you."

"But—but—" I sputtered.

"Are we going?" And before I could say another word, Sterling whisked Kevin away from me like a coyote cutting a lamb from the flock.

We pushed at the same time? I thought in shock. I'd been so worked up that night. Everything had happened in a blur. If Sterling had kept her hands low . . .

Kevin slipped his arm around Sterling's waist as they disappeared around the corner. I imagined them at the Snow Ball, just three short weeks away, Kevin wearing a tuxedo and Sterling in the Snow Queen crown, and the injustice nearly overwhelmed me. If we'd both pushed, why had Principal Ito seen only *me?* Punished only *me?* My feet moved in place as I imagined running to tell him that Sterling had pushed too.

Let her get in trouble for once! Let something be fair. For once.

Then I took a deep breath and reluctantly let it go.

Whatever minor social standing I'd recovered since Memory Lanes would surely be lost if I tangled with Sterling again. Not to mention that Kevin was certain to take her side. As hard as it was, as much as it hurt, there was nothing to be gained by opening that door again.

Sterling was born to win, and you weren't. That's the natural order of things, I reminded myself with a sigh. *The last time you messed with nature, you went from second place to last. Why take that chance again?*

After all, I had my three best friends back now. Trevor and I had called a truce. And Kevin had more or less accepted my apology.

Compared to where I'd started the week, I had a lot to lose.

A Weekend in the House Time Forgot

The worst part of being grounded is the weekends. When your parents aren't especially thrilled with you to begin with, no one needs forty-eight extra hours of togetherness. If I could have called Hayley, or fooled around on the Internet, or even watched TV, it might not have been so bad. Instead, I almost went insane. I had to do my homework in self-defense, and I even ran out of that.

In the end, I was reduced to bothering Trevor. What's worse, even *he* didn't want my company.

"It's just that I'm kind of busy right now," he said, opening his bedroom door a crack to keep me in the hall.

"I can play video games," I assured him. "You need an opponent, right?"

He let out this long, self-satisfied laugh. "No offense, Cass, but that wouldn't be much of a contest."

I was too desperate to be offended. "It's better than playing with yourself, isn't it?"

"*By* myself! And anyway, I'm busy with something else right now."

"What?" I asked, trying to push his door open.

"Something for school. You wouldn't be interested." He pushed back hard, but not hard enough.

"Is that a *sewing* machine?" I exclaimed, peering over his shoulder at the mess spread out on his desk. "Trevor! You have a sewing machine in there!"

"Shhh!" he whispered, hushing me frantically. "I borrowed it from school. For home ec. I'm making an apron for Mom and I don't want her to know."

I just stood there, blinking.

"Right," I said at last. "Because Mom wears so many aprons."

"Everyone has to sew one," he told me, annoyed. "It's part of our grade. Now get out of here."

"Just let me see it."

I pushed the door open wide enough to glimpse a length of pale pink satin flung over his bed and a mound of purple velvet lying near it on the floor. Tissue-paper patterns littered every surface, along with scissors, pins, and what looked like crumpled sketches. I was still taking it in when the door reversed directions abruptly and slammed right in my face. The lock clicked shut on Trevor's doorknob, and no amount of begging could induce him to let me in after that.

All I can say is, I can't wait till he springs this treasure on Mom and she actually has to wear it. I killed at least an hour imagining how the next time we have company I'll wait until the perfect moment to say, "Hey, Mom, you ought to wear that cool apron Trevor made you!" And she'll have to wear it, of course, to avoid hurting his feelings. I pictured our living room full of lawyers and a horrid, frilly pink and purple apron over one of my mom's chic black dresses and nearly killed myself laughing.

If that doesn't tell you how bored I was, nothing will.

By Monday, when I finally went back to school, being whispered about in the hallways seemed like a small price to pay for human contact. At least I got to see Hayley. We ate lunch together, and after hearing about my weekend, she even hung around to spend a few minutes with me after school. She was waiting in the hall when I came out of Conway's room, having just completed my first solo detention.

"Get this!" I told her. "I had to write an essay about talent!"

"You're kidding me," she said. "You didn't give Conway the theory?"

"Of course. What else?"

* * *

Hey, wait a minute! Isn't this is where you came in?
Hallelujah! You're officially all caught up.

Nine Days Later

Hi! You're Back!

So here's where we are: it's the Wednesday before Thanksgiving, and no one is looking forward to a four-day break more than I am. I'm still in solo detention—a week and two days so far—and nothing else has changed much either.

Quentin is still pining for Ros and she's still not speaking to him. (Personally, I still fail to get the attraction, but nobody's asking me.) Kevin and Sterling are holding hands all over school now. (Nauseating? The shrimp incident pales in comparison.) The winter formal is only a week and a half away. (Obviously, I remain dateless.) And Snow Queen campaigning began on Monday with seven candidates so far (although why anyone bothers to run against Sterling is a mystery to me). Instead of holding the usual special assembly for the whole school, the powers that be have announced that this year's Snow Queen candidates will give their speeches at the dance, with the voting right afterward. I suspect that's because last year's speeches were a total waste of time—all about school spirit and how much the candidates love good old Hilltop High. Besides, everyone knows it doesn't matter what gets said. The prettiest girl always wins.

Let's see . . . what else? Kevin's still speaking to me. Barely. I don't think he's mad now so much as he's just moved on. Which must be nice for him. I'd give anything to move on, but where am I going to go? People at school are finally starting to forget all the trouble I got into, but my reputation will never recover. And I'm still grounded at home. By now you'd think my mom would be bored with playing enforcer, but every time she thinks about me and Trevor out in Dad's car, and how I could have killed us both, and blah, blah, blah . . .

I'm not saying she's wrong, just all right already. Besides, I've totally learned my lesson. The problem is, the rest of the world's a bit slow to figure that out. Have you ever noticed how people never want to let you change?

So anyway, it's Wednesday, you're all caught up, and if I don't get my butt in gear I'll be late for detention with my favorite teacher. (Sarcasm. You caught that, right?)

I wonder what today's scintillating essay assignment will be. Maybe "How I Completely Screwed Up My Life." Or "What Being a Loser Means to Me." After you write enough of these things, you start seeing a definite theme. Even so, Conway has to run out of topics soon.

A girl can dream, can't she?

Detention Deficit Disorder

Mrs. Conway is pretending I'm not here. She's just sitting at her desk, zoning out, twisting one of those everpresent pencils in her bun. She's not even correcting papers.

I wonder what she's thinking about?

Whatever it is has to be more interesting than what I'm thinking about. The title for today's masterpiece is "What I've Learned from All This." Honestly, I'm pretty much out of things to say on that subject, but I'll give it my best shot.

It's not like I have a choice.

Detention Essay #13
Mrs. Conway

What I've Learned from All This
by Cassie Howard

The first thing I've learned is to think before I act. I'm totally through with being impulsive. People <u>say</u> they like someone who's spontaneous, but what they mean is they like spontaneity when it turns out well. I've learned you can't count on a good outcome. I can't, anyway.

Another thing I've learned is

Saved by the Cell

Something weird just happened. I was writing that stupid essay when all of a sudden a cell phone rang. I didn't even know Conway *had* a cell phone, and there's a rule against leaving them on inside school buildings. But wait— it's getting weirder. She's actually taking the call.

"Hello?" she says, like I'm not even here. "Yes, this is Emily Conway."

Emily! I'd have guessed a phone book full of names before I came up with Emily. Isn't it weird what we don't know about our teachers? I've never even thought of Conway as *having* a first name—other than Mrs., I mean.

"Yes?" she says, hunching over her phone for privacy.

Now Emily (sorry, but that's still cracking me up) is listening and I'm pretending not to. Not that there's much to hear. The caller is doing all the talking, with Conway only inserting a "Yes" or "I see" here and there. I doodle in the margins of my essay, unable to stop eavesdropping.

"Okay. Thank you for letting me know," she says. She doesn't actually say good-bye, which is why she catches me staring at her when she switches off her phone.

"Getting a lot of writing done?" she asks.

"Yes. Well, no. Not yet. But I'm, uh—"

"Never mind. You can go."

"Excuse me?"

"I said you're dismissed."

"But I haven't finished my essay."

Conway gestures impatiently toward the door. "Your stint in detention is over, Miss Howard. Unless you're determined to continue these sessions after Thanksgiving . . ."

"No! I mean, uh . . . no. Thank you, Mrs. Conway."

I hesitate another millisecond, unable to believe my good luck. Then I stuff my essay into my backpack and take off like a shot.

"Have a good Thanksgiving!" I call over my shoulder.

I don't wait to hear her wish me the same. Why take chances? I run full tilt down the hallway, desperate to get gone before Conway changes her mind.

So Why Am I Still Here?

I don't have a clue. I'm a free woman now—not to mention out of detention an entire hour before I'm due home for more grounding. If I had any sense, I'd be running around milking my sixty unaccounted-for minutes of freedom. Instead I'm hesitating at the end of the main hall, wondering if I should go back and double-check with Conway before I leave.

Stupid, right? She made it totally clear I was excused. The thing is, this just doesn't feel finished. It's not like Conway to leave things half done. If she'd ended my detention after I'd completed my essay, that would have seemed normal. But to let me off after only one paragraph, which she didn't even ask to see . . .

Oh, great. I know what the problem is. I ran out of there so fast I left my bio book under my seat. I should just get it later. I don't actually need it before Monday.

But what if I can't get into her room before first period? Or the janitor finds it and locks it up somewhere? I've got homework between those pages.

I knew this was too good to be true.

I creep back down the hallway. The building is deserted for the approaching holiday and it feels so weird being alone in here that I'm afraid to make much noise. Besides, I don't want Conway to hear me coming far enough in advance to change her mind.

Her door is closed. She must have already left. I sidle up and peer through the door's high window, expecting to see nothing more than Conway's compulsively cleared desktop and immaculately erased front board.

What I see knocks my errand right out of my head.

My teacher's face is down on her desk and she's crying her eyes out. The crook of her arm is over her mouth, muffling her sobs, but she's having a total meltdown. She looks so completely sad and hopeless that my eyes fill with tears too. My hand inches toward the doorknob, where the feel of cold steel snaps me to my senses.

What am I going to do? Walk in there and pat her back? She'll be so furious with me for spying that I'll probably be in detention until *next* Thanksgiving.

I waffle another second, then turn around and run.

Turkey Daze

I can't eat another bite. I had to change out of my jeans, and even my sweatpants are feeling the strain. My mom went crazy cooking Thanksgiving dinner this year, inviting the neighbors over and indulging Trevor's home ec–fueled pie-baking frenzy. On top of an enormous turkey with stuffing, mashed potatoes, and all the trimmings, we ate a pumpkin pie, an apple pie, a cranberry-rhubarb pie, and a chocolate silk pie. With whipped cream. And ice cream. And there's an actual chance I might be sick if I don't stop talking about food.

The neighbors went home an hour ago and now Trevor and I are sprawled on our living room floor, playing Monopoly. He's already got a row of hotels that looks like the New York skyline, but I don't care about winning. Much. Considering that I'm still grounded, I'm just glad to have someone to play with.

I pick up the dice and roll two threes.

"Ha!" Trevor crows, before I even move my top hat. "I own that!"

"Big surprise, Trevor," I grumble, forking over his rent money. "You own half the board."

The truth is I'd do better if I bought everything I landed on, the way he does, instead of only collecting properties with names and colors I like, but a girl has to have standards.

He rolls the dice and moves his race car. I usually use the hat, or the shoe, or the dog token, but Trev is *always* the race car. He lands on B. & O. Railroad.

"I'll buy that," he says immediately.

"Big surprise," I repeat as he handles his own transaction. Trevor is also always the bank.

"How's the game?" my dad asks, wandering into the living room and collapsing onto the sofa. He reaches back to pile pillows under his head and I notice his belt is unbuckled.

"I'm winning," Trevor reports.

"I'm letting him," I say, just to yank Trevor's chain.

Dad picks up *National Geographic* and the game goes on.

I make my next move and land on Community Chest. I read the top card, roll my eyes, and slap it faceup on the board. "Ten bucks," I tell Trevor.

"You have won second prize in a beauty contest," he reads, laughing loudly. "You get that every time!"

"It's a gift."

He hands over my ten-dollar prize, then lands on Park Place, which he adds to the Boardwalk he already owns. Things are not looking good for the top hat.

My mom comes in and sits in her antique armchair. Unlike the rest of us, she appears to have bones still supporting her body. She perches stiffly on the chair's edge, watching our game without comment. She *can't* comment, because that would be too much like speaking to me.

Fifteen minutes later, the game reaches its inevitable conclusion when I hand my last five bucks to the gloating landlord from hell. Trevor acts like he's just earned a fortune instead of a handful of pastel play money. He mimes straightening a bow tie, then knocks the ash off an imaginary cigar. I'd probably say something rude if he were my only potential source of entertainment for the next three days. "Want to play again?" I ask instead. It's only six o'clock and I need a way to kill the remaining hours before bedtime.

"Can't," he informs me. "I'm sleeping over at Bill's house tonight."

"What?" I protest. "On Thanksgiving? Mom!"

I don't know what I expect her to do. Trevor isn't grounded anymore. Still, it seems like he ought to be more appreciative of my contribution to his short sentence. After all, if I'd ever told my parents what we were *really* doing that night . . .

"Yes?" My mother raises an eyebrow at me. "You have a problem with that?"

"It's just . . ." I sigh, realizing I can't win this one. "I thought we'd all be staying home tonight, that's all."

"Well, you'll be staying home," she says.

I start to help Trevor put the game back in the box, but I can't see what I'm doing because my eyes are filling with tears. Trevor actually seems to understand; he takes some money out of my hand and begins sorting it for me.

"I can put this away," he says. "You don't have to help."

I nod and scramble to my feet, wanting to get out of there before the real waterworks start.

"Maybe Cassie would like to go somewhere tonight too," my father says to my mother. "Isn't it about time for her punishment to be over?"

I freeze in a state of disbelief. Did my father just confront my mother? Even Trevor's afraid to move.

"Excuse me?" Mom says, and her tone sends shivers up my spine. I fully expect my dad to back down instantly.

But he surprises me.

"It's enough, Andrea," he says, sitting up. "Cassie knows what she did was wrong. Don't you, Cass?"

Somehow I find my voice. "I do! I really do."

My mother is clearly stunned. This is not how things work at our house. She stares my father down. "I'm the one who grounded her and *I'll* say when her punishment is over."

Trevor eases the box top onto our game, ready to bolt if anyone glances his way.

"Then say it now," my father insists. "Honestly, Andrea, do you really want to waste a long weekend this way?"

My mother shoots me a long-suffering look. "It's not as if I *enjoy* playing policeman."

"Exactly," says my dad. "Besides, we've made our point. Wouldn't you like to have five minutes alone together again?"

He gives her a look that should *not* be seen by unfortunate teens with way too much pie in their stomachs. Believe me, I don't want to go there.

But, by some miracle, my mother does.

"That would be nice," she admits wistfully.

"Cassie, tell your mother you've learned your lesson," my father orders.

"I've learned it!" I say immediately. "I'll never take the car again, I swear. And no more plagiarizing, obviously. Mrs. Conway believes I'm reformed or she wouldn't have let me out of detention."

Dad flips his palms up toward the ceiling, putting the ball in my mother's court.

"Fine," Mom says.

"Fine?" I squeak, not sure I heard her right.

"I'll accept you at your word. And don't think I won't hold you to it."

"No way. I would never think that."

"Fine," she says again.

My feet are glued to the living room floor. I'm afraid if I move I'll wake myself up from the best dream I've had all month.

"Well? Get going!" says my dad. "Go call Hayley or something. My gut is screaming to have these pants unzipped, and that's not going to be pretty."

Trevor finally dares to stand up. I take advantage of the distraction to charge out of the room. Just as abruptly, I change directions and run back to my mom.

"Thanks," I say, hugging her neck. "I won't let you down."

"I know," she says, hugging back.

On the sofa, my father has assumed the beached-whale position. I lean across his belly and plant a big kiss on his cheek.

"I owe you *huge*," I whisper.

No More Drama

"Watch this!" Quentin says, sticking one long French fry up each of his nostrils. His fingers dab ketchup on the protruding ends, in case we're not already grossed out enough.

"I *vant* to *sock* your *blaud*!" he says, doing his best Dracula imitation.

It's Saturday night, there are about a million people in the mall's food court, and I'm starting to seriously question why I was ever attracted to him. Unfortunately, given recent events, I don't have a lot of room to complain about him embarrassing me. I remind myself to be grateful he likes me again and look away while he pulls fried potatoes out of his nose.

"That's disgusting!" Hayley says, snuggling closer to Fitz.

"True. I don't think you're helping your chances, dude." Fitz grins at Hayley, as if to reinforce the fact that he's already hit the jackpot and doesn't need to worry about a date for the Snow Ball. Because that's why we're here. The dance is a week away now, and Quentin is determined to take Ros. The theory is that she'll wander by sooner or later and he'll finally get his chance to ask her.

"You'd better not have fries in your nose if she actually shows up," I say.

At this point, however, that doesn't seem likely. It's nearly ten o'clock and the only parts of the mall still open are the food court and the theaters.

Quentin sighs and wipes his face with a napkin. "I thought she'd be here tonight. We've seen everyone else."

Not everyone, I think, but I don't say it. I'm doing my best to forget about Kevin.

"Ask someone else," I suggest. "Look, there's Cyn Martin. She'll go with you."

I know I'm right, because without food up his nose, Quentin is quite good-looking. Besides, Cyn doesn't have a date for the formal. She told me so in English on Wednesday.

"You'd like Cyn," I say, warming to the idea. "She's a little shy at first, but she's nice when you get to know her."

"*Ros* is nice when you get to know her." The look Quentin shoots my way makes it clear I should shut up.

"Well, we can't wait here forever," Hayley breaks in. "For one thing, I have to pee."

I feel myself blush, but Fitz just laughs, and I realize this is not the first time he's heard her say those words. That's how tight they are. Envy stabs me once again.

You're out of detention and you're not grounded, I remind myself. But that state of affairs is already losing its power to thrill me. Being out of detention and not grounded is like the minimum requirement for the Not-a-Loser Club. What I really want is for someone to ask *me* to the dance.

"Come on, Cassie," says Hayley. "Come to the bathroom with me."

We leave the guys behind to hold our table. Half our school's cruising the food court and seats are at a premium.

"Who would you go to the dance with if you couldn't go with Kevin?" Hayley asks me as we join the long line outside the ladies' room.

"I *can't* go with Kevin."

"Right, but . . . isn't there anyone else you'd go with?"

"Is this a hypothetical conversation?"

"I'm just saying . . . what if somebody asks you?"

"Like who?"

"Quentin! Quentin doesn't have a date either."

Her suggestion leaves me literally speechless. I stare at her, open-mouthed.

"Why not?" she persists. "You used to like him."

"Yeah, *used* to," I finally manage to say. "Besides, he'd never go with me now. Not after Memory Lanes."

"What if he's forgiven you?"

"He wants to go with Ros!"

"What if Ros shoots him down?"

"You're already three what-ifs ahead of the situation."

"Just think about it," she urges. "If Quentin doesn't ask you, you can always ask him."

"He's not going to ask me," I say.

But I *am* thinking about it. Going with Quentin wouldn't be the life-altering romantic evening I'd dreamed of, but it would be fun. I'm still thinking about it a minute later when Hayley nudges me in the ribs.

"Don't look now, but here comes SOC."

Obviously, I look immediately. Sterling and Kevin have just exited the movie theater and are headed in our direction.

"Great," I say, groaning.

She's hanging all over him, talking a mile a minute, and her face is tilted up toward his like she's so blinded by love that she's unaware of us lesser beings. That's clearly not the case, though, because a second later she spots me and Hayley and pulls Kevin off course to pass us closer.

"Wait till you see my dress for the dance!" she tells him in a voice pitched to carry. "Strapless, slinky—you're going to die."

Right now I'm the one who's dying.

"You'll need to buy me a white corsage," she orders. "Get an orchid—roses are so common."

"Okay," he says. And then he notices me.

"Hey, Cassie!" he calls, walking over.

"Hi, Kevin," I say, surprised. "Good movie?"

"What? Oh." He glances back at the theater like he's already forgotten he was there. "Okay, I guess."

"Kevin!" Sterling reproaches him. "It was a romantic comedy," she informs me in a superior tone.

"Yeah. Romantic." Kevin rolls his eyes. "Except aren't comedies supposed to be funny?"

Hayley giggles. He obviously hated it. I feel myself smiling, and Kevin smiles back.

"Come on," Sterling tells him, latching onto his elbow. "I want to get a slice of pizza before they close."

"Bye," he says as she drags him off.

"Bye," I say wistfully.

"Did you see that?" Hayley demands as soon as they're out of earshot. "He totally smiled at you!"

"So what? We're friends. Sort of." I'm not getting my hopes up again.

"That's not what it looked like. Fourteen-Karat almost swallowed her tongue."

"Are you sure? I wasn't looking at her."

"Neither was Kevin," Hayley says significantly. "Maybe he's getting tired of her. I know I would be."

"Yeah, well . . . you're not a guy."

"True," she says. "Thank God."

The line finally moves enough for us to squeeze into the bathroom with a dozen other girls.

"You really think he was smiling at me?" I ask.

Hayley nods. "Definitely."

I ponder this while toilets flush and one vain brunette hogs the only mirror. If Kevin's *really* bored with Sterling . . . if he was *really* smiling at me . . .

"You're thinking of going for it, aren't you?" Hayley asks, reading my mind.

"No! I mean . . . not seriously."

It's been three weeks since Memory Lanes, and people are finally starting to forget what happened there.

If I keep my red head down, I might be socially acceptable again by spring.

Okay, a Little More Drama

I'm sitting beside Cyn Martin in Conway's class again— except that Mrs. Conway isn't here. The room is full of whispers as a stranger in a leather skirt picks up some chalk and writes her name on the board.

"I'm Ms. Wallace," she says, for those of us in honors English who still can't read. "Ms. Conway won't be at school this week. I'll be taking her place."

Several of us cringe at her dangerous use of Ms. Before I realize what I'm doing, my hand is in the air.

"Is Mrs. Conway coming back?" I ask without waiting to be called on.

A few people laugh, assuming I'm hoping she isn't. But actually I'm remembering her crying on her desk and hoping this absence isn't related.

"Don't worry." Ms. Wallace is younger than Mrs. Conway and full of easy smiles. "Your teacher will be back next Monday. In the meantime, though, we have a whole week to spend together. What would you like to do?"

I stare blankly with the rest of the class, not comprehending the question.

"No ideas?" she asks, surprised. "Most of the classes I sub for are full of ideas."

"Is she actually asking *us* how to spend the week?" Cyn whispers to me.

"Sounds like it," I whisper back. If Conway's not already sick, she'll have an aneurysm when she hears about this.

"Computer lab!" Jeff Mann shouts, waving his hand in the air. "Let's use the library computers for independent study."

I hear a few titters. Most of the room realizes that Jeff's independent study would involve attempting to defeat the school's porn filter.

"Excellent!" says Ms. Wallace, beaming. "Do I need to arrange that in advance, or can we just walk over?"

"I can run and check with Mr. McKay," Jeff volunteers. "He's our librarian."

"Good. Do that."

Jeff is out of his chair like a shot. He obviously can't believe his good luck and neither can anyone else, since it seems about to include all of us.

"Well, then," says Ms. Wallace. "While we're waiting for . . . what was that boy's name?"

One of the guys fills her in. I can tell by his tone that we're starting to suspect the same thing: our substitute is either kind of new or kind of dim.

"Well, then," she says again. "While we're waiting for Jeff, you may talk amongst yourselves."

I feel my eyebrows leap. Has this woman *ever* been in charge of a classroom? The noise level is already rising out of control.

"I can't believe they sent *her* to cover for Conway," Cyn says across the aisle. There's no need to whisper, since there's no longer the slightest chance of being overheard. "That's like replacing a pit bull with a kitten."

"Crazy," I agree. "I wonder what's wrong with Mrs. Conway?"

Cyn shakes her head. "I'm sure she'll be back to plague us soon enough."

"Right." I wish I could tell her what I saw after detention, but it seems too private to just blurt out.

"So how about the Snow Ball?" Cyn asks. "Any new hope on the escort front?"

"Not really. You?"

She heaves a sigh. "I thought maybe Ryan Warsaw . . . but he's taking Jill Petrocelli. Everyone who's going already has a date."

I shrug. "We'll catch it next year."

I don't even sound that disappointed. After all, why

torture myself? It's not like I *need* to see Kevin and Sterling slow dancing. Besides, Sterling's sure to be Snow Queen, and that's a sight no lesser queen should ever have to witness.

"We could always go stag," Cyn says.

"To a formal?"

She sighs again. "I guess not."

It's on the tip of my tongue to tell her that Quentin is dateless when Jeff bursts back into the room, panting like a marathon runner.

"We're in!" he crows. "Hurry up, you guys, before McKay changes his mind!"

Full-Out Drama

By the time we get to the library and sit through Mr. McKay's lecture on computer-lab rules, the period is half over. Worse, there aren't enough computers to go around. I sit to one side of a keyboard, staring into space while Cyn reads Internet gossip about her favorite stars.

I can't get Mrs. Conway off my mind. I'm so obsessed with wondering about her that I even forget Kevin's in the room. When the bell rings and I notice him walking out the lab door, it's like waking up out of a trance.

"See you later," I tell Cyn, shaking off the cobwebs and heading to algebra.

The slope of a line is $\frac{y_2 - y_1}{x_2 - x_1}$, not to mention totally useless. An hour of this would make anyone crazy, and we've been studying it for two weeks. I'm ready to knock myself unconscious by beating my head against my desk. The bell finally rings and I leap to my feet, so desperate to be out of math that even Western civ looks good.

Now I'm snoozing to the classics, counting the seconds until lunch.

Fourth period ends and I'm the first one out of my seat. I've got pepperoni on my mind as I hurry down the hall, but somehow I turn right instead of left, and the next thing I know I'm lurking outside our school office. The door is open and chatty Ms. Masters is alone behind the counter, sorting papers into piles.

And suddenly I realize why I've come.

"Hi, Ms. Masters," I say, stepping inside. "Busy day today?"

She looks up. "Hello, Cassie! How's that stomach doing?"

"What? Oh. Fine, thanks." I'm embarrassed that she remembers my recent food poisoning—until I realize she's just handed me my opening. "What about Mrs. Conway? How's her stomach doing?"

Ms. Masters's brows knit worriedly. "Is something wrong with her stomach?"

"I just assumed . . . I mean, with her being out all week . . ."

"Oh, right." She goes back to her papers. "Poor thing."

"So it *is* her stomach?" I say, surprised.

"No, her husband." The secretary's hands freeze mid-sort. "Oops. I shouldn't have said that."

I glance over my shoulder, but Ms. Masters and I are still alone. "I saw her crying after school on Wednesday," I confide in a low voice. "She didn't know I was there, and I got kind of worried. Is she okay?"

Ms. Masters sighs, then decides to trust me.

"No, but she will be. Emily's tough. If she wasn't, she'd have cracked a long time ago."

"Her husband . . . ," I venture. "Did he leave her?"

"What? No!" Ms. Masters looks truly shocked. "Why would he? Emily's been a saint, an angel. . . . He worships the ground she walks on."

I must look shocked now, because she lowers her voice and starts telling me the whole story.

"Emily took early retirement five years ago. She always wanted to write—literature major and all—and the first thing she did was convert her and Ed's old garage into an author's studio. But it was barely finished when Ed's mother got sick and they moved her in with them. That studio got turned into a bedroom for Mrs. Conway—the *other* Mrs. Conway—and Emily ended up nursing her full-time."

"So she came out of retirement to escape from her mother-in-law?"

Ms. Masters gives me an incredulous look. "She came back because she's a first-rate teacher who needed the money. Taking care of someone that old and sick eats through a bank account. And Emily insisted on the *best* care, which meant insurance didn't cover much. She loved that old woman."

"Loved?" I repeat with a sinking feeling. *Love* is not a word you want to hear in the past tense.

"She died," Ms. Masters says sadly. "A couple of months ago."

"But—but—" I protest, counting backward. "We were in school then!"

Ms. Masters cocks her head as if she fails to see my point.

"She didn't say *anything* to us!"

"Well, she wouldn't. Most of the teachers don't even know. I've known Emily ten years now, and that's just how she is. Private. Had the funeral on a Saturday and kept on going."

"Wow," I say, imagining how hard that must have been.

"She's a rock," Ms. Masters says admiringly. "Not that she has a choice, with Ed unable to work for so long. And now that he's back in chemo—"

"Chemo?" My heart sinks a little further. "You mean for cancer?"

"I'm not going into details," Ms. Masters warns. "Just that they thought they got it last year, but now it's back. They found out for sure on Wednesday and he's doing chemo this week. Emily wanted to be there."

"Well, no kidding," I murmur, imagining my mother's reaction if my father was ever that sick. "Is he going to be okay?"

"I hope so. Their parents have all passed now, and they don't have any kids."

I hear the unspoken message: if Mr. Conway dies, Mrs. Conway will be alone.

Ms. Masters looks suddenly worried. "You and I, we have an understanding, right? You aren't going to repeat *any* of this. And don't tell anyone else about Emily crying, either. She wouldn't like it."

"Not under torture," I promise.

My ears ring as I walk out of the office and into the hall. It's incomprehensible that Mrs. Conway has been through so much and kept teaching the whole time. Not only that, but she's never lowered her standards, never cut a single corner, never breathed even a word of her personal problems. . . .

I think back on all the times I've accused her of demanding too much of *us* and feel ashamed. The things we don't know about our teachers turn out to be bigger than their first names.

Lab Brats

Ms. Wallace has us in the lab again. I've scored a computer to myself and I'm actually using it to finish my Western civ homework when somebody taps me on the shoulder.

"Mind if I sit with you?" Kevin asks.

"Go ahead." I'm a little confused, since our class has already been working for ten minutes. "Did your computer break?"

He takes a chair and leans back in a lazy stretch. "No."

"Just don't feel like working, huh?"

"Why should I?" he asks, nodding toward the front of the room, where our substitute is reading a magazine. "This week is a total joke anyway."

He's not wrong. I'm one of the few people actually working, and only out of respect for Mrs. Conway. The rest of her students are running wild—playing video games, talking too loud, and just generally getting away with murder. After three months under Mrs. Conway's iron thumb, having so much pressure off at once is making people giddy.

"Ms. Wallace?" a girl calls from the back of the room. I turn to see Amy Isaac's hand in the air.

Ms. Wallace looks up from her magazine. "Yes?"

"There's something wrong with this computer. I keep pushing Escape, but I'm still here."

The class explodes with laughter. Through the interior windows between the lab and the main library, I see Mr. McKay running for our door. He bursts in to find us still chuckling, Ms. Wallace standing stricken at the front.

"What's all this noise?" he demands. "This is a *library!*"

"I don't know," Ms. Wallace replies, baffled. "Apparently there's something wrong with that girl's computer."

That sets us off all over again. Abandoning my altruistic attempt at good behavior, I howl with the rest of them.

"If this class can't control itself, it will leave the library immediately," Mr. McKay threatens. The noise level drops instantly. "Now, which computer is broken?"

"My mistake," Amy pipes up. "All good now."

Snickers break out again. Mr. McKay gives us a long, dirty look.

"Can I speak to you a moment?" he asks Ms. Wallace. They step out of the lab, but I can still see them through the glass. He's clearly chewing her out, which makes me feel a little guilty. The class is quieter as it returns to independent pursuits.

"What are you working on?" Kevin asks me.

"Nothing. Western civ. Don't you have any homework?"

"I'd rather talk to you."

My heart skips a beat. "You would?"

"When I saw you at the mall last weekend, I realized how much I miss hanging out with you. You know, just talking. The way we used to. Before."

Before. There's a mouthful.

"Me too," I say.

"Sterling and I aren't getting along too well."

The admission comes out of nowhere, taking me by surprise.

"That's not how it looks," I finally say.

He shrugs. "It's just . . . I've learned a few things about her. She's not exactly how she seems."

"No kidding?"

I'm not sure turning this into a question has adequately disguised my sarcasm, but Kevin pulls his chair closer, pitching his voice to reach only me.

"When I first saw Sterling, I was blown away. I probably wouldn't even have had the nerve to say hello, except she was wearing a Newport Beach T-shirt. I told her that was my hometown and she said it was *her* hometown. . . ."

Obviously, I remember all this, but I manage to keep my mouth shut.

"The thing is, I just found out, she never even lived there. Yesterday she lets something slip about being born in L.A., and when I ask her what's up she tells me that after I transferred here, she had a friend in the office pull my file and they read all about me. Then she got a T-shirt off the Internet and *pretended* to be from Newport. The whole thing was a scam to get my attention, to make me think we had something in common."

"I knew it!" I blurt out.

Kevin looks astonished.

"Not all that," I clarify hurriedly. "I just thought she was faking about Newport Beach."

"Why?"

I shrug. "Maybe because I've known her longer than you have."

He shakes his head. "The worst part is, she thought the whole thing was funny. I mean, you'd think she'd be embarrassed, but she's laughing the whole time, like she's done something really cute. They read my *file*, Cassie."

"Yeah. That's, um . . ." I'm not sure how to fill in the blank.

Kevin doesn't notice. "When I first met her, Sterling would always ask about my plans, then show up at the same place."

"Like Quentin's party?"

He has the decency to look sheepish. "It was flattering, you know? Plenty of guys would love to be stalked by Sterling."

Plenty have, I think, biting my lip.

"But lately . . . I don't know. There's other stuff too that I'd rather not go into. She's really kind of a schemer. Her Snow Queen campaign is turning into major espionage."

What does he want me to do? Sympathize?

"*You* should run for Snow Queen," he says.

"Are you high?" The words slip out before I can censor myself. "Me? Snow Queen?"

"Shake things up," he dares me. "Give Sterling some actual competition."

It takes me a few seconds to form a suitable reply. "All right. I'm going to let you slide because you're new and obviously insane. The way Snow Queen works around here is that the prettiest, most popular girl wins. Always."

"You're pretty."

"You think so?" I'm on cloud nine . . . until I abruptly realize I'm losing control of the situation. "Wait! That's not the point. The point is, I wouldn't have a chance."

"You know what your problem is?" he says. "You sell yourself short. You ought to have more confidence."

"Well—but—" I stammer, nonplussed. "There's confidence, and then there's reality. Besides, in the unlikely event I won, Sterling would be livid. Aren't you taking her to the dance?"

Kevin shrugs. "If we're still together."

The lab spins in a very disorienting way. I blink a couple of times, then remember to breathe.

He's probably not serious.

And even if he is, it doesn't mean that we . . .

Forget it. I'm not messing with Sterling again.

Apron. Not.

Trevor is sewing again. I can hear the machine through his bedroom door. I try the doorknob. It's locked.

"That must be one complicated apron," I yell through the wood.

"It is," he calls back.

"Let me in."

"Not a chance."

I start to walk away, but Trevor's door opens behind me. "Okay," he says.

I hesitate, not certain whether to trust him. Cooperation from Trevor is inherently suspicious. We've been getting along better lately, though, and curiosity is killing me. I step into his room still expecting a booby trap, but things look reasonably safe. The sewing machine is on his desk, surrounded by a mess of fabric scraps and tangled thread. I don't see anything that looks like an apron.

"First," Trevor says, "you have to promise not to laugh."

"Ooh. That could be tricky."

"Cassie!"

He looks so serious I want to laugh already.

"All right! I mean, I'll try."

"Try hard," he says with a menacing look. He ought to realize he's setting me up for failure by making such a big deal about it. I'm two seconds from losing it right now and I haven't even seen this apron yet.

"Okay!" I say. "Hurry up!"

With one last warning look, he opens his closet and takes out a hanger. My eyes pop.

"That's a blouse."

Trevor turns the hanger around to show me both sides. The blouse's fabric is soft and white. It drapes from the shoulders in liquid folds, flowing into long bell sleeves and a deep V-neck. Round pearl buttons up the front complete its romantic look.

"You didn't make that," I say.

Trevor shrugs. "You were right. Mom never wears the apron she already has, so I got permission to make a blouse instead. She can wear it with her suits."

"But Trevor, that's . . . good."

"I know," he says proudly.

"But—but—how?"

I can tell he'd like to be annoyed, but he's way too impressed with himself. "It's sewing, not brain surgery," he says. "Granted, I'm incredibly gifted at it. . . ."

"Gifted? No. I'll admit that's a nice shirt, but your *gift* has something to do with computers."

He smiles. "Yeah, that too."

"Not too. Instead."

"Who says?" he scoffs. "Maybe I have two gifts. Or ten. Or a hundred. People aren't all one thing or all something else, Cassie. Life's more complicated than that."

"Yes, but—"

To my surprise, I can't finish the sentence. I've always believed in one main talent, one special gift, but . . .

What if Trevor's right?

I am the Queen of Second Place. But what if I'm other things too? If Trevor can sew, what else can I do? I could have talents I haven't discovered yet.

How would I even know?

"Ha! I have a point," Trevor gloats. "And you know it, too, or else you'd have something to say."

"I *have* something to say. Can I try on the blouse?"

The Nun Also Rises

This is not good. I'm digging frantically through my locker, looking for the biology handout Mr. Rich gave us last week. We have a quiz this morning and I completely forgot to study. Maybe, if I get exceptionally lucky, whatever I memorize in the next five minutes will be what's on the test. Except that I can't find my handout and I'm really starting to panic.

"Hey, Cassie!" a familiar voice calls behind me.

I turn to see Jeannie Patrick materialize out of the chaos in the hall, her cheeks flushed pink with some major news. "Have you heard?" she asks breathlessly.

I sense my chance of passing this quiz slipping away, but I can't resist. "Heard what?"

"Sterling and Kevin—they broke up!"

The noise of slamming locker doors is drowned by the sudden roaring in my ears. "You're kidding."

Jeannie shakes her head. "I just heard it from Ginger Henry, who got it from Tamara Owens, who got it from Ros, who ought to know."

"Why?"

"Because she's Sterling's best fr—"

"No. Why did they break up?"

Jeannie offers a wicked smile. "I heard he dumped her."

"Why?"

"Wouldn't you?"

She has a point. Besides, everything Kevin said yesterday is rushing back to me now.

"Well, that's just . . . wow," I say.

"I thought you'd want to know."

"Yeah, thanks. Interesting."

"Interesting!" Jeannie laughs. "Right." She's staring me down, waiting for something.

"What?"

"Have you turned into some sort of nun? This is your big chance!"

"For what?"

She rolls her eyes. "Okay. I'd love to stay and play twenty questions with you, but some of us have class."

The first bell rings, right on cue. Jeannie waves and takes off. I watch her run away, then turn back to my open locker.

Was I looking for something? If so, I can't remember what. I close my locker in a daze and head for biology.

I'm nearing Mr. Rich's door when Hayley skids around a corner and stops just inches from knocking me down.

"Did you hear?" she blurts out.

"I heard."

"Of *course* you heard—it's all over school! What incredible timing! I mean, if you still like him, and he's free now . . . Cassie, what are you going to do?"

The answer tumbles out, and it's not the one either of us expects.

"I'm going to run for Snow Queen."

Second Time

"Run that by me one more time," Hayley says, eyes wide with disbelief. "I thought you just said you were running for Snow Queen."

I nod. "Sterling's vulnerable now. I can do this."

"Are you crazy?" Her expression suggests this is a foregone conclusion. "Cassie, you know I love you, but what about the other girls? What about Angie Yee and Tamara Owens? Besides, just because Sterling and Kevin broke up doesn't mean people won't vote for her."

"No, it just means she's not *everyone's* favorite."

"Okay, okay, let's say you're right." Hayley acts like she's talking a jumper off a ledge. "It's already Wednesday, Cassie. You'd have to turn in your petition this afternoon. You'd need posters by tomorrow. Plus you'd have to write a speech, find a date, and buy a dress—all before Saturday night."

"None of that's impossible."

"I just don't understand why you want to do it," Hayley argues, glancing at the hall clock. We're both in danger of being tardy, but she obviously feels she can't leave me in this deranged state.

"Because," I say, trying to put it into words. "I just have this hunch, like it's finally my turn. No one will expect me to win, so if I lose, there's no major damage. But what if I win, Hayley?"

"It'll be the biggest upset in the history of Hilltop High."

"Exactly. All I need is a good plan."

"And a majority of the votes," she reminds me, but I can tell she's starting to come around.

"Think about it," I urge. "If I pull this off, it'll be my crowning achievement."

Hayley groans.

"I mean, you know. So to speak."

Second Wind

"Sign my petition," I tell Tate the Great at lunch. It's more of an order than a request and he accepts my pen obediently.

"You're running for Snow Queen too?" he says, scrawling his name on line twenty-three. "I've probably already signed five of these."

"Sign all you want," I tell him. "Just make sure you vote for me."

He laughs. "You're confident."

"I have my moments."

The truth is, I don't *feel* confident. But the part of my mind that thinks this is a bad idea is currently locked in a dark corner while the rest of my brain runs the show.

"Good luck," he says, handing back my petition. "You'll need it."

"You *are* going to vote for me?" I say with an imploring smile. "Please, Bryce? Those other girls will get lots of votes, but I don't stand a chance unless some of the popular people, like you, help me out."

I'm shameless. I'd bat my eyes at him if I knew how to do it. But it doesn't matter. My flattery hits the mark without any help from my lashes.

"I'll think about it," he says. "Since you asked the nicest."

I give him what I hope is a flirty smile, then hurry off in search of signature twenty-four. Lunch is almost over and I need two more people to sign my petition before I can turn it in. Well, technically I need twenty-seven, but Hayley has the other sheet of twenty-five lines and she's working the quad for me. Between her, Fitz, and Quentin, she already had a three-name head start, so I'm hoping she'll fill up her page.

I'm cruising the football field, looking for easy marks sitting alone on the bleachers, when I see a beautiful sight: Kevin Matthews all by himself.

"Hey, Kevin!" I say, climbing up to join him.

He looks up from a textbook, shading his eyes with one hand. "Hi, Cassie. What are you doing out here?"

"Running for Snow Queen. How about you?"

He grimaces. "Hiding from your competition."

It's an open invitation to ask if he and Sterling really broke up. Unfortunately, it's an invitation I'm afraid to accept. "Will you sign my petition?" I ask instead.

Kevin takes my paper. His fingers brush mine as I hand him the pen and my heart starts pounding like crazy.

"I think it's great you're doing this," he says, adding his name to my form.

"You'd better say that. You're the one who told me I should."

"I did?" He seems about to deny it. "Oh, right. I did."

"So you ought to vote for me, too. I mean . . . there's no reason you can't now. Is there?"

"Nope," he says, meeting my gaze with a smile. "No reason at all."

Seize the Date

I'm beside myself with excitement when I meet Hayley after school.

"I got thirty-one signatures!" I tell her before she has a chance to say hello. "So even if you *didn't* get twenty-five . . ."

"I got twenty-nine. And it was easy, Cassie! Everyone I asked said yes."

"Me too! Look," I say, pointing to line twenty-four. "Look who signed."

Hayley's brows twitch at the sight of Kevin's signature, but she plays it cool. "He must have signed Sterling's petition too."

"Yes, but he's going to vote for me."

"Who's his date for the dance?" Hayley asks, cutting straight to the bottom line.

I smile. I can't help it. "I'd say that's up for grabs."

A Little Support—Very Little

"That's nice," my father says, loading his plate with scalloped potatoes. "What's a Snow Queen?"

We're sitting around the dinner table and I've just informed my family of my daring campaign at school.

"What's a Snow Queen?" I repeat, unable to believe my ears. "Are you new?"

"Cassie," my mother warns.

"Yeah, but she has a point," Trevor chips in on my behalf.

"The Snow Queen reigns over the Snow Ball," I explain for my father's benefit. He still looks blank. "The winter formal? They do it every year?"

"Oh, right," he says, nodding. "Like homecoming queen."

"Only better."

"What made you decide to try that?" Mom asks. "Kind of sudden, isn't it?"

"A little," I admit. "I just felt like doing something big, you know? Something no one would expect from me."

"Good," she says. "That's progress."

"Great," Dad echoes. Our household balance of power has obviously been restored.

"I'm glad you think so, because I'll need money for a dress," I tell him.

"Oh." He glances at Mom before he answers. "I guess we can cover that. How much do you need? Fifty?"

Trevor smirks at me with his mouth full of peas.

I give my dad an aggrieved look. "For a formal? More like *two* fifty."

"Not a chance," Mom cuts in. "We're not spending that much on one dress until it's for your wedding."

"Mom!"

"One hundred," she says. "I *might* go as high as one fifty, but only if I see the dress first."

I already know what will happen: I won't be able to find

anything for a hundred dollars and I'll end up shopping with my mother. Worse, I suspect this is her plan.

"Do you really think you can win, Cass?" Trevor asks.

I listen for the mocking undertone, but it appears to be a serious question, like he actually believes I could have a chance.

"I don't know. The competition's stiff."

"It would be cool if you won, though," he says. "Everyone would know who you are then. You'd be set for the rest of high school."

I might be starting to see his angle. "And next year we'll *both* be in high school . . . ," I say, testing my theory.

Trevor tries to look innocent but he's not that sly.

". . . and so everyone will know who *you* are, too."

"Not everyone."

"Still, I suppose if I were *really* popular, it *might* help you out with next year's sophomore girls."

Trevor nearly chokes on his pork chop and I know I've hit the mark. It could have been worse—I could have used Julie's name—but I can tell by the way Mom's eyeing him that she's picked up a clue anyway.

"I'll need money for tickets, too," I announce, changing the subject to distract her. "And for a boutonniere for my date."

"Who *is* your date?" she asks.

"Kevin Matthews. I think. I haven't actually asked him yet."

"Isn't he supposed to ask you?" Dad says.

"Hal, please," my mother protests. "You'll set women's lib back thirty years."

"Sorry," he murmurs, returning to his meal.

"I think it's great that Cassie knows what she wants and isn't afraid to go get it," Mom adds, smiling at me.

My answering smile is pasted on. That *would* be great—if it were true. I have no clue what I want and even less of an idea how to get it. Not to mention that the thought of asking Kevin to anything ever again fills me with bloodcurdling terror. If he asks me first, I'll be totally thrilled.

Women's lib will survive the hit.

"Can I go to Hayley's tonight?" I ask. "We have to make posters."

" 'Cassie for Snow Queen'?" my father guesses.

"Something like that. Only hopefully more clever."

"All right," says my mom. "You can go, but I want you home by ten."

"I've got it!" Trevor says. "How about 'Cassie's Your Lassie'?"

"No thanks," I say, shaking my head. "I know lassie means girl, but people will go straight to Lassie the dog."

Trev grins with wicked glee. I'm no longer at all convinced he's sincere about wanting me to win.

"Here's one," says my dad. " 'Be Classy. Vote Cassie.' "

"Mom!" I groan. "Can I leave now?"

"All right." Her expression shows she feels my pain.

I'm carrying my plate to the kitchen when Trevor launches his parting shot: " 'Sassy Cassie's More Classy Than Lassie!' "

And we were getting along so well.

Slogan Slump

I lean my bike against the wall outside Hayley's front door, still annoyed with my parents for making me ride it. Unfortunately, the fact that I'm not allowed to drive right now—even with my parents in the car—is something I've learned it's best not to mention. At least my dad's picking me up.

I press Hayley's doorbell and Mrs. Johnson answers. "Cassie!" she exclaims. "We haven't seen you in so long I was starting to think you were a figment of Hayley's imagination."

"Yeah, sorry," I say, embarrassed. "I've been kind of . . . obsessed this year."

Mrs. Johnson smiles kindly. She has Hayley's eyes exactly, which always weirds me out. "Hayley!" she calls up the stairs. "Cassie's here!"

Hayley appears on the second-floor landing. "Let's work in my room," she says, motioning me up.

"I don't want to find paint on that floor," Hayley's mom tells her as I climb the stairs.

"You won't," Hayley promises.

"Have fun, then. Your dad and I will be in the den if you need help."

"Your mom is so cool," I say as Hayley shuts her bedroom door. "I wish *I* was an only child."

"Aren't those two separate issues?" Hayley asks with a grin. "What's the matter? Trevor bugging you again?"

"It had to happen sometime."

I shrug my backpack off my shoulders, but before I can show her the markers I brought, something catches my eye. "Is that a new bulletin board?" I ask, crossing her room.

Hayley's bedroom is huge. She has her own computer on a table beside her desk, and there's always been a bulletin board on the wall there. But now there are two, side by side, and they're both covered with photos.

"You haven't seen that before?" she says, hovering nervously behind me. "It's not *that* new."

The second bulletin board is completely devoted to her and Fitz. She has pictures of him at school and at her house, and of both of them at Memory Lanes. There are stubs from movie tickets, a note he wrote on a florist's card, and—right in the center—a big photo of him with his arm around Hayley's shoulders. He's grinning like a fool, and the way she's looking at him has completely transformed her face. I glance at the other board, the one covered with pictures of me and Hayley dating back to seventh grade, and it feels like ancient history.

"Come on," she urges. "Let's get started on those posters."

She's already spread newspaper on a patch of hardwood floor. We arrange markers, poster paints, and the biggest sheets of paper we could find on top, then sit staring at each other.

We have no clue what to do next.

"Did you come up with *anything*?" Hayley asks. "Do you at least have an idea?"

"Not really," I admit.

We stare at our blank papers.

"We could always go with 'Vote for Cassie,'" she says after a minute.

"Yeah. If we have to."

It's strange, but I'm kind of embarrassed to talk to her right now. Seeing those bulletin boards has made things different between us, like I'm still stuck on the first one and Hayley has grown up without me.

"Hey! You want to see my dress?" she offers. "My mom picked it up for me this afternoon." She's already standing, pulling a plastic-sheathed hanger out of her closet. I see the Visions logo before she lifts the plastic.

"Red!" Her full-length gown is gorgeous—sleek, simple, and cut low front and back. "That's so pretty, Hayley."

"Wait till you see it on," she says, smoothing it against her body. "What about you? Any idea what you're wearing?"

"I'm going shopping after school tomorrow. I hope there's still something left."

"Lots of stuff," she assures me.

I try to smile, but insecurity is finally getting the best of me. "I can't believe I'm doing this," I admit nervously. "Here I am running for Snow Queen, and I don't even have a dress. Not to mention a date. Or even a slogan."

Hayley hangs up her formal and sits back down. "I was wondering when you'd start to panic. Up until now, you've been way too calm."

"Wait. You *want* me to panic?"

"No. I just think it's the only normal reaction."

"Gee, thanks."

Hayley grins. "Would it help if I said I'm proud of you for trying?"

I shrug. It helps a lot, actually.

"I wouldn't have the courage," she adds. "I don't know where you're finding it."

"Maybe it's not courage. Maybe I'm just crazy."

"If you were crazy, you wouldn't be panicking." She pulls the cap off a wide black marker. "Should we get busy on that slogan?"

Poster Child

It's Thursday, still fifteen minutes before the first bell, and I'm feeling fantastic. Hayley and I are in the main hall, admiring the poster we've just taped up:

> **C** assie
>
> **A** s
>
> **S** now Queen
>
> **S** tops
>
> **I** n-Crowd
>
> **E** lections
>
> Cassie Howard
>
> A queen for the rest of us!

"Whoa!" a stranger's voice exclaims. "When did Snow Queen get political?"

I turn to see a boy wearing jeans and glasses, a shock of dark hair falling over his eyes.

"It's always been political," Hayley tells him. "It's just that the candidates are usually all from the same party."

He smiles appreciatively. "Are you Cassie?"

"No, I am. And I'd appreciate your vote," I add self-consciously.

He looks me up and down, and suddenly I'm trying to see myself through his eyes. Will he like my lace cuffs and long skirt, or should I have worn something less retro? Is my hair okay? Too short? Too red? Do I look like a contender?

Or do I just look desperate?

"Okay," he says.

"Okay?"

"I'll vote for you. Why not?"

"Hey, thanks!"

"Good luck," he says, walking off.

Hayley gives me a quick, triumphant hug. "Congratulations! Your first vote!"

Technically, he's my fifth vote. I'm about to point that out when Jeannie Patrick walks up.

"You're doing it!" she squeals, pointing to my poster. "I heard a rumor, but I couldn't believe it."

"Kind of crazy, huh?" I say, embarrassed.

"No way! It's about time someone normal runs!"

"So will you vote for me?"

"Do you have to ask?" Jeannie waves and wanders down the hall, which I suddenly notice is filling up. A few people smile as they read my poster.

"They like it!" I whisper to Hayley, elated. "You know

what? I'm starting to believe I might actually have a chance!"

"Come on, Your Highness," she teases. "Let's put up the rest of these posters."

Feeling Lucky

I walk in late and spot Kevin already seated behind a monitor in the lab's back corner. I hesitate half a heartbeat, then head directly for him.

"Hey, Kevin," I say, dropping into the nearest chair. "How's it going?"

The lab is packed with Mrs. Conway's English class, but I'm not worried. Let them listen. I'm bulletproof this morning.

He smiles. "Hi, Cassie. I saw your posters."

"Yeah? What do you think?"

"I think Sterling's probably hoping you get hit by lightning."

I laugh. It feels good. Heads turn, and that feels good too. "I'm only saying what everyone already knows," I tell him.

"Sure. Just look both ways when you cross the street."

We're both laughing now. Our eyes meet and neither one of us looks away.

Say it, I think. *Ask me to the dance.* I can tell he wants to. I can almost read it in his face.

"So, doing anything Saturday night?" he teases, right on cue.

"I have this thing to go to. No big deal." I try to play it light, but my heart has started racing.

"Anyone going to that thing with you?"

He's flirting! My heart speeds even faster.

"That depends on why you're asking," I say, daring to flirt back.

Part of me thinks I should stop being coy and grab this chance to ask him. But he's so close to asking me . . .

"Cassie?"

I stop breathing. "Yes?"

"What if—"

"Excuse me! Class?" Ms. Wallace has chosen the worst possible moment to interrupt. "There's way too much talking in here."

Heads swivel. We all look around in amazement. Not only have we been yakking all week, she's the one who said we could.

"Mr. McKay has informed me that if there are any more disruptions, we will be asked to leave the lab and return to our regular classroom," Ms. Wallace says. "Since I've only got today and tomorrow left with you people, I don't want to come up with a new lesson plan. That means that starting today, there will be only one person per computer. Students who don't get a keyboard will work up here at the front table. There will be no talking, no laughing, no fooling around—in short, no interaction of any kind. Do I make myself clear?"

We're all too stunned to answer. It's the longest speech

she's made since we met her—and it smacks of Mrs. Conway. I can't help wondering if they've been in communication.

"Good," says Ms. Wallace. "If you don't have a computer to work on, come to the front of the room. Everyone else, start researching something."

She seems serious. I risk whispering to Kevin anyway, counting on the noise of people changing seats to cover me.

"I guess I'd better go up there," I say.

"Yeah, sorry. See you later."

I pretend to adjust a backpack strap, hoping he'll remember what we were talking about.

"All right, then," I say, scooting to the edge of my chair. "I'll see you."

"Definitely," he says, with a meaningful smile. "I will *definitely* see you."

Okay, So He Didn't Ask Me

But he wanted to. If only Ms. Wallace hadn't interrupted!

I obsessed about that missed opportunity all day, and now I'm in bed, still obsessing about it. If I don't get some sleep, I'll be useless tomorrow when I need to be my best. The problem is, I can't stop analyzing every word Kevin said this morning. And when I force myself to stop thinking about him, I remember all the other people I talked to today. People I didn't even know came up and said they hoped I'd win Snow Queen.

Those posters hit a nerve. It's like all of a sudden the entire school realizes they don't have to choose one of the usual girls. Voting for me is the new form of *social* protest. By the time I left school this afternoon, my cheeks ached from smiling so much.

Granted, it wasn't a *perfect* day. If it were, I'd have a date with Kevin right now. And a dress to wear on it. Because despite what Hayley said about there still being plenty of dresses, when I took the bus to the mall this afternoon I couldn't find anything in my price range. I finally picked a red lace, midcalf number, but it's forty bucks over my limit, so I had to put it on layaway until I can take Mom to see it. Obviously, I'm not looking forward to that. Plus I'd hate for Hayley to think I was copying her color. I may still change my mind and get something else.

The dress I *really* want is a floor-length, pale pink satin halter. Very 1930s Hollywood glamour—I saw it at Visions and fell in love. But it's vintage and costs five hundred dollars, so there's no point even showing Mom that one tomorrow. Assuming I end up taking her. Which I probably will.

And then there's my speech. Have I mentioned the speech? All Snow Queen candidates have to make one, and I'm so traumatized by public speaking that I'm still having flashbacks about an oral report I gave three years ago.

The entire seventh grade met in the auditorium, and five of us had to present the results of our classes' science projects. For the record, I got the shaft. My class voted for Marly Mitchell to give our report—I was only the runner-up. I should have been in the clear, but then Marly developed this totally convenient case of laryngitis and I got stuck covering for her. I'll never forget walking out on that stage. I was so petrified that this muscle in my butt started spasming and didn't let up the entire ten minutes. The only thing that kept me from fleeing in shame was that leaping butt cheek.

At least Snow Queen speeches are short. Which is good, because I have no idea what I'm going to say. Hayley thinks I should stick to what's on the posters, how a vote for me is a vote against the status quo. I'm not so sure. The posters are great, but I don't want to sound bitter. It might be better to go the standard rah-rah route and say how cool our school is and what being Snow Queen would mean to me. Besides making Kevin want me, I mean. Because he *is* the one who said I should run.

So why didn't he ask me to the dance today?

You know what? I think this bed is getting harder. Can that happen? When mattresses get old, do they stiffen up, like people?

Anyway, whatever my speech is about, when I give it I'll definitely try to make sure no one is anywhere within view of my rear end.

You know. Just in case.

This Is Weird

Kevin hasn't looked at me all period and now the bell's about to ring. He was late today, so he's reading at the front table while I'm on a computer in back. But he could still smile or wave or *something*. He's had his eyes on his homework ever since he came in, like it's the most interesting thing in the world.

Granted, Ms. Wallace is acting hard-nosed again, trying to convince us she's gotten tough. This week has worn her out, though; I can tell by the bags beneath her eyes. I'll bet she's thrilled it's Friday.

I know I am.

Except that the Snow Ball is tomorrow, and if I want to go with Kevin I have to ask him today. Oh, great—there's the bell. I have to ask him *now*.

Everyone is up, rushing the lab door. Ms. Wallace is lying about what a pleasure it was, but no one's listening. There's a big crowd between me and Kevin. He slips through the doorway up ahead, and it's all I can do not to push my way out. I finally squeak through the lab door, only to see him leaving the library. At this rate, I'm in danger of losing him altogether. By the time I run out through the main exit, he's already on the lawn, walking ridiculously fast.

"Kevin!" I call. He doesn't hear, although other people turn their heads to watch me trot past.

"*Kevin!*" I shout again.

He finally stops. But when he turns to face me, his freaked-out expression makes me forget why I'm running him down.

"What's the matter?" I ask, worried.

"Nothing." He's lying. I can tell by the way he's not meeting my eyes.

"Did something happen?"

"I'm in a hurry, that's all. I don't want to be late to third period."

"Well, neither do I. Come on, let's walk."

He bolts off in the direction of the main building, leaving me to follow.

"Listen, Kevin." It's hard to sound casual when you're jogging, but I do my best. "I was wondering . . . I mean, tomorrow is the Snow Ball. And I was thinking . . . I mean, since you and I are both—"

"I'm taking Sterling."

"What? Since when?"

He stops walking, and I finally realize *this* is what is wrong. He didn't want to tell me this.

"Since last night," he says, embarrassed. "I mean, we were already going. And then we weren't. And now we are."

"Of course," I say sarcastically. I feel my cheeks flaming, but for once it's with anger. "That all makes perfect sense."

"It's just . . . Sterling and I have a history. And she was counting on me to take her. I guess I always kind of knew we'd get back together."

Which explains why you were flirting with me *yesterday.* But I don't accuse him out loud. Anything he says to deny it will only make me madder.

"That's great," I say instead. "Congratulations."

"You're not mad?" he asks dubiously.

"What for? I mean, you didn't think *I* was going to ask you, did you?"

"Well . . ."

He obviously did.

Because I obviously was.

You know what? So what.

"You'd better hurry," I tell him. "You don't want to be late for third period."

"No . . ." He looks longingly toward the building, then back at me, like he's trying to figure out if there's a catch. "Okay. I'll, uh . . . see you later."

Not if I see you first, I think.

I watch him walk away from me, like he's walked away so many times before. The difference is, it doesn't hurt this time. In fact, I'm kind of glad to see him go.

Why shouldn't I be? He led me on, he went running back to Sterling, and he wasn't even man enough to tell me until I forced him to. If he's that weak, she can have him.

They deserve each other.

Whatever

It's lunch and I still don't care. Much. Besides, with Snow Queen elections tomorrow, I have bigger things to worry about. I find Hayley in the quad with Fitz and Quentin and I don't even mention Kevin.

"Are we going to buy pizza?" I ask. "Because I should probably eat fast, then spend the rest of lunch trying to get more people to vote for me."

"How are you going to do that?" Fitz asks.

I have no idea. "Which pizza line is shorter?" I counter.

"*I'll* get the pizza this time," he says. "I'm sick of you guys always buying it without me."

"I'll stand in line with you," Hayley offers heroically.

Quentin and I exchange a look, but neither one of us argues. Apparently he's not hungry either.

"We should take bets on whether he'll get back before the bell rings," Quentin says as Hayley and Fitz walk off with our money. "We could start a pool."

Except that Quentin doesn't look ready to start anything. He's slumping on our bench, his legs stretched out in front of him and his arms crossed over his chest like he's settling in for a good long sulk. One of his high-tops is untied, but either this detail has escaped his attention or he just doesn't care.

"So. Snow Ball tomorrow," I say. "Did you buy tickets?"

"Yeah. Not that I'm likely to use them."

So that's the problem. He's still moping about Ros.

"Look. If you really want to take Ros, get up off your butt and go ask her. Forget about Sterling and whatever you think she's saying."

Quentin doesn't move. "It's probably too late."

"You'll never know unless you ask." I sound too much like my mother for comfort. "What have you got to lose?" I add in my normal voice.

"Forget it. She hates me."

"Don't be such a baby. What's the worst thing that can happen? She'll say no and you'll be no worse off than you are now. In fact, you'll be *better* off, because at least you'll know you tried."

"Thank you, Dr. Phil," he says sarcastically.

Quentin can be so stubborn sometimes. I don't know whether it's better to push him or just give up. I'm still trying to decide when Ros appears at the edge of the quad, completely Sterling-free.

"Look! There she is," I say, pointing.

Talk about bad timing; the second I raise my finger, Ros looks directly at us. I whip my hand behind my back, but it's too late. With a distinctly wounded glance at Quentin, she tosses her head and begins stalking off.

"You *have* to go after her now," I say. "She thinks we were talking about her."

"We were."

"No, but . . . just go!"

Amazingly, he rises to his feet. The sullenness has left his face, and now he just looks nervous. "Okay, I'm going," he says. "Wish me luck."

I cross two sets of fingers as he hurries through the quad and taps Ros on the shoulder.

She turns around and her face lights up. For a second I think Quentin has it made. Then her chin juts out, she crosses her arms, and I realize he's in trouble.

Quentin seems to know it too; he's talking a mile a minute. I do my best to follow the conversation by interpreting his arm gestures. I have a sinking feeling he's trying to explain about Memory Lanes and how everything that happened there was really all my fault.

Sure enough, their heads turn in unison and look right at me. How embarrassing. I offer a tiny, apologetic wave.

They look away again, and I'm pretty sure Ros is sneering. But wait—she just uncrossed her arms and laughed. I swear Quentin grows two inches.

Now, I think. *Ask her now.*

It looks like that's what he's doing. He's smiling for the first time in days. His expression is seriously hopeful. . . .

Say yes, I think, focusing my full powers of ESP on Ros. Okay, technically I don't have ESP. But I'm trying.

Quentin is nearing the end of his pitch; I can tell by the way he rocks up on his toes.

And now it's up to Ros. Everything hangs on her answer.

Quentin holds his breath and so do I. Time freezes. This is one of those moments where two lives could change forever. . . .

Ros hesitates, then shakes her head. Quentin and I both deflate. She's talking, but Quentin isn't listening—all he wants is to get away. My heart breaks for him as he backs up, shrugging like she hasn't just shattered his world.

Ros takes a tentative step forward. Then she stops, shakes her head, and walks in the opposite direction.

Quentin shambles back to our bench, his face saying it all.

"I'm sorry, Q," I say, feeling his pain. "I shouldn't have told you to go over there."

"No big," he says, plopping back down at my side. "Whatever."

"Did she say why she—"

"It doesn't matter." His tone makes it crystal clear he doesn't want to talk about it.

"I just wondered if—"

"She said no!"

I wish I could hold his hand or put my arm around him—anything to make him feel better. Instead I sit a foot away, completely useless.

"I really am sorry," I say at last.

Quentin winces. "Whatever," he says again.

Pityfest for Two

I've waited until the last possible minute to buy my Snow Ball tickets. All right, ticket, if you have to get technical. There's not much sense buying two at this point. School's let out for the day and I'm not going to snag a date walking down the main hall.

Great—there's a line out the office door. I should have come at lunch instead of hanging around trying to cheer up Quentin. Not only did I fail miserably, it's going to be humiliating standing in line behind all these people. I stop fifty feet from the end, trying to figure out what I'll say if someone asks who I'm going with. And this is the *easy* part. What will I say at the dance?

I should drop out. I *could* drop out. I could just not show up, then say I got sick or something. Food poisoning—that's a brilliant excuse!

Except that if I back out now, I'll be an even bigger loser. I *want* to be Snow Queen. All sorts of people are cheering me on. Besides, can you even imagine how Fourteen-Karat would gloat? No, I'm in. And if that means walking into the dance alone, I'll do it with my head held high and pretend that was my plan all along. After all, there's no Snow King.

It's not like I *need* Kevin.

I raise my chin, just for practice, and start forward to join the line.

"Hey, Cassie." A morose voice stops me. "What are you doing here?"

I turn around and see Quentin, two dance tickets in his hand.

"I was going to buy a ticket," I admit. "What are *you* doing here?"

"Selling these back. I hope."

He tries to look like he doesn't care, but after Memory Lanes I know exactly how he feels. It's the reason I didn't buy tickets in advance this time.

"Hey!" he says, perking up. "Why don't you buy my tickets and save us both from that line?"

"I would, but . . ." He seems to have missed my humiliating admission. "I only need one. I was hoping to go with Kevin, but . . . let's just say he made other plans."

Quentin smiles ruefully. "We're a pair, aren't we?"

"Pretty pathetic," I agree.

"That Kevin—he's not good enough for you."

"I could say the same about Ros."

"She's not how you think," he says sadly. "We could have been really great."

"I just still don't understand how you jumped to her from Sterling."

Quentin thinks a moment. "Sterling is kind of . . . blinding. When she's in the room, she makes it hard to see anyone else."

"I've noticed," I say, piling on the irony.

"But Ros and I, we just clicked. As soon as we started talking, I knew. I can't change why I first asked her out. I just wish she'd forgive me."

"She still might. I mean, in a month or two. If you still like her . . ."

"No, I blew it. I'm so stupid."

"You're not stupid. I fell in love with Kevin the very first second I saw him. Love at first sight—*that's* stupid."

"Love?" Quentin looks surprised. "You love the guy?"

I feel my face heat up. "Honestly? I thought I did. Now all I feel is lost."

"Lost," he says, nodding. "Me too."

"I mean, I'll be okay. Eventually." I don't want Quentin thinking I'm completely sad. "Life goes on, right?"

"I guess." He looks down at the tickets in his hand. "In the meantime, though, I'd love to cut my losses. You want to buy just one?"

"Sure. Unless . . ." I catch my breath as the obvious solution hits me. "Quentin, would you want to go to the dance with me? And not because I need a date—okay, I kind of do—but I *want* to go with you. If you want to, I mean. Why shouldn't we?"

He looks shocked. I hope I haven't just made a complete fool of myself. I rock up on my toes, waiting for his answer.

"Why not?" he says, smiling. "I want to go with you too."

"Really?"

"You and I have been friends a long time. Let's find out if we're . . . more."

My old feelings for him spark up from their ashes. I grab

him by both shoulders, totally in the moment. "We're going to have fun," I promise.

"I know. We always have fun."

"You're the best." And without any further warning, I press my lips to his. I don't know what I'm thinking. I'm not thinking. I just need to kiss him now.

Quentin's mouth is warm and sweet and perfect. I relax my grip on his shoulders and his arms circle my waist. My quick, impetuous peck stretches out until people waiting in the ticket line start advising us to get a room.

We break apart at the same instant. "We have an audience," Quentin murmurs.

I can barely look at him. What seemed inevitable a second ago now feels incredibly awkward. It's not that I'm sorry—not in the least. I just think my timing could have been better.

"You want to get out of here?" he asks, looking a bit uneasy himself. "Now that we've got this ticket thing solved, there's not much point hanging around. Hey!" His face crinkles into a grin. "Way to get out of buying a ticket!"

"Quentin!" I exclaim, shoving him playfully in the chest. "I'll gladly pay for my ticket. What I *really* want is to arrive at the ball in that styling minivan of yours."

He laughs and puts an arm around my shoulders. "Come on. If it's that big a thrill, I'll drive you home in my chick magnet."

Dress Stress

"I'm sorry," says my mother, shaking her head, "but that color does nothing for you."

We're in Visions, and I've just come out of the dressing room wearing the red lace dress I put on layaway.

"Mom!" I whine. "I tried on everything and this was the best one!"

"It's no good," she insists. "Red makes your hair look orange."

"News flash, Mom," I say testily.

Trevor laughs. You might think that bringing my mother to the mall was bad enough, but no. Trevor insisted on coming too, to squander his allowance on some new video game.

"Let's just see what else they have," she says. "There has to be something you'll like even more."

My head jerks up hopefully. "Well, actually . . . it's a little expensive. . . ."

I lead the way to the vintage section, my socks slipping on the high-polished floor as I rush to see if the pale pink gown is still there. I catch a glimpse of satin and actually start to run. It's a miracle I don't take down the rack as I slide to a clumsy, windmilling stop.

"This one!" I say, snatching out the halter gown and holding it aloft. "I *love* this one."

My mother gives it a glance. It's pretty clear she doesn't share my enthusiasm. "How much?"

"I warned you it was expensive. . . . "

"*How* expensive?" she asks, reaching for the tag. "Five hundred dollars! Are they insane?"

"It's not even worth it," Trevor says. "Satin only costs like ten dollars a yard."

"How much does *used* satin cost?" my mother asks.

"It's not used—it's vintage!" I protest. "There's a difference."

"Right. Vintage satin's been used a *lot*," says my angelic little brother.

"Forget I mentioned it," I tell my mother sulkily. "You're the one who asked."

"That dress isn't even hard to make," Trevor persists. "It's just an A-line—all straight seams."

My mom and I both stare at him. I at least know about his clandestine sewing, but since he's saving Mom's blouse for Christmas, she's totally in the dark.

"Home ec!" he says in self-defense. "It was on the test."

"Let's just get this one," I say, pointing to the dress I'm wearing. I don't even like it anymore, but it's Friday night and too late to find something better.

"Don't be so impatient," Mom says. "We've barely even looked yet."

I see where this is heading. She'll make me try on a dozen dresses I can't stand "just to see how they look on." I've told her a hundred times that I'm not going to love it on my body if I hate it on the hanger. But it's no use. She's

265

back at the new formals now, considering dresses I wouldn't look at twice.

"What about this one?" she says, pulling out something long and black.

"I don't want black," I say automatically.

"Black is gorgeous. Black is *classic*." All of my mom's party dresses are black.

"It's the *Snow* Ball," I remind her. "I either want a pretty holiday color or white."

"Black is appropriate for every occasion," my mother answers, undeterred.

Trevor sniggers. "Yeah. Especially funerals."

It's going to be a long night.

Cassie+Quentin?

Hayley and I are on the phone. I've just finished telling her what happened with Quentin, so I can only pray we're speaking privately.

"I can't believe it!" Hayley squeals. "You and Quentin?"

"Maybe," I say nervously. "I'm not sure."

"How can you not be sure? You kissed him in the main hall!"

It wouldn't be possible to overemphasize how seriously I hope Trevor hasn't managed to sneak onto another extension somewhere. I crack open my bedroom door to make sure he isn't listening in the hall.

"I know," I say. "I was there."

"But you were in love with Quentin forever! And if Kevin is stupid enough to go back with Sterling . . . I don't understand why you wouldn't want this."

"It's not just what *I* want, Hayley—Quentin's likely to have an opinion too."

"But he kissed you back?"

"He did."

Hayley huffs impatiently. "What else do you need to know?"

"It's complicated, all right? And I don't want to get my hopes up for nothing again. We're going to the dance, and after that . . . we'll see."

"Fine. You play it cool. But this is going to be so fun! You and Quentin, and me and Fitz, all hanging out together . . ."

"It is," I say, forgetting about Trevor long enough to smile. "But right now it's late and I'd better go. I'll see you tomorrow night."

I hang up the phone still smiling. Hayley's right: it'll be a ball hanging out with her, Fitz, and Quentin. I mean, you know, so to speak. Even if I get my butt kicked in the election, I'll have my three best friends around me.

And as far as Cassie+Quentin . . . who knows?

I'm sure not ruling it out.

Speech Impediment

This is bad. Four-cavity-trip-to-the-dentist bad. It's three o'clock in the afternoon and here's what I have for my speech tonight:

Hi, I'm Cassie Howard, and I want to be Snow Queen because

That's it. I've finished that sentence ten different ways, and all of them are bad.

I shouldn't have slept in. But all I had to do today was write this stupid speech. And it only has to be two minutes long. Maybe if I'd been able to fall asleep last night, it would have been easier to get up today. But I've barely slept at all since I decided to run for Snow Queen.

Which I want to be because

This is hopeless. The problem is, I can never admit the real reason I want to be Snow Queen. Can you imagine?

Hi, I'm Cassie Howard, and I want to be Snow Queen because I want you all to like me.

That's it, if I'm honest. That's what popularity is—having people like you. Or pretend to, anyway. Except that I don't want them to pretend.

I want to be Snow Queen because

What could I have been thinking? In what universe could someone like me ever win Snow Queen? I should get out while I still have the chance. Food poisoning—that was a *great* idea.

Except now Quentin's counting on me. And I'd be crazy to let him down after everything we've both been through.

I just have to concentrate.

Hi, I'm Cassie Howard, and I want to be Snow Queen because

Who am I kidding? I'm doomed.

Paint It Black

"Cassie!" my mom yells down the hall. "Quentin just pulled into the driveway."

I freeze in front of the mirror on my closet door, my eyes spilling over with tears. I'm ruining my mascara, but it hardly matters. I couldn't look much worse.

"Are you ready?" my mom calls.

"Not yet," I choke out.

I don't want her to know I'm crying—it will only make her feel bad. But I really, really wish I hadn't let her talk me into this black dress. Everyone at the stuffy store she took me to after Visions told me how sophisticated I looked, but here, alone in my own room, I finally see the truth. I look like I raided my mother's closet. I grab a Kleenex off the dresser and wipe my eyes, but it's no use; the tears well up as fast as I can dry them.

I have to stop being such a baby. This dress isn't bad, it's just not me. Kind of severe. And black.

Too late now.

I blow my nose and it sounds like a foghorn. Very regal.

The truth is, if a black dress were my only problem, I'd be in pretty good shape. I can't blame Mom for forgetting I had to buy Quentin's boutonniere this afternoon, cutting ninety minutes out of the time I'd set aside to get ready. Or for wasting so many hours trying to write a speech that there was no time left to paint my nails. Or for the fact that my rush-job curls came out all crooked. The entire day slipped away and now Quentin is here and I'm a mess and I don't think I can go through with this. If I don't pull myself together—

Oh, great. Someone just knocked on my bedroom door.

Second Helping

Trevor is standing outside my room with a load of laundry in his arms, looking impossibly smug. I can't begin to deal with him right now.

"What do you want?" I ask impatiently.

"Quentin's here."

"I know. I heard. How about going away so I can finish getting ready?"

He scrunches up his face. "Honestly, Cass? You look a long way from ready."

I *hate* to cry in front of him, but fresh tears spill instantly.

"Hey!" he says, surprised. "I didn't mean it like *that*."

"How else *could* you mean it?" I turn my back on him. "This night is a disaster! First my speech and now—"

"Stop freaking out," he says, following me into my room. "Look, I brought you something."

I look in time to see him remove a tangled bedsheet from around the bundle in his arms. Instead of the dirty clothes I'd imagined, he's left holding something pink.

"I know it's late, so maybe you won't want to wear this now," he says, letting his bundle unfurl. "I meant to have it to you by lunch, but I ran into a problem. . . ."

I blink hard, trying to clear my teary vision. I can't be seeing what I'm seeing. Trevor is holding up the pale pink gown from Visions!

"How did you *get* that?" I start forward, then freeze in horror. "Oh, no, Trevor. You didn't . . . you didn't *steal* it?"

He throws back his head and laughs, so completely proud of himself that the truth hits me like a bolt. Rushing over, I snatch the gown from his hands and give it a closer look. There's no tag, and uncut threads still dangle from the inside seams. It's *not* the dress from Visions—it's a brand-new satin knockoff.

"You *made* it!" I breathe, awed.

"I told you it was easy!" he crows. "Except for the zipper." The thought of the zipper brings him back to earth. "I had to put it in three times, but nobody's going to notice."

I flip the dress over and can't see a single thing wrong with the short, hidden zipper centered in its low-cut back.

"Get out," I tell him.

"Hey!" he cries, offended. "If you don't like it, fine. You don't have to be rude."

He reaches for the dress, but I snatch it away.

"No, Trevor. I meant get out and let me try this on! I don't even know if it fits."

"Oh, it'll fit," he says, smiling again. "I made the pattern off that green dress you wore all summer."

I look at the gown with new wonder, noticing its similarity to my favorite sundress for the first time. "Please, Trevor," I beg. "If this fits, I'll give you anything you want. Just let me try it on."

He allows me to push him into the hall, where I can hear my dad gabbing with Quentin in the distance. "I'll be out in a minute," I yell before I shut the door.

The black dress is off in a flash, a dark puddle around my ankles. I pull Trevor's gown over my head, trembling as the long sheath of cool pink satin slides into place. And now I'm crying again, but these are tears of joy. The reflection that meets my eyes this time is exactly what I dreamed of— pretty, delicate, feminine. Actual Snow Queen material.

"Trevor, you're a genius!" I cry, throwing my door open. "I could *kiss* you!"

"Let me see," he says, walking in. "And keep your kisses to yourself."

He walks a slow circle around me, giving the dress a long look. "Perfect," he declares at last, yanking up on the zipper.

And it is. Totally, completely perfect.

"Thank you, Trev!" I trap him in a hug despite his frantic squirming. "I can't believe you did this for me! You're the best brother ever!"

"Obviously," he says, breaking free. "Get a grip on yourself. I have conditions."

Conditions. I should have known. I take a deep breath, bracing for his worst.

"Okay," I say. "Let's hear them."

"Number one: that dress is your Christmas present. I worked on it all night and I'm not getting you anything else."

"Agreed. More than fair."

"Number two: you have to get me into a high school party and Julie Evans has to be there."

"All right." That won't be easy, but at least it's legal. "It might take a few weeks, but I'll work it out somehow."

"You have to make sure we're *both* at the party. Then you have to bring her over and introduce her, like you don't realize we know each other."

"Okay."

"And you have to act like I'm cool. And don't remind her I'm in eighth grade. And don't tell her or anyone else that I sew!"

"*Okay*, Trevor. What's number three?"

"Number three?"

"Your third condition?"

"Oh." He shakes his head. "No number three."

"That's *all*?" I say in disbelief.

"Merry Christmas, Cinderella. Knock 'em dead."

I almost push him down with the force of my second hug, landing a couple of wet ones on his cheeks despite his loud protests. He's wiping off lipstick with both hands when I finally turn him loose.

"Tell Quentin I need five more minutes, okay, Trev? And ask Mom if she can come help me fix my hair."

Falling to my knees, I paw through the stuff on my closet floor, looking for my white platforms. The dress is floor length, so my feet won't show much. I just need something better than the black shoes I have on.

"Cassie!" Mom says at my back. "It's not polite to make Quentin wait."

I spot the platforms and yank them out, then stand to face my mother.

"What are you wearing?" she asks, astonished. "How did you get that dress?"

"From Trevor. It's not the one from the store—he made it."

I'm not sure if Mom is on the list of people I'm not allowed to tell about Trevor's sewing, but I can't have her thinking he's a thief.

"You're kidding!" She walks over and grabs one side of the bodice, checking his workmanship. It's a little embarrassing, considering where her hand is, but at least it's keeping her attention off the black dress on the floor.

"Listen—don't make a big deal," I say. "He's a little shy about it."

"But this *is* a big deal! I had no idea!"

"I'm pretty sure that was his plan. So instead of embarrassing him, do you think you can help me with this?" I point to my lopsided curls. "My hair looks even worse tonight than usual."

Mom shakes herself out of a trance. Her eyes find their way to my hair and eventually focus.

"Come to my bathroom," she says. "We're going to need some serious hair spray."

(Second Helping)^2

I'm redoing my ruined makeup in my parents' bathroom mirror while Mom tries to comb some sense into my hair.

"Sit still," she says. "You're making this harder than it has to be."

I pause with a lipstick in my hand. "No, I'm not. It's always hard."

"Just hold still! And close your eyes."

I barely comply in time to avoid being blinded by a cloud of hair spray. I start coughing, but Mom continues tugging on my curls despite the pollution. She sprays again and again, and when the air finally clears, I'm amazed by what I see. My once lopsided curls are now perfect shiny rings set off by blossoms of baby's breath she took from a vase on the counter.

"You're good!" I gasp.

"And you're late," she returns with a smile. "Quentin must be the most patient boy on earth."

I finish my lipstick in one quick stroke. "What time is it?"

Mom checks her watch. "Seven fifty-nine."

My heart misses a beat, then starts pumping double-time. "No way! I was supposed to be there at eight!"

"I thought you said eight-thirty!"

"The *speeches* are at eight-thirty. Principal Ito told us candidates to be there by eight." I scramble up in a panic. "How did it get so late?"

"You don't really want me to answer that."

She's right. I'm already running to my room. The clutch I chose earlier is black, but there's no time to swap purses now. I grab it and sprint to the kitchen, where I find Quentin and my dad leaning against the counter, drinking sodas.

The sight of Quentin in a classic black tux stops me dead in my tracks. He's a good-looking guy. I've mentioned that, right? But in that suit, he's Prince Charming. I stand there blinking like I've never seen him before.

My father notices me. "There she is! Don't you look pretty?"

I hope so, because Quentin's doing a major double take. He seems as surprised by me as I am by him.

"Cassie! You look . . . that dress is . . . wow," he finally says.

"Thanks," I say, blushing. "You look nice too."

My mom walks in behind me. "You'd better give Quentin his boutonniere so the two of you can get going."

"Right!" I turn toward the refrigerator, but she's already opened its door.

"Here," she says, handing over the white rosebud I bought earlier.

My hands shake as I remove the pearl-capped pin and

approach Quentin with it. "Do you want me to pin it on or . . . ?"

"Wait. I have something for you too," he says, wrestling a corsage out of a cellophane box on the counter. I smile when I see it—white rosebuds.

"Great minds think alike," I tease.

We laugh and it breaks the ice enough for me to pin the rose on his lapel. He slips the corsage's elastic band around my wrist and we stand there looking at each other, like we're waiting for something more. . . .

"Hadn't you better be going?" my mom breaks in. "Here, take my cell phone so you can call and tell us how the election goes."

I would obviously prefer to have my *own* cell phone, but they won't buy me one, so I tuck Mom's into my clutch. I'm snapping the purse shut when the phone on our kitchen wall rings.

My dad answers it. "Oh, hi, Hayley. Yes, she's right here." He holds the phone out to me.

Mom points to her watch.

I hesitate, torn, then grab the phone. "I thought you'd be at the dance by now."

"I am!" Hayley says. "Where are *you?*"

"We're just leaving. I'll be there in ten minutes."

"Cassie, you don't understand. You're supposed to be here *now.*"

"There was a hair situation. And I had to change clothes. I'm running a few minutes late."

"You don't understand," she repeats, and I can hear Fitz

talking frantically in the background. "All the other candidates are here, and Principal Ito—I *know*, Fitz—Principal Ito just announced that it's eight o'clock and anyone who isn't in line to check in is disqualified."

"What?" The air drains out of my lungs. "That's not fair!"

"He says he told everyone to be here at eight. I'll bet Sterling put him up to this. He thinks she walks on water."

"It's not fair!" I repeat, my voice rising into a wail. "He's only doing this because of Memory Lanes!"

"What's going on?" my mom interrupts.

"Principal Ito just disqualified me because I'm not in line to check in!"

My mother's face goes oddly expressionless. "Give me the phone."

I hand it over, too upset to argue.

"I'm sorry, Cassie," Quentin says softly. "I should have been here earlier."

I shake my head, blinking back tears. We both know he was plenty early.

"What's this about, Hayley?" my mother asks. She listens a minute, then rolls her eyes. "Are you on a cell? . . . Good. Put Principal Ito on the line."

"No, Mom!" I lunge, trying to grab the phone away. "He already hates me!"

She holds up one finger, cutting me off. "Principal Ito? This is Andrea Smythe-Howard, Cassie Howard's mother. I understand there's some confusion about the Snow Queen check-in this evening."

She listens quietly, the picture of calm.

"That *is* unfortunate. And of course it would be better if

Cassie had been on time. But we had a few holdups here, and since the speeches don't start until eight-thirty, I can't see what harm it will do if—"

She stops talking. Principal Ito has interrupted her; I can tell by the slow simmer in her eyes.

"Perhaps you can explain the necessity of having all the girls check in at once," she says pleasantly when he's finished. "Since they can only speak one at a time, I'm afraid the problem still eludes me."

I find myself smiling through my tears. Ito has no idea what he's up against.

"Is anyone else disqualified?" my mother asks. "No? Because that could cause a reasonable person to conclude that you're doing this specifically to exclude my daughter."

Quentin snorts, then quickly clamps a hand over his mouth. His eyes shine with admiration.

My dad leans over to whisper to us. "Go on. You've got the cell phone, right?"

I hold up my purse.

"Just get over there as fast as you can. Without crashing," he adds for Quentin's benefit.

My mom's still on the phone but she motions us out of the kitchen like she's heard every word Dad said.

"Come on!" I grab Quentin's hand and charge for the door.

"What's going on?" he asks, confused.

"My mom's teaching Principal Ito the basics of debate."

(Second Helping)³

"Do you think she can change his mind?" Quentin asks, backing his minivan out of our driveway. "I don't want to be negative, but if he's already made an announcement . . ."

I take Mom's cell phone out of my clutch and stare it down, willing it to ring. "If anyone can win this argument, it's my mother."

Quentin nods and turns his attention to driving to the gym by the fastest possible route. It's dark, it's late, my heart's beating far too fast, and with every corner he takes I'm only getting more nervous. I honestly don't know whether to hope Mom wins or not.

"At least if I'm disqualified, I lose with some dignity," I say. "If Principal Ito keeps me out, I can't get humiliated in the voting."

"That's not going to happen," Quentin tells me. "You might not win, but you won't be humiliated."

"I don't know. I'm the least popular girl running."

"*I* know," he says with a significant look. "Have you *seen* you?"

I smile uncertainly. "Yeah?"

"Yeah. Definitely."

The phone rings in my hand, launching me halfway out of my seat. I fumble for the button. "Hello?"

"It's me," Hayley says breathlessly. "Your mom made Principal Ito promise that so long as you're in line before he finishes checking in the other candidates, he'll let you participate."

"She did it!" I tell Quentin. "We're in!"

He slaps the steering wheel.

"No, listen, Cassie," Hayley says. "The line is flying. He's just making the girls sign some sort of agreement and he's already halfway done."

"We're really close. I'll be there in five minutes."

"That's too long! You'll miss the whole thing!"

"I have to be in a line," I tell Quentin desperately. "And the way it's moving, I'm going to miss it."

Quentin thinks a second and comes up with gold. "Not if Fitz gets on the end."

It's like a door bursts open and fresh air starts flooding in. "Ask Fitz to stand in line for me," I tell Hayley. "He can say he's holding my place."

Hayley laughs—she feels the fresh air too. "Cassie wants you to hold her place in line," she tells Fitz.

"You people are crazy!" he complains loudly. "I don't know how this myth got started."

"Just go!" Hayley says. "Prove us wrong."

"You owe me, Cassie!" he yells.

"Is he doing it?" I ask Hayley.

"He's going," she reports. "Okay, he's on the back of the line. He looks so cute in his tux!"

"How many girls are left?"

"Two. Plus Fitz."

"I have to hang up before I puke."

"Nice," Quentin teases as I switch off the phone. "Very romantic."

"This whole thing is too much pressure," I say, rolling down the passenger window. "I feel like I'm going to pass out."

"We're almost there," he assures me.

I see the lights of the high school up ahead, blazing in honor of the dance.

"Turn in at the main entrance," I say. "It'll be fastest to park by the library and run across the grass."

"Not as fast as parking at the gym."

"We'll just drive in circles! That lot's been full for an hour!"

Quentin smiles. "Then it's time for someone to leave."

I close my eyes and take a deep breath, trying to stay calm. I understand his confidence, but this isn't the best occasion to test his parking gift.

Quentin turns in at the gym, the front of which is completely covered with twinkling icicle lights. A dark blue banner over the door welcomes everyone to the Snow Ball. It's all so beautiful I almost don't notice that the lot's packed tighter than a box of crayons.

Then I do.

"Turn around!" I beg Quentin. "We don't have time to look for the best parking place!"

He shakes his head. "It hurts that you have so little faith in me."

"It's not about faith. It's about—"

"Talent," he supplies.

I can't see an empty space in any direction. My hand clenches Mom's cell phone as I fight the urge to call Hayley for an update. We're almost all the way up to the gym. The only open slots are handicapped spaces—and one lone space directly next to them.

"Classic!" Quentin says, pulling in. "One blue line and people freak out. I've seen it a hundred times."

The minivan stops. My door flies open.

"Hey! Wait for me!" Quentin calls as I leap out onto the pavement.

(Second Helping)[4]

It's hard to run in platforms—waiting for Quentin was definitely the right move. He's got me by one elbow and is practically levitating me over the sidewalk. We burst through the gym door together, returning the looks aimed our way with as much dignity as we can.

"Cassie! Over here!" Hayley cries.

She's waving from the doorway of the basketball office. We change directions to join her.

"Are we in time?" I pant.

"What a cool dress!" she exclaims. "I thought you said it was black!"

"The first one *was* black. It's kind of a long story."

"Tell me later," she says, pushing me into the office.

Principal Ito is seated at the coach's desk and Tamara Owens is standing across from him on the desk's other side. Fitz is behind Tamara, tugging miserably on his bow tie. The other Snow Queen candidates sit in chairs against the walls, looking beautiful and put upon. Sterling stands out in a shimmering white gown, a diamond headband gracing her hair like a prediction of better things to come.

"This is ridiculous! Coach Harris must have *something* else to write with," Principal Ito says irritably, digging through desk drawers as I hurry to take Fitz's place. "*None* of you girls has a pen?"

"Still no," says Mindy St. Croix, snapping her gum.

"I'm here," I say softly, tapping Fitz on the shoulder. "What's the story? Fill me in."

"I can't believe how lucky you are!" he whispers, stepping out of line to let me have his place. "Apparently there's only one pen in the entire gym, and if it hadn't run out of ink—"

"Oops! There it goes!" Tamara says, scrawling loops on a piece of paper. "It must have been an air bubble."

"Finally," huffs Principal Ito. "Sign the pledge and let's get moving."

Fitz hands me a half-sheet of paper. "Here. You're supposed to read this and sign it in front of him."

SNOW QUEEN CANDIDATE'S PLEDGE

I, _____ , hereby affirm that my Snow Queen speech this evening will contain nothing of an inappropriate, obscene, or libelous nature. I acknowledge that my participation in this event is voluntary and I agree that Hilltop High School, its educators, and its administrators cannot be held accountable for any irregularities in the voting. I pledge to conduct myself throughout tonight's festivities in an honorable, sporting way, reflecting the best traditions of our school and community.

Signed: _____

"Is he kidding us with this?" I whisper to Fitz, just as Tamara steps aside and leaves me facing Principal Ito.

"You have a problem signing the pledge, Ms. Howard?" he asks icily. "Perhaps you'd like to call your lawyer about it."

Ouch.

"No. No problem," I say quickly. "It just seems a little . . . Fine." I snatch up the pen, scrawl my name on both lines, and push the pledge across the desk.

He extends his hand, palm up.

I stare at him, baffled, then pick up my paper and place it on his hand.

He heaves an enormous sigh. "No, Ms. Howard. I want to see your speech. If you'd been here on time, you would know that."

"My—my speech?" I stammer. "Don't you have to *hear* a speech?"

Someone snickers. Sterling.

Principal Ito winces like he's just taken an ice pick between the brows. "Your *notes*, Ms. Howard. I assume you've jotted down something relative to your speech tonight."

"Oh. Well . . . um . . ."

"I'm checking all the candidates' notes, for adherence to the pledge."

Opening my purse, I take out a three-by-five card and reluctantly hand it over.

Hi! My name is Cassie Howard, and I want to be Snow Queen because

He looks at that card a full thirty seconds before he hands it back to me.

"That's all you've got?" he asks.

"That's it. I'm pretty sure it adheres."

Principal Ito shakes his head. "This ought to be interesting."

(Second Helping)[5]

Fitz, Quentin, Hayley, and I have all just entered the gym. Entered the Snow Ball, I should say, since technically we were already in the gym. The place looks amazing—all fixed up with midnight blue streamers and twinkling white lights. There's a stage at one end draped with dark blue velvet and edged with fluffy cotton snowdrifts. Hundreds of lacy white-and-silver snowflakes glitter against the dark drapes and hang on long silver threads from the ceiling. It's like being inside a giant snow globe.

"Wow," I say.

"I know," says Hayley. "She's all over him."

"Huh?"

I follow her gaze and find Sterling on the edge of the crowd, both arms wrapped around Kevin. The gym is packed with cute couples, but those two still stand out like a spotlight is pointed at them. Kevin looks heartbreakingly handsome in his tux, and Sterling shines in her strapless white gown as if she's the source of the light.

"How does she do that?" I wonder out loud.

"Do what?" Quentin asks at my elbow. I look into his smiling face and feel the need to change the subject.

"Nothing. Wow, this place is crowded!"

"You saw the parking lot."

Hayley pokes me in the arm. "You'd better go wait by the stage, like Principal Ito said. We'll all go, so we can stand in front for your speech."

The word *speech* fills me with dread. Despite the fact that I never succeeded in writing one this afternoon, somehow I'd managed to convince myself that inspiration would still come. None has, though, and now Principal Ito knows it.

How many minutes before the rest of the school discovers I'm a fraud too?

"Can I talk to you?" I say, pulling Hayley away from the guys.

"What's going on?" she asks.

"The speech, Hayley. I can't do it."

"You're just nervous."

"No, you don't understand. I'm about to make a total—"

"Will you be joining us for the speeches, Ms. Howard?" asks a chilly voice at my back. "Or should you be exempt from that requirement too?"

Hayley's eyes go round. She's the one facing Principal Ito.

"Yes. I'm . . . uh . . . I'm right there." I give Hayley a desperate look as the principal stalks past us.

"Go!" she says. "You'll be fine."

"Hayley, I don't *have* a speech! I tried to write one, but . . ."

She blinks with shock. "You're kidding. No speech at all?"

"None. Nothing. Zip."

"Cassie! What are you going to do?"

"That's what I'm asking you!"

I'm praying she'll use that straight-A brain to come up with something brilliant, like a believable explanation for a sudden attack of fake laryngitis, or a clever way to "accidentally" break a microphone. Anything. I'm desperate.

Hayley looks me in the eye. "You want my advice? Take a deep breath, get your butt to the stage, and when it's your turn to speak, just say whatever comes out. You've come too far to give up now."

I stare in disbelief. She's serious! As if to make that more clear, she starts pushing me toward the stage.

"Don't ramble," she advises, bulldozing me along. "Keep it short and sweet."

"Short won't be a problem."

"You're going to be fine." She sounds so certain I almost believe her. "You can do this, Cassie!"

"Hayley?"

"What?"

"You're the best friend ever. I don't know what I'd do without you."

She stops pushing. I turn my head and catch an amused smile on her face.

"I know," she says. "You're a lucky girl."

"No, I mean it. You're the best friend anyone ever had."

"I love you too, all right? Let's talk about it *after* your speech."

She sees me off with a final shove that sends me stumbling through the crowd. I catch my balance and keep walking, afraid I'll lose my nerve if I look back.

By some miracle, I'm not the last girl at the stage. The gym is so packed that a few candidates are still trying to fight their way over. From here I can't even see the DJ set up at the other end. He's playing Christmas carols, so the mob of people between us is mostly standing around talking.

Principal Ito climbs the stage stairs and walks to the microphone stand at its center. There's nothing else up there except the fake snow and a row of eight chairs behind him. I gulp as I realize the other girls will have an up-close view of my backside the entire time I'm speaking.

This is bad. I can feel my gluteus muscles warming up already.

Ito taps the microphone with one finger. Thuds echo through the gym until the DJ cuts the music.

"Good evening," our principal says, in this phony master-of-ceremonies voice. "Welcome to the Hilltop High School Snow Ball!"

He pauses for applause, which is not as thunderous as he probably expected. My palms are sweating. I wring my hands nervously.

"As you know," he continues, "one of the traditions of the Snow Ball is to elect a Snow Queen. This year we have eight candidates vying for your support. In a moment, they will each get the chance to address you. After that, we'll start the voting."

More lukewarm applause.

"So, without further ado, let me introduce your candidates!"

He turns and motions for us to come up. The problem is, we're not in any kind of order and no one's sure who should go first.

Leave it to Sterling. Adjusting her rhinestone headband, she springs up the stairs and hits the stage like Miss America, her smile turned up to "stun." Both arms stretch above her head as she gives the crowd a beauty-queen wave.

The funny thing about popularity is, you don't have to be nice to be worshipped—at least, you don't have to be nice to me. Not if you look like Sterling. The applause that eluded Principal Ito erupts at full volume, making the snowflakes tremble overhead. I close my eyes and gulp for breath. I can't follow that. *No one* could follow that.

But Mindy St. Croix's going to give it a shot. As Sterling takes a chair at the end of the stage, Mindy parades along its edge, doing her best with smiles and poses to get the same amount of applause. I'm pretty sure she doesn't, but it's close.

One by one the other contestants climb onstage and wave to the crowd: Tamara Owens, Claire Everhart, Tiffany Moralez, Shondelé Smith. The only girls left are me and Angie Yee. I move toward the stairs, not wanting to be last, but Angie scrambles up in front of me.

I hesitate a few seconds, then climb the stairs anyway, hoping to avoid my full share of scrutiny by dividing the crowd's attention. Angie makes a runway turn, frowning as she sees me already up and waving from the opposite end of the stage. I lunge for a chair and sit down fast. Angie glares as she takes the remaining seat, obviously assuming I was trying to steal her moment instead of just forfeiting mine.

"Your Snow Queen candidates!" Principal Ito shouts, to a final burst of applause. Then he turns and points at Sterling, crooking his finger to call her forward.

The speeches are about to begin.

Sterling sashays forward and shimmies behind the microphone stand. "Hi, I'm Sterling Carter," she announces. The resulting cheers make clear how many people already know this.

"Being Snow Queen is a special opportunity," she says when she can be heard again. "It's a chance to represent the entire school, to show how proud I am of Hilltop High and display my Hilltop spirit."

People scream as if she's just said something brilliant instead of recycling last year's tired clichés. Then again, at least she *has* a speech.

"Even on my first day here, as a lost little freshman, I already knew our school was the best in California," she continues.

I have no idea how she arrived at that conclusion, but it doesn't matter. People are cheering for whatever she says. She could probably read the phone book and get the same reaction. She's still talking, but the words are flowing past me now, lost in my ever-increasing sense of desperation.

"So vote for me!" Sterling says. "Because I want to be *your* Snow Queen!"

What? Is she done already? She must be, because Mindy is taking the mike. Does this mean we're going to speak in the order we were introduced? I'll be last! There won't be any good clichés left!

"Hi, I'm Mindy St. Croix, and I want to be your Snow Queen because I can't think of a more perfect way to show my school spirit and love of Hilltop High."

Time is slipping. Not only is it moving in fast forward, I'm losing entire minutes. I catch only snippets of Mindy's speech: "So proud . . . a golden opportunity . . . if you vote for me . . . Hilltop High forever!"

Tamara Owens is up next. Claire Everhart follows and I swear they read the exact same speech. I don't think my brain is getting enough oxygen. Tiffany Moralez sounds like she's speaking underwater. Shondelé Smith is one long burst of static with only a few key phrases breaking through: ". . . the ultimate expression of school spirit . . . a dream come true . . . the best tradition at Hilltop High . . . school spirit . . . school spirit . . . school spirit . . ." And, phenomenally, ". . . a chance to give back for everything Hilltop High has given me."

Is Angie Yee speaking already? I'm going to pass out. Wait—maybe I already have! How else could I have missed so much of the speeches?

Principal Ito is at the microphone again. Oh, no! He's pointing at me!

I'm on my feet. I think. My legs are completely numb. I stumble forward and stare down the barrel of the mike, afraid to look anywhere else. I *can't* look anywhere else, because if I move my eyes even a fraction of an inch I'll be faced with an entire gym full of people, all waiting for a speech. And I have nothing to say. There's nothing I *can* say that hasn't already been covered seven times.

Help! I just looked up. Everyone's staring at me. I'm completely paralyzed. I can't move. I can't speak. I can't even swallow. If I don't come up with something to say in the next two seconds . . .

Did my butt cheek just twitch?

"Come on!" a voice in the crowd yells. "Let's get this over with!"

My lungs shrink to the size of lentils. I hold on to the microphone stand to keep from falling down. Remembering Hayley's advice to just say whatever comes, I suck down a breath and open my mouth.

Nothing comes.

I'm doomed.

Suddenly, a sound slices through the gym, the most welcome sound in the world. It's Hayley, she's whistling the "Charge!" theme, and this is how gifted that girl is—she actually sounds like a trumpet.

*Dud-dle um dun da-*da! Hayley whistles.

"Charge!" voices yell.

It's like a reflex; people hear that tune and yell "Charge" automatically. Okay, it's mostly just Hayley, Quentin, and Fitz—but they're yelling really loud.

Hayley goes again: *Dud-dle um dun da-da!*

This time about half the gym yells "Charge," and a smile cracks the ice of my frozen face. Oxygen floods my brain. It's a Snow Ball miracle.

*Dud-dle um dun da-*da!

"Charge!" Ninety percent of the gym this time, easy.

"We love you, Cassie!" Hayley, Quentin, and Fitz tack on in unison.

And just like that, the words start pouring out.

"Hi, I'm Cassie Howard and I want to be your Snow Queen," I say all in a rush. "But you already know that, right? Everyone up here wants to be Snow Queen. Except for Principal Ito. I mean . . . I assume."

I barely know what I'm saying, so I'm kind of surprised by the laugh that gets. I plow ahead, encouraged.

"I had an awful time coming up with a speech for tonight. I kept thinking I needed to tell you *why* I want to win. But I've just realized I don't. You already know that too. My reasons aren't different from anyone else's. And—if we're being honest—they don't have a lot to do with school spirit."

Another laugh. I take a deep breath.

"So why should you vote for me? Well, because you can, I guess. And because I'll appreciate it. In fact, I'll probably appreciate your vote more than anybody up here. Because let's face it—over the course of their lives, *all* of these girls have been voted for. A lot. The queens of the school are on this stage. The queens of the school and me. And Principal Ito, of course. I didn't mean to imply . . ."

Too late. The whole gym is laughing again. I'm not exactly frowning myself, even though I'm perilously close to violating that pledge I signed earlier.

"Anyway," I break in, "what I meant to say is, you have the power to make me a queen too. Just for tonight. And I promise not to let it go to my head or to milk it past Monday. Much. But it would mean a lot to me. Because long after you've all forgotten who was Snow Queen this year, I'll remember. I'll remember for the rest of my life. And if you want me to, I'll look back on this night and smile."

I've done it.

I can't believe it!

I've just given a speech and it didn't suck!

I gaze out over the gym in a state of thrilled amazement. People are clapping and cheering. A triumphant whistle sails above the commotion and there couldn't be a more beautiful sound. This is quite possibly the best moment of my life. I throw my arms overhead like a rock star. "Thank you, Hilltop! Good night!"

And now I'm backing away from the microphone with a completely spasm-free rear. I still can't feel my legs, but it's because I'm walking on air. Principal Ito steps up and starts explaining the voting procedure, but I don't hear a word he says. I've pulled it off! I'm in the running.

I might actually win this thing.

Second Chance

"Do you want to dance?" Quentin asks.

It's like he's reading my mind. Not that it isn't fun having people I don't even know congratulate me and say they hope I win, but it's kind of nerve-racking, too. Especially now that the voting is over and all I can do is wait.

Quentin leads me across the floor into a relatively uncrowded corner. The music isn't as loud here, and a mirror ball I didn't notice before casts flecks of light around the walls and ceiling. The suspended snowflakes come to life as sparks skitter across them.

A slow song starts and Quentin folds me into his arms. "Are you having fun?" he asks.

"Yes. Aren't you?"

"Of course."

I settle my head on his shoulder, one of my cheeks resting against the warm skin of his neck. He smells fantastic— all soap and shampoo and cute boy.

"Are you worried about the voting?" he asks.

"There's nothing I can do about it now."

It feels good being in Quentin's arms. Like old times. Not that we ever got this far. But I wanted to. As we move around the floor together, I'm gradually overwhelmed by the memory of how badly I wanted to.

"I was totally in love with you last year," I say, just throwing it out there like a comment on the weather. "I really thought we were going to be together."

"What?" Quentin pulls back to look at me and I can tell he's stunned. "We were just friends!"

"No, *you* were just friends. It's okay," I tell him, recapturing my place on his shoulder. "I got over it."

Quentin is quiet a long time. When he finally speaks, his voice is deeper than usual. "What if I don't want you over it?"

"Well . . ." I relax up against him. "Maybe I could get back under it."

He pulls me closer. "Maybe I could get under there with you."

Maybe. The word hangs between us. Not a promise. Just a . . . maybe.

We make slow circles on the floor, and when the music speeds up, we don't. I see Hayley and Fitz across the gym and smile. This night really is a dream come true. Not the dream I had back in October, when I foolishly announced that I'd be at this dance with Kevin, but just as good, in its own way. Who'd have guessed then that I'd be here in Quentin's arms tonight, let alone that I'd be an actual contender for Snow Queen?

Maybe things happen for a reason.

Quentin's back stiffens, interrupting my reverie. I feel him catch his breath. He lets it out quickly, but I'm not fooled. He's obviously seen something he doesn't like.

I pretend not to notice, but as soon as I'm facing the way he was I give the crowd my full attention. I spot the problem in two seconds: Ros Pierce has finally made an appearance, and she's dancing with Tate the Great.

Did I say dancing? It's more like she's propping him up while he gropes her buns. He's drunk or high or something, and Ros is mortified. She looks like she doesn't know whether to slap him or burst into tears.

"You want to go over there?" I ask Quentin.

"What? Go where?" He's a terrible actor.

"I see her, Quentin."

"Oh." He sighs. "Well, I'm not going over. Why should I?"

"Because she looks like she could stand to be rescued."

"That's her problem."

"Uh-huh. Okay." Like I said, a terrible actor.

"She didn't want to come with me," he says defiantly,

dropping his arms to look me in the eyes, "so let her enjoy Tate."

I'm not prepared for the intensity of his gaze. "Okay," I say meekly.

"I'm here with you," he says, pulling me close again. He holds me tighter than before, so tight I feel his heart beat through his lapel.

"I'm with you," he repeats.

I wonder which of us he's trying to convince.

Second Best

"I just heard," Hayley squeals, running up to me and Quentin. "They're announcing Snow Queen in fifteen minutes."

"I have to go to the bathroom," I blurt out.

Everybody looks at me as if I've shared too much.

"I want to check my hair!"

"Well, hurry," Hayley says. "We'll wait for you by the stage."

I rush toward the exit doors, trying not to make eye contact with anyone who might stop me to talk. Quentin and I have been dancing half an hour now, and my hair has no doubt reverted to its former lopsided state.

The girls' room is packed; the line stretches into the atrium. I hesitate, wondering if I can take cuts since all I want is the mirror, but it won't be worth it if someone gets mad. The school trophy case is down the hall and I'm pretty sure it's mirrored. I start in that direction, then remember the bathroom in the basement, off the locker rooms.

My platforms clunk on the concrete stairs as I jog to the lower level. I have to hike my dress above my knees to keep from tripping, but there's no one down here to see me—the whole floor is so empty it echoes. It suddenly occurs to me that the bathroom might be locked, but the door swings open to my pressure and I breathe a sigh of relief. I have the place to myself—a long, unobstructed line of mirrors over six slowly dripping sinks.

To my complete amazement, my hair looks nearly the same as when I left home. I bend close to the nearest mirror and tweak a couple of strands, making a mental note to buy a case of whatever Mom sprayed on it. I'm blotting my forehead with a paper towel when a muffled noise from one of the stalls makes me freeze.

I'm not alone after all.

My heart thuds in my throat. What kind of psycho hides in the girls' bathroom? I back silently toward the exit, my eyes fixed on the toilet stalls and my pulse pounding in my ears. No one will hear me scream down here. I calculate the distance back upstairs, afraid if I turn and run for it I'll be tackled from behind.

"Who's there?" I ask shakily. My voice sounds like someone else's. I hold my breath in suspense until somebody finally speaks.

"No one. Go away."

I'm no expert, but I'm pretty sure your average perv doesn't sound like a tearful teenage girl. I heave a sigh of relief and step back toward the sinks.

"You scared me!" I tell a closed stall door. "I thought I was alone in here."

"So did I."

The voice is still choked up, but there's an edge to it now—a snobby, soc-y edge that's impossible to miss. I'd be positive it was Sterling if I hadn't just passed her upstairs, hanging all over Kevin. . . .

"Ros?"

She sucks in her breath and clams up, as if keeping silent now might throw me off her trail.

"I know it's you. You might as well come out."

Nothing happens for at least thirty seconds. Then, slowly, the stall door swings open and Rosalind Pierce walks out, a wad of wet tissue in her hand and mascara streaking her cheeks.

"Satisfied?" she asks, gesturing to her swollen eyes. "Is this what you wanted to see?"

"Not really. I just wanted to make sure you were all right."

Ros snorts and walks past me to the sink. She looks in the mirror, grimaces, and begins splashing water on her face. Her dress had to cost a fortune. The fabric's like liquid silver, and rhinestone straps crisscross her bare back.

"I, uh . . . I guess I'll be going," I say.

Ros's reflection pretends I'm already gone.

"It's just that I saw you with Bryce," I venture. "And if I were you, I'd be crying too. No girl wants to be treated that way. He's lucky you didn't deck him."

Ros's lips press together. "The night's still young."

'And then she does the last thing I expect—she smiles. A small, wounded smile that yanks my heartstrings hard. "Although he'll probably pass out before I have to beat him up. Last time I looked, he was out puking in the bushes."

"What's wrong with him?"

Ros dries her hands and finally turns to face me. "The guy calls himself Tate the Great. One adjusts one's expectations."

"Huh?"

"I knew what I was getting into when I agreed to go out with him," she says impatiently.

"Then why did you?"

"I'm not discussing that with *you*," she says, her face turning sour again. "I don't even know why I'm talking to you. I'm *not* talking to you." She tosses her head and walks toward the bathroom door.

"Ros, wait!"

She freezes a foot from the exit.

"Just tell me this: why did you come with Bryce when you could have come with Quentin?"

She stands there so long I don't think she's going to answer. "Bryce asked me first," she says at last. And just like that, she's out the door.

"What?" I scramble out behind her, trying to catch up. "Did you tell Quentin that? Because he thinks you just don't like him."

"Maybe I don't," she says coolly.

"Yeah, and maybe you *do*." I grab her by one arm, stopping her at the foot of the stairs. "Why are you doing this? I mean, if I hadn't opened my mouth at Memory Lanes you guys would be together right now. Quentin's ripped up about you."

"You think so?"

"Duh! How many times has he tried to apologize?"

The little smile is back. "A lot."

"He made a mistake; he asked you out for a stupid reason. But otherwise he might never have gotten to know you. He couldn't care less about Sterling now."

Her smile flicks wider. Then her eyes narrow suspiciously. "Why are you telling me this? He's your date."

"He's also my friend. And if there's any chance I can set this right . . ."

It's truly lousy timing, but I owe Quentin this much.

"I know Sterling's talking trash about him," I plunge ahead. "At least, that's what Quentin thinks. How come you always listen to whatever Sterling says?"

"I don't. Always. But other people do. And she's talked him down so far now, she's the only one who can talk him back up." Ros's lip twitches into a sneer. "Which will probably happen the second Kevin dumps her again."

"Yes!" I exclaim, dumbfounded that she actually grasps the situation. "Sterling was *using* Quentin!"

Ros gives me a look that makes me entirely reassess her intelligence. "Like I don't know that? Everyone thinks I'm so stupid—even Sterling. But I do have a brain cell to spare."

A *brain cell to spare*. Where have I heard that before? Oh, no! No way! But it all makes sense now. . . .

"A brain cell to spare and a shirt that covers your pair?" I ask.

Ros blushes and my guess is confirmed. She's the one who placed that ad in our school paper!

"I can't believe it! *No one* suspected you!"

"No one ever does. My therapist says I need to work on expressing my feelings more clearly."

"Seemed pretty clear to me." I'd laugh if I weren't so shocked. "Does Sterling know?"

"No! And you can't tell her!" Ros's irritation turns into panic. "I was angry about Quentin when I did that. But Sterling's my best friend. Please, Cassie."

I've still got her by the arm and now she grabs one of mine. We stare each other down and something weird happens between us. There's a definite connection, the glimmer of an understanding. . . .

A cheer rolls down the stairway like a wave from the gym up above. The walls tremble as people stomp their feet, adding to the noise.

I look up, baffled. The cause hits me all at once.

"Come on!" I cry, towing Ros up the stairs. "They're announcing the Snow Queen!"

Queen Catherine the Second?

"Where have you been?" Hayley asks frantically as I pop out of the crowd beside her, Fitz, and Quentin. "We've been looking all—"

She notices Ros and abruptly falls silent. Quentin is staring, equally speechless.

I give Ros a final tug and a push in his direction. "Talk to him!" I urge.

"What's going on?" Hayley whispers, distracted.

Principal Ito is up at the mike.

"Did I miss it?" I ask. "Did he announce Snow Queen?"

"No, he just called for the crown. I swear Cassie, if you'd been ten seconds later . . ."

Her words are drowned out by more cheers as Mitch Madsen, the senior class president, walks onto the stage carrying a rhinestone crown and scepter. Behind him Lori Vidal, the vice president, holds a bright red envelope. My stomach squeezes with anticipation. I wish I had X-ray vision.

Lori hands the envelope to Principal Ito. He opens it, peeks inside, then waits for the noise to die down. I've stopped breathing. Anything not on that stage has temporarily ceased to exist.

"It was a close race this year," Principal Ito announces. "Closer than I can recall in a long time."

"Who's the winner?" some guy yells. "Get to the point!"

My thoughts exactly. Besides, I can't hold my breath forever. Principal Ito shoots a poisonous look in the direction of the disturbance, then pulls a white card from the envelope.

"I will announce the runner-up, then the winner," he says. The DJ hits a drumroll effect. "This year's Snow Queen runner-up is . . . Cassie Howard!"

"Cassie!" Hayley squeals. "Cassie, that's you!"

Someone slaps me on the back. Hands push at me from all sides. Quentin steps out of the chaos and offers me his arm.

"Congratulations!" he says.

If I didn't have Quentin to cling to, I wouldn't make it up

the stairs. My legs feel like Gummi worms in platforms. He gets me onto the stage, then walks me slowly along its edge.

"Wave, or smile, or *something*!" he whispers.

I wave like a zombie, but when the crowd below us cheers, my smile is genuine.

"Go, Cassie!" someone yells, and this time it's *not* one of my best friends. Happy tears pool in my eyes. I wave again with my heart full of thanks.

"And your Snow Queen is . . ." Principal Ito pauses for dramatic effect. "Miss Sterling Carter!"

Sterling seems to levitate onto the stage. Kevin follows a few steps behind, standing to one side as Mitch pins the crown on Sterling's head. Lori hands her the scepter, and the newly crowned queen of Hilltop High bounds to the microphone and waves for all she is worth.

"Sterling! Sterling!" The crowd screams, eating her up.

"Thank you so much!" she gushes. "I'm so proud to be your queen!"

I slump against Quentin.

"Are you okay?" he whispers.

"Fine. A little dizzy. I mean . . . second place is pretty good!"

He smiles, and it's all I can do to keep from kissing him again. "You're right," he says. "Besides, this girl I know told me we all have to go with our strengths."

All That Glitters Is Sterling

We're still onstage and the DJ has just started the music for the Snow Queen's first dance. I watch enviously as Kevin takes Sterling's arm to escort her to the floor. But just as they reach the stairs, Sterling spins Kevin around and makes him parade her along the stage again. Quentin and I have to step back to let them pass in front of us, Sterling waving to the crowd like she doesn't even realize we're there. Before they can snub us a second time, Quentin leads me down the stairs and out of Her Highness's way.

"She's supposed to start the dancing," I grumble, watching Sterling soak up the spotlight.

"Want to start it for her?" Quentin asks with a mischievous grin.

"Oh! That would make her crazy!"

"I will if you will," he offers.

I'll tell you the truth—I'm tempted. Seeing her drag Kevin around that stage . . . it would totally serve her right. But I restrain myself, clapping with the rest of the crowd when she finally descends to our level. She sails past me and Quentin like we don't exist again, but this time Kevin gives us an apologetic look.

"Ah, the pressures of serving the Crown," Quentin drawls to me as they pass. I giggle with appreciation. He's being so nice tonight. And then I remember.

"Did Ros talk to you?"

"She said she wanted to, but we didn't exactly get a chance." He glances over his shoulder, to see if she's still with Fitz and Hayley. "Do you know what she wants?"

"You'd better ask her."

"I will. When I can."

Sterling and Kevin are finally in position on the dance floor. The song is slow and Kevin reaches to pull Sterling close, but she sidesteps and puts one of his hands on her waist. Grasping his other hand, she maneuvers it out to the side. Her right hand, the one holding the scepter, alights on his shoulder and she takes a few expert steps, more or less forcing him to follow. He looks as confused as I am.

"Are they *waltzing?*" I ask Quentin.

"Poor sucker. Then again, that's what he signed up for. He could have been here with you."

I shrug, not wanting Quentin to guess how jealous I am.

"Come on," he says, taking my hand. "They've had the floor to themselves long enough."

He leads me out near Kevin and Sterling and wraps his arms around me. I snuggle up against him as we move with the music, just swaying to the beat. We're no match for Sterling's fancy steps, but at least we both know what we're doing. Judging by the embarrassed expression on Kevin's face, that's something to be grateful for.

Oh, great. Kevin just caught me looking at him and now he's coming over here. Sterling is trying to push him in the opposite direction, but he's actually backing her up. I can't help smiling at her lame attempt to pretend this is part of their dance moves. Kevin lets go of her hand and reaches to touch my bare arm.

"Congratulations, Cassie," he says. "Your speech was really good."

Sterling gives him a deeply unappreciative look.

"Thanks," I mutter into Quentin's shoulder.

"Really good," he repeats. He might be trying to make up with me, but I don't trust him anymore.

"Thanks," I say again.

"Of course, not good enough to *win*," Sterling puts in condescendingly. "But nice try, anyway."

My jaw drops. Kevin looks mortified. But Sterling is all smiles again as she whisks him off across the floor.

"That was low even for her!" Quentin growls. "Someone ought to tell her off."

"Someone, but not you," I beg, holding on to his lapels.

A new song starts, a fast one, and the floor immediately fills with couples who've been waiting to dance.

"Go talk to Ros," I tell Quentin. "Now, before she chickens out."

"I'm not—I can't just *leave* you here."

"I'll be fine. I'll hang out with Hayley."

I push him in Ros's direction, and with a last worried glance, he goes. He's halfway there when I suddenly realize I can't hang out with Hayley because she's started dancing with Fitz.

Perfect.

Edging off the floor, I press my back to the wall in the darkest spot I can find. I'll just watch for a couple of songs. Then if Quentin's still tied up with Ros, I'll find someone else to dance with. People will start switching partners soon. I hope.

I can see Quentin and Ros beneath the scoreboard, having an intense discussion. If I'm reading their body language right, she's the one begging this time. Quentin tries to act like he could go either way, but I think she has a good chance of winning him over.

Call me crazy.

Oh, look at that! Unbelievable! Sterling is dancing with her scepter, bopping the girls on their heads and knighting the guys on their shoulders. She's totally stealing my Halloween dance! And since most of these people weren't at Quentin's party, they don't even *know* what a fake she is. Copycat!

You'd think Kevin would remember, since he was dancing with me that night. Sterling's so impressed with herself right now she's probably forgotten that part. Or maybe she thinks Kevin just won't care. Maybe she's right. I'm starting to wonder if he cares about anything except the way she fills out a strapless gown. I swear that thing's staying up by magic.

Where did Quentin go off to? Oh, there he is, dancing with Ros. They look overjoyed, so I guess it's official—Quentin and I aren't meant to be. I sigh, remembering our kiss in the hallway, but we both knew that was a random thing. An experiment. Not like if he'd kissed me here tonight . . .

Besides, I can't be mad at Quentin when I'm the one who hooked him up. No, I'm happy for him. Mostly.

"Cassie! What are you doing by yourself?" Hayley and Fitz have just shown up, flushed and winded from dancing.

"Sitting one out," I say. "You know, taking a rest."

"Come on," says Fitz, reaching for my hand. "Come and dance with us."

I can only assume his offer means he's noticed Quentin with Ros, but I let myself be towed along, happy to be included. The music changes, and it's a song I really like. I throw myself into the rhythm, dancing with Hayley and Fitz and trying not to worry about whether anyone's counting partners.

Hayley and I do the bump, which is truly silly and therefore fun. We trap Fitz in the middle and bump him from both sides. We've got him going like the pendulum in a runaway clock when Quentin and Ros dance over and start trying to bump with us.

Bumping with three takes timing; bumping with five is a major production. We try to make it happen by lining up girl-boy-girl-boy-girl, and everyone agrees that should work—the problem is we look like complete dorks while we're trying to figure it out. We give up and start dancing freestyle in kind of a mob of five.

The floor is packed and we're all just letting fly. Nobody's paying attention to who's technically with whom. Besides, technically Quentin's with me. But every time he looks at Ros, I know how technical that is. The two of them are obviously smitten, just like Hayley and Fitz. There's all this very significant eye contact, and by the time the next song starts, I'm wondering if Bryce is still out in the bushes and whether he can be sobered up enough to dance with me.

Except that would be desperate, and I'm *not* desperate—I'm the runner-up! The only thing Sterling has that I don't is the crown. And the scepter.

And Kevin.

"I'm going to get a drink," I shout to Quentin over the music. "Stay here and dance with Ros."

"Are you sure?" He's sweet to look so conflicted.

"I can entertain myself. Go for it, Q. I want you to."

His face clears into a grateful smile. I dance away and lose myself in the crowd. The gym is probably full of guys who wouldn't mind dancing with a runner-up, at least for one or two songs.

I just have to find them.

If Three Is a Crowd, Then Five Is Just Pointless

It's actually a relief to be on my own. I'll get something to drink, and that will give me time to plan my next move. Because I absolutely refuse to be pointless tonight. I just need to regroup, that's all.

The line for punch is ridiculously long. I join it anyway, then change my mind and decide to head for the drinking fountain. I step back and turn around—only to find myself face to face with Fourteen-Karat and Kevin.

"Why, hello!" Sterling exclaims, as if finding me in the gym is an unexpected delight. "What are you doing over here all by yourself? Where's Quentin?"

The malicious glee in her eyes shows she knows exactly where Quentin is. I avoid looking at Kevin or anyone around us as I reply.

"Quentin and I are friends, so it's fine with me if he dances with Ros," I say, striving for a suitably dignified tone. "*Friends* want each other to be happy."

It's a dig, but it sails right over her head. I knew it would.

"Still, it's got to hurt, losing twice tonight," she says with a pouty smile.

"I didn't lose him—it's *fine* with me. In fact, it was my idea."

"Sure. Okay," she says soothingly.

She's humiliating me, and she's doing it in front of a huge crowd. The people packed around us are hanging on every word. I glance at Kevin, but his sympathetic expression looks more like a grimace. He's not coming to my rescue.

"I have to go," I say, trying to act as if nothing she's said has bothered me. "See you both around."

I start to walk away, but Sterling launches one last shot at my back: "Don't feel bad, Cassie—that's just the way you are. Some girls couldn't keep a guy in a cage."

People gasp. I can barely believe my own ears. I wheel around to see Sterling hanging on Kevin, rubbing salt in my wound.

You know what I just realized? There's karma and not hating and all that, but sometimes you have to stand up for yourself. I open my mouth to let Sterling have it.

Kevin beats me there.

"You're unbelievable!" he exclaims, shaking her off. "Someone should put a padlock on your mouth."

Snickers erupt around us, but it's a nervous sort of laughter. Nobody's smiling.

"Kevin!" Sterling looks totally shocked and nearly as angry. "That wasn't a nice thing to say."

"No, it wasn't," he agrees, not backing down.

She seems to sense that she's losing control of him. She tries to take his arm again, but he yanks it away, brushing off his jacket sleeve like there might be some of her on it.

"You know what, Sterling?" he says. "If you're so good with guys, go find yourself another one. I'm through with this."

A lesser girl might have hysterics, maybe even faint. Being dumped is bad enough, but being dumped while wearing the Snow Queen crown, in front of a gym full of people . . .

But Sterling doesn't cry. She simply shakes her head as if she can't believe what's happening. Honestly, I'm having a hard time believing it myself. I'm just part of the crowd standing here with my mouth hanging open, wondering what to do next.

"Can I talk to you, Cassie?" Kevin asks.

"I . . . I guess so."

"Outside, okay?"

And before I can reply, he takes me by the elbow and escorts me out of the gym.

If I Knew What I Wanted, I'd Know What to Do

But I don't have a clue. Besides, this is all pretty sudden. I let Kevin lead me around the outside of the gym to a deserted patio on its darkened back side. Music seeps through the building's thick walls, and I can just make out Kevin's face by the glow of a security light.

"Is this all right?" he asks, glancing around to make sure we're alone.

"I guess. It's kind of cold out here."

"We don't have to stay long."

He takes off his tuxedo jacket and drapes it over my shoulders. The fabric is still warm from his body, the lining silky against my bare skin. I inhale by reflex, smelling him on the coat, remembering being in his arms on Halloween. . . .

"Better?" he asks.

"What? Oh. Fine."

"Good." He looks like he wants to say more, but he can't seem to spit it out. He shifts back and forth in his polished black shoes, then paces a circle around me.

"I'm so sorry," he blurts out. "I ruined everything."

"You did?"

"I wanted to come to this dance with you, and I thought you wanted to come with me. If I hadn't let Sterling talk me around . . . again." He shakes his head, disgusted. "The dumbest part is, I thought I was doing the right thing. She said she was counting on me, but she could have found another date. Guys are just accessories to her anyway, like, 'I'll be wearing a white dress and Kevin Matthews.' "

I shouldn't smile when he looks so bitter, but it *is* kind of funny.

"You think I'm pathetic," he says, interpreting my expression.

"Not pathetic, just . . ."

"Weak?"

That pretty much sums it up.

Kevin shakes his head again. "Ever since I moved to

Hilltop, my life's been upside down. It's like I saw Sterling and just went insane. I'm not usually so shallow and . . . lame." He offers a pained smile. "I guess that's hard for you to believe, that someone could just suddenly wake up stupid one day and spend entire weeks acting like a person they barely recognize."

Hard for me to believe? He's preaching to the choir.

"I don't know," I say, pretending to give the matter deep thought. "I heard about this girl at our school who plagiarized a play just to impress some guy. Quite a nice girl, normally. But one day she woke up stupid."

"I heard about that girl too," Kevin says with a smile. "What ever happened to her?"

"Well, it took way too long, but eventually she woke up smart again. Relatively, anyway."

His gaze locks with mine. "I can only hope for the same."

It's hard to be clever when he's looking at me that way, but I give it my best shot. "Maybe you just got your wake-up call."

He reaches a hand toward my cheek, then pauses, like he's not sure he's forgiven. Honestly, I'm not sure either. But I like him better now than I did ten minutes ago. I give him a tentative smile. Encouraged, he reaches past my face and touches one of my curls.

"You're so beautiful tonight," he says. "That dress is incredible. I voted for you, like I promised. I really wish you'd won."

I shrug because I'm afraid to believe him. "I should have known I wouldn't. I have this love affair with second place."

"What?"

"Well, not a love affair, exactly. More like a committed relationship."

"What are you talking about?"

It suddenly occurs to me that I've never explained my theory of talent to Kevin, not even during one of my many apologies, when it might have helped him understand the driving force behind those disasters.

"I'll tell you someday, but not tonight."

"Just tell me this," he says, moving closer. "How committed is that relationship? Is there room for anyone else?"

His breath tickles my cheek. My heart pounds hard enough to break a rib.

"Maybe," I manage to say. "If the right guy comes along."

"Or what if he just comes to his senses? I blew it, Cassie. I know that now. Will you give me a second chance?"

An enormous smile spreads across my face. I'd rather look mysterious, but I can't help myself. Because all of a sudden, I *do* know what I want.

"You've come to the right girl. Second chances are my specialty."

Kevin's grin is as wide as my own as he reaches out to hug me. I lace my fingers behind his neck and pull myself even closer.

"Now let me ask *you* something," I say. "In the spirit of starting fresh and all . . . Did you kiss my hair on Halloween?"

"Hmm. Like this?" His cheek nuzzles my head. Then, with the slightest twist of his neck, his lips graze through my hair, trailing warmth against my scalp. I melt against his body, finally certain I didn't imagine it, that he felt something that night too.

"*Kind* of like that," I say. "But weren't you holding me tighter?"

One arm squeezes me closer. The other slips to the small of my back. "Like this?"

"It's hard to be sure. Maybe if you did that thing with your lips again . . ."

"Why don't you let me show you what I *really* wanted to do?"

His lips run through my hair, but this time they keep moving. His mouth glides down my cheek, a whisper of skin on skin. My eyes drop closed with longing just as Kevin kisses me.

One of my feet lifts off the ground. My other knee is Jell-O, but Kevin's arms keep me from falling. I run my hands up into his hair, sighing as I return his kiss. It's such a romantic moment, I can almost hear music playing.

Wait a minute. I *do* hear music. The DJ in the gym has just cued up my favorite song. I can't believe his timing. I can't believe any of this. I lean back to look at Kevin, to see if he's as amazed as I am, and suddenly I notice that the sky is full of stars. There's a pillow of stars behind his head, a blanket of stars all around us.

"I love this song," I say.

"Want to dance?"

So we do, just the two of us under the stars, slow dancing our way into our new lives. Because everything's going to be different now.

I mean, that's just obvious. Right?

If the Glass Slipper Fits . . .

"I'm keeping you away from your adoring subjects," Kevin teases, kissing the tip of my nose. "Do you want to go back in?"

We've been dancing outside for so long that I've lost track of the time.

"In a while," I say, reluctant to leave our private oasis. "I like it better out here with just us."

"I like us too," he says. "I just thought, this being your big night and all, you'd want to go back inside before the ball is over."

"Over?" I lift my head off his shoulder. "What time is it?"

"Eleven thirty-two," he says promptly.

"What?" I glance around to see if I've missed some obvious clock, but all I see is stars. "You're just guessing."

Kevin shakes his head. "It's eleven thirty-two. Well . . . thirty-three now. Check me, if you have a watch."

I don't. As far as I can tell, neither does he. He hasn't looked at it if he does, because both of his hands are behind my back.

"How do you know?" I ask.

He shrugs charmingly. "I just know. I can tell time in my head."

"In your head?" I repeat, stunned. "You always just know exactly what time it is?"

"Pretty freaky, huh? Don't ask me how I do it, because I have no idea. Just born that way, I guess."

I grin and wrap my arms around his neck.

"Interesting! Tell me more."

Don't You Just Love Happy Endings?

Or maybe this is a happy beginning. One thing's for sure: school looks like a different place this Monday, with one of my hands in Kevin's and the other holding my final detention essay for Mrs. Conway. I know she said I didn't have to finish it, but today is her first day back, and I want to give her something. Just a little token, to show I care. Things between us are going to be different from now on.

That's my plan, at least.

"Move your seat again," Kevin says as we walk down the hall toward her classroom. "Come sit in back with me."

"Ooh, I don't know about that," I tease. "People might think we're into each other."

Kevin rolls his green eyes.

"After all, I *am* the second most popular girl in school," I can't resist adding.

"And you promised not to milk it," he reminds me.

"Au contraire. I promised not to milk it past Monday, which means I still have fifteen hours. Besides, that was if I won. Runner-up should have a longer expiration date."

"You're crazy," he says, smiling.

"Crazy like a runner-up."

He wraps his arms around me, stopping me feet from Mrs. Conway's door. Anyone who wants to go into English has to walk right past us. He stares into my eyes until I feel weak in the knees.

"What are you doing?" I ask breathlessly.

"Blowing your cover," he says. "Come on, you might as well sit with me now."

"Kevin!"

I try to push him away, but somehow my arms collapse and we end up chest to chest, laughing. And now I'm staring into his eyes, our breathing rising and falling together. I can tell he's feeling exactly what I am, and believe me, that's a lot. Hall traffic gradually clears, but I don't want to move.

"What time is it?" I ask, expecting a to-the-second answer.

"Time for this," he says, kissing me.

Plus There's Always One Last Happy Bit

"Hi, Mrs. Conway!" I say, rushing into her room behind Kevin. I have a ridiculously happy grin on my face and it must be contagious, because instead of pointing out that the tardy bell has rung, she actually smiles back.

"Hello, Cassie," she says. "And congratulations on your near victory Saturday night. That must have been very . . . routine for you."

There's a funny sparkle in her eye. Is she actually making a joke?

"A girl goes with her strengths," I say. "But what about you? Are you all right?"

"Why wouldn't I be?" she snaps, instantly crabby.

"No reason! Just that you were out a whole week. And our sub was a nightmare. And it's good to have you back."

"Thank you," she says, relaxing. "I'm fine."

She thinks I don't know anything. But I know this: I'm going to cover her like a blanket from now on, just in case I can help her out.

"I brought you something," I say. "You can read it later."

She accepts my essay with obvious surprise. Her expression suggests I might want to lie down until I come back to my senses.

"Oh, and one more thing," I add, pointing to the seating chart taped to her roll book. "If it's okay with you, I'll be sitting by Kevin from now on."

"I see," she says with a smile.

And I really think she does.

Voluntary Essay #1
Mrs. Conway

What I've Learned from All This
by Cassie Howard

What I've learned from all this is that when it comes to talent, I didn't quite get it before. Not completely. I still believe every person on earth is born with one special gift, but I'm not so big on the "one" part now. Based on what I've seen lately, you can't assume it's just one at all.

You also can't assume you know what it is. A person may have some obvious talent, something that screams to be recognized, but it's a mistake to get hung up on that. You never know what you might be overlooking in the process. A person you've decided is a computer genius, to give a random example, could turn out to be a budding fashion designer. A teacher with a talent for intimidation, to be even more arbitrary, might also have a selfless gift for helping other people.

Honestly, it's a lot more confusing than I realized.

But it's more exciting, too. For all I know, I could wake up tomorrow morning and discover I'm a tremendously gifted ukulele player or something. Obviously I'll be hoping for the "or something," but that's not the point. The point is that the possibilities have been blown wide open.

And here's the most important thing I've learned: it's silly to make judgments about a talent's glory factor. There's no such thing as an inglorious talent when it's the one coming to your rescue. Hayley's whistling, Quentin's parking, Fitz's ability to stop any line, even my mother's arguing . . . every one of those things is beautiful under the right conditions. Even my gift for second place is something I'm seeing in a whole new light.

Talent is a mysterious thing, but it's never a limitation. I have to believe there's some bigger plan too, because when a bunch of oddball talents join together for a common goal, it's amazing what they can accomplish. It's actually kind of staggering to imagine how much better off the world will be if the human race ever gets over itself and agrees on a good plan.

Maybe after college, I'll be a talent agent. Not your normal, singing-and-acting-talent agent, but an all-talents-welcome agent. I'll help figure out what people's gifts are and where they can make the biggest impact. That would be cool. Do you know what I'd major in for that?

Anyway, these past two months have been a

rough ride, but the destination was worth the trip. I wouldn't trade where I am now for anything.

One last thing I've learned?

If you have to live in Second Place, it's good to be the queen.

Can't get enough of Cassie? Her story continues in <u>Queen B.</u> Here's a sneak peek. . . .

This new year is my year to shine. For the first time in my life, I have an actual shot at being someone at school. I've always been more of a Queen B than a Queen Bee—you know, B as in not A. Second tier. (Fine, if you have to get technical, sometimes even lower.) But now I have a chance to be a real Queen Bee.

There's just one teensy problem: What good is being popular if all your friends are mad at you?

<u>Queen B</u>

Summer 2006!